Homegrown

By

Dave Wickenden

Printed in the United States of America

FIRST EDITION / R1

ISBN: 978-0-9977949-1-5

Published by:

Crave Press

www.cravepress.com

Chapter 1

Ninety seconds, do or die. Dalton glanced at the scoreboard — there was less than a minute and a half to break the tie for the State Hockey Championship. The ice's chill gave no relief from the heat his body emitted as he shook the sweat from his eyes. Using the break the offsides play gave him to recover, he tried to get his breathing under control as his chest pumped like billows from exertion.

This is it. We either end it here or take a chance in sudden overtime. Got to get the puck out of our zone. What would Dad do? Dalton looked up in the stands and the empty seat beside his mom played on his mind. The first tremor of concern rippled through him because it wasn't like his dad to miss a game this important. *Where the heck is he?*

"Okay, guys, let's do this," Dalton said, the letter "C" on his jersey heavier than it had ever been. Being captain of the team was a heavy responsibility for a 17-year-old, but Dalton shouldered it well.

"Jaxson, we got this," Dalton yelled to the goalie.

Jaxson shifted nervously on his skates and banged each post with his stick to center himself, his trapper raised at the ready. The linesman slid up to the left faceoff circle, scanning to see if the players were in their positions. Both Dalton and the opposing centerman faced off, their muscles tense and their hockey sticks quivering.

The puck dropped. Dalton scooped it behind him to Daniel. As the puck rebounded behind the net, Dalton didn't hesitate but instead left his opposite standing there watching the play. Dalton drove towards his own blue line, his eyes following the puck as his teammate raced up along the boards.

As the puck barreled towards Dalton, he dug in his skates, accelerating down the ice. Facing the two defensemen, he made a split-second decision to fake a surge towards the space between them. When they tightened up, they left the right side clear.

It was the right move, considering Dalton's speed. He cut behind the defenseman closest to him who was already turning around to give chase. The other defender angled towards Dalton. *He's going to try to run through me if I cut in front of the net.* It was the same maneuver Dalton had used in the second period, and the hit would have been savage if Dalton had not seen it coming.

Keeping his sight fixed on the goalie, Dalton's opponents saw what he had planned and they all reacted. The goalie tucked in tighter, his body compressed against the right hand post, ready to follow Dalton's lead, while the defensemen built up more speed for the hit. All eyes focused on the goalie, ignorant of Dalton's left winger who followed just behind the play.

The team had practiced this maneuver countless times from every angle, so it was second nature. Still facing forward, Dalton dropped the pass behind the opposition defensemen so there was no time for them to react. The puck slid smoothly across the center of the attack zone, and Ian converged on the slot without slowing down. He snatched up the puck and let fly a hard wrist shot. With a sniper's accuracy, the puck made for the net. Blinded by his defensemen, the goalie threw out his right pad, but the puck flashed past him. The red light lit up as the referee pointed to the net to indicate the goal.

Dalton screamed, "Yeah!"

The arena exploded with a roar as the fans screamed in excitement. Dalton looped around the net, whooping as he made for Ian who looked like a ballerina on steroids doing a victory dance. The two met in a crushing hug, mangled by their teammates.

"Just like we practiced," Ian said.

"At least you hit the bloody net," Dalton said with a laugh.

Dalton was pummeled from all sides by teammates.

"We did it!"

Gloves and helmets flew through the air. Benched players swarmed the ice. The press of bodies was the only thing keeping Dalton upright as his skates left the ice.

"Was it worth all the extra practices?" Dalton asked as he fought for balance.

But his friend's reply was lost beneath his team's mismatched chorus of "We are the Champions."

Dalton stepped off the ice onto the thick rubber mat. Again he scanned the crowds for his dad. No luck.

In the dressing room, the celebration continued as water and stick tape flew across the room like black flying snakes. Dalton was laughing when the coach stuck his head into the room.

"Dalton," he called out from the door, his expression serious.

"Yeah, coach?" Dalton said, looking up.

"Finish getting dressed and get out here."

Dalton shoved his gloves into his bag. *Must be for a statement for the school paper.* He pulled his shirt over his head and ran his fingers through his hair, sweeping it out of his face. He had to duck to avoid Daniel's jockstrap which was aimed at his head. Dalton stepped through an obstacle course of equipment bags and helmets to get to the door.

As the door closed the noise off behind him, the coach nodded and said, "Follow me."

Dalton fell into step behind the coach as they marched to one of the arena's offices down the hall. At the door, the coach turned and patted him on the shoulder.

"I'll be here for you Dalton," he said as he opened the door.

Dalton frowned at him before turning to the room. A tall police officer stood there, his bulletproof vest making him look like a gorilla in a suit too small. Another man stood there in a dark suit, nervously pulling on his sleeve.

Beside Mr. Dark Suit sat Dalton's mother, looking small and scared in a foldout chair. Her eyes were glassy, her mouth slack, and, for a moment, Dalton was terrified she was having a stroke. She sucked in her lips at the sight of him, her grey eyes filling with tears. He rushed to her and pulled her to him. As she wailed, her body rocked against his chest; the scent of his mother's perfume made him heady. It was usually so comforting, but today it was suffocating.

“Why are you crying?” he said to her. “We won. You should be happy.”

His comment caused her to cry even harder. He was confused and looked at the others in the room.

And where’s Dad? He never misses my games. Never...

Chapter 2

Dalton lay on his bed, one arm across his forehead, as he listened to his mother's sobs coming from the next room. Part of him was saddened by her tears, her loss. He hated to see her in pain and he was helpless to fix things for her. He felt so useless, so inept.

Another part of him was jealous, hearing her cry, listening to her express the pain he was unable to. He felt the sadness and pain like a heavy, cancerous tumor in the pit of his stomach, but try as he might, he couldn't shed a single tear. What the fuck was wrong with him? What kind of son can't cry for his father?

In anger, he sat up. In the gloom, the posters on his walls, all of his favorite rock stars, seemed to stare at him with disgust. It was a trick of the light, but Dalton felt it was deserved.

He crossed to the window and looked outside for the hundredth time, wishing without hope that his father would be returning from work. The street stood empty, the only movement the insects swarming the street light.

The sobbing finally stopped, and Dalton put his ear up to the wall that divided his room from his parent's — no, he corrected himself, his mom's — bedroom. He could her steady breathing, and hoped her sleep would be dreamless and allow her to rest.

At least one of us should get some sleep.

It had been a long couple days for both of them. With yesterday's viewing and today's burial followed by the wake, they were both spent. But there would be no real break as tomorrow there were three other funerals followed by more over the next few days.

Regardless of how tired he felt, Dalton's mind would not stop long enough to fall asleep. Except for some power naps which he suspected was him just passing out while sitting up, he had not slept since he was told about the accident that killed his father. On impulse, Dalton decided to go out, to get out of this house where he saw his father everywhere he looked. Dragging on his runners and a hoodie, Dalton eased his window open and stepped out into the night. He took his time closing the window so there was no noise.

Following the driveway down to the street, he was painfully reminded of all the street hockey games he played with his dad. Dad was as much a coach and friend as he was a father. Dalton felt his eyes burn at the memory; he felt certain the tears would finally give him some relief and wash some of the pain away, but they continued to betray him. Frustrated, he started to run. He concentrated on the steady rhythm of his feet pounding the pavement. At first, it acted like a salve covering the endless thoughts of his over-tired mind, but eventually the thoughts began to intrude, denying him any relief. His mind replayed the conversation of the company man who had explained what they knew of the accident.

His father operated a huge crane used to build high-rise buildings, lifting supplies and steel beams into place. Any mistake could rain the material down on the streets below, putting numerous people at risk of being crushed, including his co-workers. There was an electrical problem that caused the crane to smolder, filling the cab with toxic black smoke. As his father left the cab for the safety of the ladder, the flames started to consume the console. The cab became unstable and plunged, crushing his father before continuing 67 floors to the street below, taking 23 construction workers with it and killing an additional 18 civilians. The compounded shock and the grief of all the others who died, some of whom they knew, was made worse by the whispers and looks of accusation that seemed to blame the accident on his father even though the investigation hadn't even started.

"He's dead. Hasn't he paid enough even if he was at fault? Haven't we paid enough?" Dalton wanted to scream at those accusers, but had no choice but to swallow his anger. It would do no good.

Then there was his own buddies Ian and Daniel. It was a relief to see them yesterday at the wake, and he wanted so bad to take a break and just chill with guys that loved Dad as much as he had. But when he turned around, he found they had bolted from the funeral home as fast as they could. Not only did they forget about all the advice Dad had given them both on and off the ice, but when Dalton needed them the most, they left him standing by himself.

He pounded past a stop sign and jumped up, slamming his hand against the sheet metal. It made a rebounding echo that briefly eclipsed the city's nighttime noise. Better, it caused his hand to sting, clearing his mind for a moment. He looked around and realized he had wandered into an area of the city that was unfamiliar. He pulled out his phone and realized he'd been running and walking for over two hours. *Shit, had he been asleep?* Looking back the way came, Dalton could see he had already past the Washington Hospital Center, so it meant he was almost in the Columbia Heights area of Washington, D.C. This was no place to be after dark.

He turned again, this time looking for threats, and was in time to see two shadows break away from a clump of trees and move his way. He started backing away, and the two figures broke into a run, coming straight at him. With no conscious thought, his feet started moving until he was running full out towards the lights of the hospital. The slap of pursuing feet on the pavement slowly faded as he got closer to the large facility, bathed in bright flood lights that pushed back the night. He looked over his shoulder and the two continued to follow, but at a walk. There were a number of police and emergency services vehicles parked in a side parking lot, and a couple uniforms looked up as he slowed to a walk. That in itself might be the reason the hunters had slowed down, but they were obviously not that intimidated by the police to stop completely. The cops eyed Dalton as he passed them and entered the hospital, but they said nothing.

Blinking at the harsh lights, he walked through the main lobby and past the admission desk as if he knew where he was going. Once around the corner, he ducked down another corridor. He didn't think his pursuers would continue chasing him into the hospital, but he preferred not to take chances. The last thing his mother needed was to find out he had been beaten, or worse. Following the long hallway, he saw a sign over the next section that announced that he was entering the Washington Cancer Center. He glanced back, and there was no sign of anyone following him. He continued on, now looking for an exit so he could head home before he ran into more trouble.

A group of doctors and nurses in multicolored scrubs came out of a room further down the hall and turned towards Dalton as they animatedly discussed some case. Rather than fall under their scrutiny, Dalton ducked into the next open room, which turned out to be a chapel.

The room was not overly large, but it held about 15 chairs facing a small altar that held a lone pedestal. The lighting was soft in a relaxing way. He quickly sat in one of the chairs as the group of staffers walked past the chapel's entrance. There was a pamphlet on the seat, and he picked it up instinctively and opened it in an attempt to make it seem like he actually had a reason to be there. As the group passed the room without even acknowledging his presence, Dalton shoved the pamphlet into the hoodie's front pocket. He waited until the voices died out and left the room before he continued through the building.

In short order, Dalton found himself at another entrance to the building and headed back out into the night. Checking the area for any sign of his two followers, he continued south towards home, feeling the adrenalin wear off and the fatigue set in. The walk back home was uneventful, except for the growing exhaustion that caused him to stumble at times over bumps in the sidewalk while navigating through a marathon of yawns.

Dalton climbed through the window and listened for any sign his mother was awake, but the house's silence told him she was still asleep. He turned on his bedside lamp before pulling the hoodie over his head and dropping it over his chair. As he kicked off his shoe, the pamphlet fell out of the sweater's pocket and onto the floor. He snatched it up and glanced at it in the lamp's light as he planned to toss it in the trash. The words at the top of the paper stopped him, and he had to re-read them: "Have you lost a loved one? Are you in pain? We can help."

The line was repeated in a number of different languages. At the bottom of the page, a Washington address as well as a web page were displayed. A faded picture of a building unlike anything he'd seen before with a high tower stood off to one side. Pulling his laptop off his desk, he sat on his bed and powered it. Minutes later, he typed in the website's address, and the site loaded: "Grief. Depression. Stress. Allah has the answers to all that affects mankind."

Chapter 3

Aazam ibn Abd al-Muttalib crouched low beside a pump house for one of the many gigantic oil tanks that stood under the blazing sun. The refinery and storage farm was situated outside of Baiji, an industrial town north of Baghdad. The wind brought Aazam the faint cry of the mu'addhin, those appointed by the mosque to call the true believers to prayers. Amplified by bullhorns mounted at the top of the mosque's minaret, the distance rendered the words unintelligible but the cadence was recognizable by every Muslim in the area.

Aazam lifted his binoculars and scanned for the front element of the enemy force. He could see the cloud of dust kicked up by the tank treads as the force made its way around the town. His scouts were following the progress and would fall back before the enemy was committed. Aazam heard the radio behind him squawk, and minutes later his second-in-command and best friend, Najib, scurried over and placed his hand on Azam's shoulder.

"Rasha has verified that the battle force has stopped for morning prayers, Aazam."

"*They* may have, but not the godless American pigs," Aazam said, lifting his chin to indicate the incoming coalition jets that hugged the desert floor heading towards their position. Aazam and Najib watched as missiles launched from the two lead jets. Aazam knew the Americans used lasers to guide the Maverick missiles to their targets, so it was unsurprising when two of the small rockets made straight for the half-buried launcher set up before his position. What did shock him was that the battery was able to launch two of its own rockets before the launcher disappeared in a double ball of flame. The rockets, two streaks of silver escaped the explosion by seconds, rising like Hamian arrows. Both locked onto one of the intrusive aircraft and gave chase, forcing the intruders to litter the sky with flares and other countermeasures as they ran for the horizon.

Around Aazam, his men cheered wildly. It wasn't often that forces of the Islamic State of Iraq (ISIS) could put the run on the Americans and their allies. The Iraqi forces with the help of the Americans had forced Aazam and his men to withdraw from Baiji after weeks of vicious house by house fighting. Aazam grinned callously as he recalled the number of enemy soldiers killed by the traps left by his men as they pulled back. It created fear and hesitation which ground the assault to an almost complete standstill.

"Are the oil tanks rigged to blow?" he asked over his shoulder.

"Yes, my friend, everything is set," Najib said. "Are you that confident the enemy will do as you wish them?"

"Yes. They think we are finished, and they will be looking for a quick victory. As long as our men keep up the deception, the enemies will enter the trap." He laughed aloud and turned to his friend. "It's like I told the men, we are safer here in the tank farm than out there. They think we are beaten so the Americans will never risk the oil. It's the only reason they are here."

Najib laughed and said, "Well, I for one am happy you assigned me to the convoy, so I can get as far away as possible before you release your trap."

"Then give the word to move north to Hawija," Aazam said, his teeth flashing in contrast to his sun baked complexion.

"Don't wait too long!"

"Allahu Akbar[1]," said Aazam.

"Go with God, my friend," Najib said, slapping Aazam on the shoulder as he hurried off to the rear of the plant.

Aazam had set this trap up more than a week ago, when they were pushed back through the central courtyard of the city. Rather than keep setting tripwires and explosives for the advancing soldiers, he ordered his men to slowly stop with the traps. He wanted the enemy to think that they were abandoning their positions in panic. In fact, he had ordered his men to abandon the last few neighborhoods without any resistance at all. As the Iraqis passed by the last of the town's buildings, they saw the remnants of the ISIS army racing across the desert floor towards the oil tank farm. His hope was that the enemy believed they were beaten and routed.

Behind him, the radio squawked again, but Aazam didn't require an update to inform him that the prayer time was over and the enemy had resumed its march. He could hear the rumble of the heavy diesel engines and see the trail of dust in the distance.

As they broke cover, Aazam was able to see the front rank consisted of four American made M1A1M Abrams tanks. They were there to protect the variety of armored personnel carriers which followed behind. Normally, the Abrams would have struck fear in Aazam and his men, but he was certain they would not attempt firing their main guns among the oil tanks. No, they would come in with close battle weapons rather than heavy ordinance.

He was betting his and his men's lives on it.

Aazam waited until the range closed on the incoming tanks to signal to one of his men. There were multiple thuds of mortar rounds being launched. He kept his binoculars trained on the enemy as more rounds were fired. Moments later, four explosions threw up dust and smoke in and among the armored personnel carriers.

In a choreographic maneuver, the tanks split apart. The long column of armored personal carriers (APCs) broke into two separate lines and continued following behind the more heavily armored vehicles in a hope of shelter. There was a steady barrage of explosions landing around the vehicles, but except for smoke and flying shrapnel that clattered harmlessly against the armored troop carriers, it did little to slow the enemy.

Aazam gave another command, and seconds later two anti-tank guided missiles were launched almost simultaneously. Traveling at such a high speed, Aazam saw only a flash of light leaving a gust of white exhaust in its wake. Both hit their targets — the lead Abrams. The first missile hit just under the turret in a massive explosion that left the vehicle fully engulfed in flames. The tank and its crew died instantly. The second projectile hit low and tore the right tread off the machine, leaving it stranded like a crippled turtle.

For a moment, the APCs slowed almost in unison as the realization that Aazam and his men had weapons that could inflict real damage hit home. It gave the mortars a more stable target, and there were a couple direct hits and Aazam let out an unconscious cheer. It was taken up by those close to him, and he forced himself to concentrate on the bigger picture.

Flashes of high speed jets crossed the sky directly above Aazam's position. He could hear the staccato reports of their 20 mm multi-barrel guns to the north and knew they were targeting Najib's convoy. They would also be radioing the Iraqi ground forces telling of the ISIS soldier's abandonment of the tank farm, he hoped.

The two enemy columns continued their run to get behind the massive oil tanks as cover so they could unload their infantry. The lead elements disappeared from view, and Aazam gave the signal to pull back. His men began to run for the vehicles that were strategically positioned for a fast exit. They came barreling down the roadway that ran between the two rows of oil tanks, totally ignoring the massive force spreading out to either side of them.

The last two vehicles slowed enough so Aazam and his few remaining men could jump on board. Then they raced for the gate at the rear of the facility and the highway leading north. Aazam felt helpless sitting in the rear seat as he urged the vehicle to go faster. It was absurd, he knew. The driver was pushing the SUV as fast as he could. The helplessness came from not being in absolute control, and he silently scolded himself for not trusting his men.

The first of the enemy shots searched for their vehicle, and they all crouched lower in their seats, praying today would not be their last.

The gate filled the windshield, and the driver put the vehicle into a hard drift, the centrifugal force pushing them all to one side before the tires bit into the highways hardtack, causing them to bounce back across the interior of the SUV.

"The control box," Aazam commanded as the highway raced up a hillside. He looked back and could see the enemy forces stretched out the length of the tank farm, knowing there would be a second column mirroring it.

The man beside him pulled a hard yellow box from the floor and passed it over to Aazam.

Aazam opened the case, exposing the remote detonation control panel. He quickly powered up the unit and lifted the small antenna. He switched the large knob from safe to the armed position. Glancing through the windshield he saw they were just about to cress the hillside and knew they would be protected on the other side of the red sandstone mountainside.

Turning in his seat, Aazam saw the lead Iraqi forces were milling near the fence trying to bear their weapons on the fleeing vehicles. As the SUV crested the hilltop, he pressed the transmit button and felt cheated as the tank farm disappeared from view behind the slope. They felt the explosion rather than saw its effect. The ground shook so badly that the driver had to fight the wheel, slamming on the brakes to gain some control. Behind them, a massive mushroom of flame reached skyward, stretching past the hilltop before consuming itself. The heat followed the blast and, if not for being below the hill, Aazam was sure they would have been cremated with the SUV acting as an oven. Sheets of flaming twisted metal, globs of burning oil and the odd clump of smoking body parts rained down all around them.

Aazam left the relative safety of the SUV and climbed the hill they had just descended. He had to see. Slapping at the heated, yet unburnt oil that dropped like a toxic rain as it burned his arms, he labored up the grade until he could just see over. He was panting and coughing on the foul air, but he forgot his discomfort as he peered over the crest. Aazam could only look for a couple of seconds as the radiant heat threatened to burn his eyes out and forced him to duck behind the hilltop, but the snapshot was enough that it would haunt him for the rest of his life.

The entire scene was flame and smoke. Shadowy outlines of what might have been vehicles were scattered across the landscape, and the desert was on fire. Nothing moved except the greedy tongues of the fire reaching to devour the sky. From his one glance, it seemed a river of flame was working its way to the city which lay lower than the tank farm. He had killed hundreds — no, thousands — of men, fellow Muslims at the push of a button. He had created Jahannam, or an afterlife for punishers, on earth, and it was filled with hell fire to burn those who defied the Islamic State.

Chapter 4

Aazam and the remaining ISIS soldiers raced north to catch up with the main force, leaving the devastation behind. The massive silo of black, oily smoke stayed visible the entire time, a constant reminder to Aazam of the atrocity he committed on his fellow Muslims. He was a soldier, damn it, but what he had done was mass murder. Those men had been his fellow Iraqis. What purpose did it serve? We were ordered to destroy the facility rather than allow it to fall into the hands of the government. But to kill so many.

His men sensed his dark mood, and for the most part, the ride was done in silence, each man's thoughts his own. It was interrupted by the driver who pointed out another smaller column of smoke, this one to the north.

As they came closer, Aazam recognized a number of burning vehicles in flames as part of the convoy of his soldiers that had retreated north. The smoke lifted in a furious boil, blackened by fuel and rubber. The vehicles, a pickup and another SUV, had been pushed to the shoulder. A third vehicle was parked further up the road, and a soldier jumped out as they came even with the wreckage, waving for them to stop. Aazam was relieved to see no other evidence of his ragtag army.

"Aazam, its Najib," said the man in a rush.

Aazam felt his heart lurch. *No. Not Najib.* They had been together from the beginning. Aazam kicked the door open and ran to the pickup that stood apart from the inferno.

"We were strafed by the American jets," said the soldier, but Aazam heard him as if through a long tunnel.

He clambered up the back of the truck's bed and knelt beside his friend's prone body. Hope swelled in Aazam's chest for a second when Najib's eyes found him, but when Aazam saw the ragged hole in the man's stomach, he shuddered with despair.

"That bad, eh?" Najib said, blood dribbling down his cheek as he spoke.

"No. We'll have you patched up in no time," Aazam said, keeping his eyes locked on his friend's gaze. He grasped Najib's hand in his, feeling only a slight pressure in return.

"You were never a good liar my friend."

Aazam swallowed and cursed himself for allowing his feelings to show. They had shared so much together, and they were more like brothers than friends.

"Did the trap work?" Najib asked, coughing up more bright red blood which Aazam recognized as lung blood.

"Yes, my friend. It worked. The Iraqi army is no more."

Najib smiled a tight grin that may well have been a grimace. He closed his eyes and gave a weak nod. A sudden coughing spasm seized Najib, sending a spray of blood across Aazam's face and beard. Aazam held his friend as his body convulsed, cradling the man to his chest. The labored breath slowed and finally stopped with a suddenness that caught Aazam unprepared. He had so much to say. He wanted to talk of the early days as soldiers in Saddam's army, so young and so proud. Or the night Najib introduced him to Shasmeen, who Aazam would later marry, and how the three of them spent the entire night on the rooftop talking about a future that would be stolen by the American invasion of Iraq.

Instead, Aazam said, "Go with God, my friend." He reached out and closed those dark eyes that were already glazed over, not feeling the stream of tears that silently fell and hid in the coarse hairs of his beard.

His sorrow was replaced by a cold hatred that froze out all other feelings, leaving him numb. The Americans had stolen another person from him. First Shasmeen and now Najib. Aazam's hand that still clutched his friend's hand began to ache, making him realize that in his anger, he was squeezing their hands together until his knuckles turned white.

"I promise you Najib, I will make them pay for what they have done to us. As Allah is my witness, I promise."

***

When Aazam entered the central mosque in Hawija, he placed his rifle on a table at the entrance so as not to insult Allah. On the long, frustrating journey from Baiji, his convoy had been harassed by coalition aircraft, but he'd been numb to it. His thoughts circled around one thing: how to hurt the Americans and the coalition countries that followed them. It wasn't until they reached the surface-to-air weapons set up around Al Fathah that his soldiers could fight back. The coalition jets left them alone after that.

It went against his nature to give up, and pulling back from the refinery had been difficult. It still bothered him that he had killed fellow Muslims rather than what he saw as the true enemy — the Americans.

Aazam knew his friend was now in the palace of God, a reward for following the faith; however, Aazam was now completely alone. It was unsettling. From the beginning, Najib had been with him. They entered the Iraqi military together and had sworn allegiance to Saddam Hussein. They both spent time at the Guantanamo Bay detention camp in Cuba after the second invasion of Iraq by the Americans. After suffering the humiliation and repeated torture by the American military, Aazam and Najib were released in 2009 and returned to their home country with no charges. They had been soldiers of the regime, not leaders.

Both also served time in Iraq's Abu Ghraib jail when they were able to escape during a prison break in 2013 which began when a suicide bomber drove his explosive-loaded vehicle into the prison gates. Insurgents stormed the prison freeing most of the senior members of the al-Qaida terrorist group who had been sentenced to death. They, with the freed leaders, would form the nucleus of the Islamic State.

The loss of his friend was a bitter pill, but Aazam had to go on, assured that it was Allah's will. Perhaps Najib had to die to give him the strength to take the fight to the coalition countries.

Aazam removed his footwear and prepared himself to pray. The tall plain walls were broken by a simple strip of blue and white tile work of geometric patterns. Most was lost to the shadows, the only light coming from through the arabesque styled metal window coverings. It was past the traditional Isha, or evening prayers, but he had to postpone it as a safety measure. So he was here to perform Qadaa — to make up for the missed prayer session.

He first made his intention in his heart to pray to Allah and then recited two rak'ah (prayer units) aloud, his voice echoing in the empty room amid the swish of his clothing as he bowed as prescribed. The last two rak'ah he recited internally, praying from his heart. He thanked Allah for the safe arrival of his men and for the soul of his good friend. After his thanksgiving to Allah, he rose to find the imam — the mosque's worship leader — waiting for him, his arms folded within the sleeves of his jacket. Aazam nodded and strode to meet the religious leader.

"Aazam, I thank Allah for your safe return."

"Thank you."

"I have heard about Najib. May Allah reward him for bravery in the face of the infidel."

Aazam bowed his head humbly, accepting the blessing and kind words. "Your kindness holds true to the Prophet, may peace and blessings of Allah be upon him."

The old cleric nodded. "Have you reported to headquarters? One of the leaders, Abu al Meshedani, is here to personally hear your briefing of the conflict."

Aazam stiffened, wondering if he would be held responsible for the loss of the refinery. Others had been executed for lesser mistakes.

His anxiety must have been evident on his face, because the imam placed a hand on his shoulder, "Allah holds you in the palm of his hand and knows you are his warrior. He will not see you harmed."

Aazam relaxed and nodded his thanks. "If you will excuse me, I will report at once. May peace and blessings of Allah be upon you."

"Go with God, Aazam."

Aazam left the mosque and crossed the courtyard, the market stalls empty for the night. He knew tomorrow the square would be loud and busy with vendors hawking their wares. He paused outside an unremarkable building, chosen specifically to avoid detection, to gather his courage. He steeled himself and entered the building. He was immediately recognized, and a cheer went up. The administrators and planners greeted him as a hero.

Other soldiers still covered in dust with ragged, tired faces came forward to congratulate him, shaking his hand and slapping him on the back. He felt like a fraud. The commotion brought a superior officer to the entrance who waved Aazam to a back room.

The superior officer led Aazam through a dark communication room where rows upon rows of computer banks were set up. A discordant mix of conversations overflowed the busy room. The headquarters supervised an entire sector of the Islamic State, and Aazam was heartened to see the news was not all doom and gloom. Although chaotic from his point of view, the calm professionalism he witnessed was mixed with smiling faces illuminated by the monitors. Aazam and the officer entered a large room, the walls covered with maps of all the areas that ISIS controlled and those it planned to control. The door closed behind them, trapping the light. Light was an enemy that satellites searched for.

An older man detached himself from a nearby group and held out his hands to Aazam. "My friend, I thank Allah you have returned safely."

Aazam took the hands warily.

Abu al Meshedani managed the operations in this part of Iraq and Syria, and held the power of life and death over those under him. Although Aazam was ready to die for the cause and in Allah's name, he was anxious to hold onto life as there was so much for him to offer. And, of course, so many enemies to kill.

"I thank you for your concern, but I have failed to hold the refinery," replied Aazam.

"We did not expect you to, Aazam! With the forces against you, we knew that the fall was inevitable. However, from the preliminary reports, you made the Iraqi troops pay for the now useless plant with their lives. By delaying the detonation, at no little risk to yourself, the explosions killed almost their entire force." He slapped Aazam on the shoulder, "You have done more than we had ever expected."

Resentment flared throughout Aazam's core, Najib's dried blood still staining his face. "My men died for nothing?"

A hard edge transformed Meshedani's voice. "Your superiors and betters will determine how the war is to be fought." He tugged on his full beard and then leaned against the wall, appraising Aazam. "So you can understand and have confidence in my leadership, I will explain."

He walked over, sat down on the corner of the desk and said, "With the air support of the coalition, we have changed our tactics. We have begun to slowly pull back, but we are making sure the Iraqi forces pay for every step they take. This is demoralizing them and reducing their numbers. It also lessens the progress of the coalition force which increases the opposition they face at home."

He spoke simply, as if he were talking to a child. Aazam flushed but bowed his head. "Thank you for taking the time to explain your exalted reasoning to one as low as I." Aazam bowed low and then raised his eyes to meet his commander. "I have a suggestion on how to hurt the coalition, if you are interested."

Meshedani tilted his head and said, "I am listening…"

Aazam explained the foundation of his plan which hatched on the northern journey as he sat in the open bed of the pickup with Najib's lifeless body for company. Abu al Meshedani allowed Aazam to fully expand on his plan. While they talked, an aid brought them stiff black coffee which went cold as they discussed the details. Meshedani systematically tried to find fault in the plan, but Aazam countered every argument with sound reason. After a time, Meshedani nodded and said, "You are the desert Jinn[2] the Quran speaks of. You will smite our enemies with ease. Please seek out Abdullah Ali al-Anbari, who leads up the recruitment of the Western jihadists. As you make progress, I will try to clear all obstacles from your path."

Aazam shook the man's hand, "Thank you for your support."

"Do not thank me. I might be sending you to a hell worse than the battlefield."

Aazam pressed his palms together and bowed. "As Allah wills it."

Chapter 5

Although the sign said everyone was welcome, Dalton moved cautiously as if he were trespassing in some sacred shrine where his mere presence would cause the gods to rain down their wrath. He wasn't blind. He'd seen the news reports of the attacks by Islamic extremists all over the world, and no one could forget the September 11, 2001, attack on New York City's World Trade Center; but you couldn't paint all Muslims with the same brush.

"If you believe that, then why are you so nervous?" he thought to himself.

Dalton pushed further into the lobby, his head on a swivel looking for someone he could talk to. The door closed behind him, striking a bell. The sudden noise made him freeze momentarily. The building was fairly new but the architecture design was definitely of Arab origin with the soft rose colored walls. The lobby was wide and airy, the windows tall and curved at the top allowing a lot of natural light into the building.

The website he visited last week left him with more questions than answers, so he decided to meet and speak with someone face to face. Although the pamphlet had made promises to help him deal with the pain, the website did not drill down to the core answers he hoped to find. It had taken a week before he could find the time and opportunity to make the hike to the mosque. With the remaining funerals for his father's other coworkers behind him and his mother dealing with legal matters, he was finally able to make the trip.

An older, heavier man with a full beard came out of an office that stood to one side of the entrance. He wore a very simple robe that dropped to his shoes and a small skull cap covered the top of his head.

"Good afternoon. Welcome to our mosque," said the man, his voice deep and warm. He placed his hand over his chest and bowed slightly towards Dalton. "I am Ali Arwani, the imam, or leader, of the mosque. And you?"

"Dalton Westree. I was at the hospital the other night," he said as he pulled the folded pamphlet from his pocket, "and found this in the chapel."

The imam took the paper and reached for a set of reading glasses which hung across his chest by a chain. "Oh yes," he said, looking over his glasses at Dalton. "How can we help you? Are you interested in Islam?"

Dalton looked at the floor and said, "It said you could help with the pain of losing a loved one." He took a deep breath to steel himself before he looked at the man and continued, "I just lost my father."

The man's eyes widened and he clasped his hands together. "I am truly sorry. Come. Please, come inside so we can talk."

Dalton allowed himself to be ushered inside the office. There was a woman at a desk, her head covered in the Muslim custom. The imam said something in Arabic before guiding Dalton into an inner office. The room held a large desk, but to Dalton's surprise, he was led to a corner that was covered in a beautiful rug with geometric designs. Scattered over the mat was a large number of pillows. A low table was the focal point of this sitting area. The imam took off his sandals and pointed to a position along one side of the table while he lowered himself on the other side. Dalton hesitantly removed his shoes and sat where the man pointed.

"In Islam, we speak our intentions to ourselves so that we are sure of why we do something. For example, before we pray, we cleanse ourselves and announce our intention to speak with Allah. Do you understand?"

Dalton nodded.

"So, before we discuss your issue and how we might assist you, we make that intention known to Allah and to each other." He raised his hands with his palms open and closed his eyes. "Allah, this is your servant. I am here with Dalton, who has recently lost his father and has turned to us for help. Grant us the wisdom to ease his pain." He lowered his hands to his lap and nodded to Dalton, "Tell me what has happened."

After a faulting start, Dalton did just that. He sat there calmly and explained how his father had been killed, how people seemed to be blaming his father for the accident, his mother's pain, the inner turmoil he was feeling, and the fact he couldn't even cry for his father. He emptied his heart to this stranger from a strange religion he had no knowledge of and, for the life of him, he couldn't explain why he emptied his heart out, even to himself. But just telling someone about his feelings made him feel better. It was like having a burn blister that stretched the skin so tight that it throbbed as the fluid beneath pushed for escape. Then at the prick of a needle, that pressure is released and it is at that very moment you realized just how much pain it caused.

Surprised, Dalton said, "I feel…more relaxed. How did you do that?"

The imam smiled, "I did nothing but listen. Sometimes, that is all that is required. But do not be fooled. The pain you've felt will return. It's natural, but now you know that by holding it inside, it can hurt you. Let it out. As for shedding tears for your father, when you are ready, they will come."

A small bell rang in the outer office, and the imam rose to his feet. Dalton stood as well.

"That signals Asr[3] prayer time is almost upon us. Would you care to join us?"

Dalton, feeling better than he had for days, nodded and said, "Yes, I would like that."

"Good. Let us prepare to meet the others," said the imam and they headed for the main mosque area.

Back in the lobby, the imam showed Dalton where he could store his shoes. "For us, the shoes keep dirt off us, so we remove them and cleanse ourselves so there is nothing between us and Allah." He smiled at Dalton. "It also helps when it comes to cleaning the hall."

The room opened up to a large hall that was covered in carpeting that was patterned to create multiple lined areas running horizontally across the expanse of the hall. Some kind of altar was positioned to the center of the back wall with a staircase that rose to, well, nowhere. It ended higher up the wall.

"As a guest, you can observe from back here," the imam said, gesturing to the back wall where there were a few chairs set up. "The prayers, which are in Arabic, will last about 15 minutes. Afterwards, if you have any questions, we can discuss them. I would suggest you just listen to the tone and rhythm of the prayers. Some find it very soothing."

Dalton was left sitting there. He watched as the worshipers began arriving, some giving him questioning looks while others smiled and nodded a welcome before finding a spot on the open floor.

As the imam had told him, all the praying was done in Arabic so he was unable to follow it. He closed his eyes and concentrated on the sound as he'd been directed. At first, his ears picked up clusters of individual words, but it soon became something like a chant. The sounds crossed his consciousness like waves, pushing him first one way and then the other. He let himself float in the ebb of those waves and felt as if he was expanding like a huge balloon. He felt content, even happy.

Dalton opened his eyes as the prayers ended and the men all rose and started to converse with their neighbors. He felt refreshed and relaxed. Dalton stood up as the imam made his way towards him.

"I saw that you followed my advice. How do you feel?" asked the imam, his dark eyes dancing as if he already knew the answer.

"Actually very good. Do you think I could come again?"

The man put his hand on Dalton's shoulder and said, "Our doors are always open. You may come whenever you wish. I am glad I was able to help."

"You did. I feel much better," Dalton said with a smile. "Thank you again. I think I will come back."

"In that case, let me introduce you to someone your own age who can help introduce you to Islam and answer any questions you might have." The imam walked him over to a small group of young men who were talking.

"Maajid," he called. A handsome, clean shaven man of about twenty looked up from the group and seeing the Imam walking towards him, broke from his friends. He had dark straight hair that was cut short and a lighter complexion than others in his group.

With one hand on his chest, he inclined his head, all the while studying Dalton.

"Maajid, this is Dalton," the imam said. "He is interested in learning more about us, and I was wondering if you might assist him as you are about the same age."

Maajid smiled a contagious grin and said, "I am honored, Imam." He turned to Dalton. "Would you like to join me and my friends for coffee?"

Chapter 6

Dalton scrubbed the shampoo out of his hair, the steaming water causing his skin to tingle. Excitement coursed through him as he thought about the upcoming ceremony that would welcome him into the Muslim faith. In the three months that passed since he first attended the mosque, Maajid and his friends had coached and mentored him to the point where he was ready for the next step — the shahada or Muslim profession of faith, the first of the five pillars of Islam. Dalton would be proclaiming Allah's oneness and his faith in Islam. The imam and his new friends would witness his pledge and assist him in following the Muslim lifestyle.

Dalton had been concerned about the conversion and what it might mean with regards to his family. He worried he might be turning his back on his father who had not been a follower of Islam.

"The Christian and Islamic religions are one and the same," said the imam. "Jesus was a prophet as was Muhammad, may their names bless us all. Jesus said, 'Whoever believes in me, believes not in me, but in he who sent me.' That 'he' is Allah, no matter his name." The older man smiled and continued, "Even Jesus is telling us that there is but one God, just as Muhammad has told us. They spread the same message. They are one and the same."

Dalton, not being raised in a church-going family, saw the logic of the statement, but what the imam said next settled Dalton's doubts.

"Both religions speak of the mercy and forgiveness of God. What God would separate a child from his father because of different beliefs in theology?" he said, putting his hand on Dalton's shoulder. He looked him in the eye with a kind expression. "You will be reunited with your father when the time is right. Allah is merciful."

Toweling off, Dalton wiped off the mirror and combed his blond hair off to one side. Running a hand over his chin, he sighed at the lack of facial hair. Maajid's cousin, Dilawar sported a full, lush beard. With a towel around his midriff, Dalton checked to make sure his mother didn't return home from work unexpectedly and then ducked into his own room. A guilty part of him realized he was keeping his impending initiation to Islam from his mother, but Maajid had made him promise not to tell her. It had to do with the negative feelings sweeping the world in light of the Muslim extremist attacks against the West. Still, this was something he wanted to share with his mother.

Imagine if the fellows on the hockey team found out he joined a mosque. What would be their reaction? Would they accept it or would it gain him resentment and grief? Not that it mattered lately. Since the accident, his friends were rarely in his thoughts. It was like his father's death had severed that part of his life. At school he sat alone or took walks alone. He knew he had closed himself off, but seeing those guys brought back all the times his dad helped out with the hockey practices, fundraisers, and tournament trips. Whenever they were around, it was like a huge collage of his dad. And it hurt. God did it hurt. It was easier to just stay alone.

Dalton dressed in a pair slacks and a golf shirt. Maajid advised him to dress humbly. That wasn't a problem. He was never one for dressing up. Jeans and a t-shirt was his style, and a hoodie if it was cool.

He locked the house and started the long walk to the mosque.

At least the new apartment he and his mother would be moving to were closer than the house was to the mosque. He didn't mind the exercise, but traveling over an hour five times a day was a little extreme. Of course, he wouldn't be able to attend all the prayer times, especially when his mother was around. She would definitely notice and demand answers.

Having to sell the house crushed his mother, but without a steady income, her hands were tied. The insurance company kept stalling because of the investigation and pending lawsuits. She had found a job, but it was only mornings, so she was still looking for something else.

With two months left before graduation, Dalton needed to start looking for a job as well. College could wait. He was at least going to help get things settled before thinking about school. His mother would balk at this, but she couldn't do it alone.

***

Dalton stood before the imam, his head bowed. Maajid, Dilawar, and Maajid's friends Parsa and Ubayd stood to either side as witnesses to Dalton's conversion to Islam.

"Dalton, you have observed our ways and have learned what it takes to be a Muslim," said the imam.

Dalton nodded nervously, "I have."

"And are you ready to become one of us? To hold Allah as the one true God?

"Yes."

Then recite the shahada after me: "La ilaha illallah, Muhammadur rasulullah."

Dalton, his eyes closed, repeated the words that translated to, "I testify that there is no other god but Allah, and Muhammad is God's messenger." As Dalton spoke them, he felt the familiar warmth fill him as it had the first time he was exposed to this beautiful religion. This time it was overwhelming, and tears sprung up without warning.

The old man smiled kindly at him. "You feel the power and love of Allah," he said. He put his hands on both of Dalton's shoulders. "It is done. You are one of us now. To help you follow the principles of Muhammad, please accept this Quran."

Dalton was taken aback by this gift. Holding the book reverently, he traced the intricate gold embossed filigree over the indigo blue backing. He smiled through the tears that continued to flow, not trusting his voice. The imam laughed and hugged Dalton to his chest.

"Welcome, Dalton," said Maajid, clapping him on the back. The others joined in and he laughed as he wiped at his face self-consciously.

"I, too, have a small gift for you, Dalton," Maajid said, "but you must come out to the lobby as my sister is not allowed in the men's area." Dalton followed his friend to the entrance. Maajid stopped before a group of women and motioned one of them forward.

"Dalton, this is my sister Daanya. I had asked her to make a prayer rug for you."

"Thank you," Dalton said, his voice trailing off as his eyes locked onto the two dark eyes that stared back at him. Her face was framed by a soft yellow hijab that covered her hair and neck. Her large doe-like eyes twinkled as he stammered. Her full lips pulled back in to read a smile that was stunning.

To avoid standing like a gawking fool, Dalton stepped forward and examined the rug which she held folded over her hands. The mat was fine stitched, and Dalton saw the geometric designs were blended to create a rich piece of art. He reached out and placed his hand on the fabric so his hand brushed hers in between the fold.

"It is exquisite," he said looking her straight in the face.

She didn't pull away or turn her gaze; her smile widened, causing her high cheeks to become more prominent.

"The rug or my sister," Maajid said with a sharp tone that caused Daanya to take a step back, breaking the spell.

Dalton felt himself blush and said laughing, "Both." He turned and smiled at his friend. "Honestly, thank you for the thoughtful gift, my friend. And thank you for all your help preparing me to make my shahada."

Any resentment disappeared from Maajid's expression, and he smiled back, "You are welcome, Dalton. Now, my mother has prepared a small meal to celebrate your conversion to Islam. While we walk to my home, I will explain the rules of Muslim courtship."

Chapter 7

It would take Aazam three months of travel time to reach the home of Abdullah Ali al-Anbari in Dubai. The travel arrangements were designed to disguise Aazam's importance. He crossed from Iraq to Syria to Turkey as one of the thousands of refugees fleeing the fighting. Once in Turkey, arrangements and a passport allowed him to take a roundabout journey to the United Arab Emirates.

As the taxi drove him through Dubai, Aazam was almost suffocated by the crowded towering high-rises, especially after the open battle fields of the north. He was dropped off in front of a mammoth building which overlooked the inner harbor. He inquired at the lobby's front desk and was directed to a bank of elevators.

His contact owned the entire 87th floor. The entrance was humble, but the apartment was outfitted with a cascading waterfall, tropical plants, and Japanese koi. Row upon row of rich amber liquor lined the far wall. Leather and cherrywood furniture was strategically placed around the room with an eye on style rather than practical use. Modern art, including a nude that Aazam hurriedly averted his eyes from, dominated every wall. The entire room was an assault on his beliefs. Although Aazam had seen plush living quarters when he worked under the Saddam regime, he was shocked that a member of ISIS would allow himself to languish in such a cesspool of debauchery.

"Welcome, my friend. We have been expecting you," said a voice off his left. Abdullah Ali al-Anbari stood behind a huge desk as Aazam approached and raised both arms in welcome, but Abdullah stopped short when he saw Aazam's stiffness. "What troubles you?"

Aazam gestured to the entire room. "All of this is an insult to teachings of Allah."

The large, swarthy man lowered his arms and tucked them behind his back, "Aazam, all of this is a disguise to fool our enemies. It hides our real purpose," Abdullah said.

The answer caught Aazam off guard, and he bowed head. "I am sorry. I sense the truth in your words, my friend. I will attempt to master myself."

"While you are here, you must not bring any attention to me or my holdings. Yours is only one mission, while the work I do here supports many different needs of the caliphate," Abdullah said, his voice shaking with suppressed anger.

He walked back to the large, hand-carved desk. Reaching into a top drawer, he pulled out two bundles of cash stilled bound together with the banker's paper band. He handed them to Aazam, "Here is some pocket money. Go buy some clothes that are suitable for high-fashion clubs. Here in Dubai, image is everything. I will introduce you to this strange and magical city."

Aazam was shocked to find the bills were American currency; both bundles were of five $100 bills.

Abdullah gave him a toothless grin. "I'll have my driver take you shopping. He'll know where to go."

"You do me great honor," Aazam said, feeling self-conscious. He wasn't comfortable with all this money, and he wanted nothing to do with Dubai nightlife.

"I also suggest you shave your beard and get a modern haircut. With your light skin, you could pass for an Italian or Frenchman. It may aid you in the future."

"That makes good sense. Thank you," Aazam said, suddenly frustrated that this man had so quickly made him subservient. This never happened on the battlefront.

"Good. Now let me take you on a tour."

They luxuriated in the rear compartment of a stretch limousine as the driver negotiated through the streets of the city. Dubai had grown out of the desert, built by the vast profits of the

oil industry. Other than the simmering heat, there was no evidence of that desert in the city. Some of the world's most fantastic buildings had transformed this quiet village by the sea into an architectural wonderland, with each new building attempting to outshine the last.

Aazam gawked at the endless storefronts which sold everything from lavish Muslim headdresses to precious gems. Women in the traditional garments with proper coverings mingled with others who dressed in the Western style, flaunting their sexuality. With some effort, he swallowed his disgust and kept his expression neutral.

As they traveled away from the sea, the architecture and its purpose changed first to a residential and then to a more industrial area with warehousing and service providers. Abdullah's driver pulled into the parking lot of a typical two-story warehouse, its brick and metal-clad exterior unmarked by any logo. Leaving the comfort of the air-conditioned vehicle, they were assaulted by the searing heat. The entrance was password-coded with a video camera mounted over the doorway. Upon entering the building, Aazam found the real security, was just inside the entrance. Two armed guards gripped wicked looking automatic weapons at the ready until Abdullah entered the room.

Abdullah explained, "Only those cleared can enter. Once inside, anyone who is not identified is given a one-way ride to the desert."

One of the security people was seated before a computer console that monitored a number of live video feeds. Aazam appreciated the military manner of the facility. At the next door, Abdullah pressed his face up against a retinal scanner and then laid his hand on a second scanner that compared his prints to those stored in some database. Once satisfied, the door buzzed and he pushed it open. Only then did the guards relax.

"We will have you scanned before we leave so you have access," Abdullah said, leading the way further into the building. The entire warehouse was filled with four rows of metal shipping containers with a stairwell and walkway that ran the length of the row to access a second level. What Aazam found curious was that some of the containers had a light illuminated above the doorway of the container. He raised an eyebrow at Abdullah.

"The light means that the unit is live and must not be entered. We will enter one that is not lit so you can see what we do here."

Abdullah tapped the door of the nearest unlit container. When no response came, they stepped from the warehouse and entered a bedroom. The scene shocked Aazam, and his eyes roamed around the room. Up against one wall with a picture of an American football player reaching to catch a ball in mid-air lay an untidy bed, its sheets tossed haphazardly. On the opposite wall, there was a computer desk with a modern computer. A young, thin man of Arab descent with a scraggly beard stood and bowed as they entered.

Abdullah waved his hand at the young man and said to Aazam, "This is Kalib, one of our recruits from America. Kalib is my nephew and will probably replace me as the head of recruitment due to his computer skills and his dedication to our cause. His knowledge of American society makes him an asset in recruiting more to our cause."

Aazam nodded his understanding.

"I will leave you with Kalib."

Abdullah moved towards the entrance, "My driver will pick you up in time for Asr prayer. You and I can dine together afterward. Kalib, please see that he is scanned for access to the building."

When the heavy steel door closed behind Abdullah, Kalib stood and said, "If you do not mind, I will show you the building while we discuss what it is we do here. It will give me a chance to stretch my legs."

The two left the makeshift room and began to walk along the row of containers. Waving his hand across the huge room, Kalib said, "We recruit across the world. To date, we have successfully recruited between 20-30,000 warriors for our cause."

"How does someone, especially an American, become involved with ISIS?" asked Aazam, unable to keep the suspicion from his voice.

Without taking offense, Kalib said, "I was raised in a small town outside of Los Angeles. Even though I was born there, I was an outsider. The Americans treat all non-whites with disdain. When the Islamic State was formed, I figured that this may be a place to call my own, where I would be treated with respect and have purpose."

"A wise choice."

"I am content with my decision," Kalib said, nodding. "There are many Muslims like me who feel the same, and these are the easiest to recruit as they look for greater fulfillment from their religion." He gestured to computer, "However, many of our recruits are not even Muslims when they reach out to us. It is my job to convince them to join Islam and then to encourage them to help us in our fight."

At the end of the row of containers, a huge bank of electronic machines stood by themselves, multiple lights blinking at regular intervals. From these, multiple bands of cables rose towards the ceiling and then snaked through the roof girders to the different container rows. Single cables dropped down to each unit.

"Our internet servers," Kalib said, seeing Aazam's eyes following the leads.

"And you have had success?" said Aazam. Part of him was wondering why Kalib and all the others in this facility weren't fighting for the homeland they profess they want to be part of, especially when they're so often short on soldiers.

"I can name a few. The first incident is the Canadian who slew a soldier at a war monument and then stormed the Canadian Parliament Buildings in 2014," Kalib said, counting the attacks off with his fingers. "Recently, the three attacks — one in France at an American owned compressed air and gas plant, one in Kuwait, and the other in Tunisia at the beach resort. The latest was the killing of four marines in the States. These were our recruits."

"How do you find these recruits?"

Aazam noticed the smug look as Kalib continued with confidence, "Most are on social media such as Facebook. We look for people who are discontent, angry, or alone. There are others who are looking for an adventure which, of course, we can arrange. We offer them a way to feel that they matter, that they can bring about change, or that they can belong to a loving family within Islam. When they are ready, we assist them with travel information and even money to bring them to one of our training bases in northern Syria. Once they are there, my job is complete and the training camp prepares them for the battle-ground."

Ahead of them, three young women left one of the containers. Two of them were casually tying hijabs over their hair while the third did not bother. All three were beautiful, but the heavy makeup reminded Aazam of prostitutes. He eyed Kalib, the question evident.

"Do not underestimate the sexual drive of a teenager. They make our best suicide bombers."

"Really," Aazam's tone dripped with disdain.

"We have learned over time what works and what doesn't. We originally modeled our recruitment techniques after al-Qaida. As you can see, we've turned the infidel's social media into a weapon against them. We have 120 recruiters in this facility alone and others set up in Turkey and Kuwait. Also, we have live recruiters scattered worldwide who work through different mosques."

Aazam thought for a moment. "What has Abdullah told you of my mission?"

"Just the basics."

"I am thinking of a small team of three to four, all willing to die for the cause in each of the international coalition countries[4]. They must be prepared to learn explosives."

Kalib nodded. "We have people all across the globe. I have taken the opportunity to put together a number of potential recruits for your mission."

"And do you have recruits in America?"

"Yes, I have one special recruit that should be ready," Kalib said with a smirk.

"What is so special about this one individual?

"He is white. A true-blue American. Think of the fear the Americans will face if one of their own is found to be involved in an attack on American soil. It would throw them into chaos. They would not be able to trust each other."

Aazam smiled at the thought. It was more than he could expect.

Kalib brought up a photo of a white male, a typical American teenager with a scattering of acne across his forehead and a soulful, sad look in his eyes.

Kalib read the file aloud, "Dalton Westree. Eighteen. Lost his father a few months ago to an industrial accident. The mother works two jobs to provide for them. No other family noted. Just graduated from high school. Prior to his father's death, he held exceptional grades and is looking for summer employment. Plans to attend college but has not decided on a major. He was captain of his hockey team until the death of his father, when he quit playing. Suffering from depression. He has confided to his handler that since losing his father, he feels empty and has nothing to live for but his mother. He is left alone often due to his mother's work schedule, and he spends a lot of time online.

"He came to us while trying to cope with the loss of his father. Fortunately, the recruiter is a member of the mosque he attended. He was very receptive to the teachings of Islam and performed his shahada two months ago."

Although Aazam could see the rationale of this approach, it stank of being unworthy. Here was a young man who became, a believer and this coward would use him as cannon fodder. It gave Aazam the creeps. He judged people by what they stood for and how they performed on the battlefield. Manipulation stunk of lies and cowardice, but to advance his plan and, more importantly, to place an American at the heart of the attack, he would sell his very soul.

"This recruiter. Tell me about him."

Kalib scrolled down the report. "Maajid Nasry. You might recognize the name. His father was Colonel Nasry of Saddam's palace guard," he said, looking up. Aazam shook his head.

The younger man shrugged his shoulders and continued. "Just before the second invasion by the Americans, Nasry sent his family to America for safe keeping. He was killed in the subsequent bombing. Maajid has worked for us for a few years." Kalib spun the monitor so Aazam could see a photo of an Iraqi youth — a handsome man with a winning smile. There was a photo part way down the screen that caught Aazam's attention. The photo was of Maajid. Beside him was a young woman with large dark eyes and a smile that reaches those eyes.

"Who is the girl?" There were enough similarities between the two that Aazam answered his own question, "Sister?"

Kalib nodded.

"If he hasn't introduced her yet to the American, tell him to do so."

"She is not part of us," Kalib said his eyes wide in alarm.

"She is now," Aazam growled. "I want him totally dependent on his new friends. And nothing makes a man more pliable than the desire for a woman."

"But…"

Aazam glared at the young computer technician. "Do you know how we are able to get a soldier to charge into battle without regard for danger?"

Kalib swallowed and shook his head.

"Because he knows that if he doesn't follow orders," Aazam said leaning forward. "I'll shoot him in the head."

He allowed the message to sink in. "You will issue the order."

The man nodded. Aazam could see the fear in his face, and although he didn't believe in wasting lives so frivolously, he needed to ensure that his orders were followed to the letter. He would not permit failure by a non-combatant because of fear.

"Anything else?" Kalib asked.

Aazam thought for a moment, "Will this Dalton be ready in time for the mission?"

He pushed his glasses tighter on his face. "With the progress we've seen, it shouldn't take long. Is there are any preparations required in advance of the mission that he could carry out that will allow him to prove his worth during the trial period?"

Aazam thought for a moment and then said, "Have him trained as a bus or truck driver. Either would be beneficial to us."

Both men nodded.

For Aazam, he felt he needed to wash himself to get rid of the duplicity and lies.

Chapter 8

Maajid and Dalton sat at a low outdoor table shaded by canvas awning outside Maajid's home. The closed backyard featured a beautiful cultivated garden with a small but musical water fountain. The sound of the falling water added to the peace of the garden.

Dalton tossed the dice across his side of the Backgammon board and looked at his stones. A double five was a great throw, but he refrained from showing it. This was the game match against Maajid, and it was the first time over a number of encounters that Dalton actually stood a chance of winning. He had four primes hindering Maajid's stones and had been able to move the rest of his into his own house. Trying to keep from being over confident was an effort because Dalton had seen his friend win in the past with less chance. The double fives would allow Dalton to move two of his primes forward without exposing himself to attack. As he reached to move his pieces, a garden door further down the back wall opened and a Daanya came running towards them. She stopped suddenly when she saw Dalton and, with a look of horror, tried to cover her head with her arms.

"Maajid" she cried, "I did not know you had company."

Her distress bothered Dalton. He found that he wanted to help her, to shield her, but at the same time he understood he was the one causing her anxiety. He averted his eyes to allow her some respect. Even though he had looked away, it would be a long time before he would ever forget that wave of dark brown hair. Short of breath and sweating suddenly, he hoped she didn't notice. He had gone out with girls in the past, but he never had a reaction like this.

He heard Maajid move towards Daanya and hiss a reproach at her, but Dalton could not make it out. "But Mother told me to come get you. That it was urgent. She did not tell me that you were entertaining. I had just returned from the market," Dalton heard Daanya sob, and then he heard her feet moving across the grass towards the door she had come from.

"My apologies, Dalton, and my thanks for your consideration for looking away. Daanya has embarrassed a guest and brought dishonor upon my family by her lack of modesty."

"Maajid…it's okay man, hell, it was obvious she didn't know I was here."

"Dalton, a Muslim woman must always show modesty in the presence of others, as Muhammad told us. The fact you saw her without her hijab brings dishonor upon her and our family."

"How can it bring dishonor? Is the wearing of the hijab not a statement by a woman's faith to Allah? How could it reflect on your family? And furthermore, if we believe that Allah is all knowing, does he not see her true feeling for the faith in her heart?"

Maajid gaped at him and then smiled. "Who have you been talking to, my friend? You almost sound like a scholar."

"Well," Dalton admitted, "I have questions and I use the internet to find the answers. There are a lot of sites that explain the teachings of the Quran."

"Dalton, I commend you for your desire to learn and your fortitude to search for the truth. I would suggest you avoid the internet as anyone with an opinion can voice their views, even if they are contradictory to the true teachings of the Prophet; may God's peace and blessings be upon him."

"So which is real? And how can I tell?"

"Why don't we talk to the imam tonight?" he said with a smile. "Now, you must excuse me, but I must attend to my mother for a moment. I will be right back."

As Maajid left the patio, Dalton's mind went back to Daanya. "Wow, I thought she was beautiful the last time we met," he thought, "I hope I see her again." He shook his head, surprised at the mixture of emotions he was feeling.

The garden door opened and Maajid stuck his head out, "Would you like an iced tea?"

"Yes, please," Dalton nodded.

His friend spoke to someone inside and then came out and sat down at the table. Looking at the board, he smiled to himself and said aloud, "I guess you are waiting to finish me off and win the match?"

"The game's not over just yet," Dalton said cautiously.

"Spoken like a true pessimist," laughed Maajid.

They resumed their game, and Dalton ended counting his stones off the board first, winning the game. He felt elated.

"Congratulations, my friend. You have learned well."

Dalton was about to thank his friend, but when he looked up he saw Daanya, this time with her head covered by a light blue hijab, carrying a tray with tall glasses of iced tea. Even with her hair covered she was stunning, and he was a captive to her gaze. He moved forward to assist her with the door, knocking over the Backgammon board in his haste. "Please allow me to help."

"Tha…Thank you," she stammered.

As he closed the door, she moved gracefully to the table to place the tray down. She was as tall as Dalton with a slim, yet not scrawny figure. Turning back to the patio, he saw the expression on Maajid's face and was taken back. He was looking at his sister, and there was a cruel, bemused look that was nothing Dalton had expected from his friend. It creeped him out. This was a side of his friend he'd been unaware of. The expression changed in an instant and the kind hearted, easy going expression was back. Dalton wondered if he'd imagined the look, which made him more uncomfortable.

"Maajid, can your sister join us?" Dalton asked suddenly. His request caught his friend off guard.

"Uh…if she would like to," Maajid said hesitantly, clearly annoyed. He was obviously off his game and not enjoying it.

"I am pleased see you again, Dalton," Daanya murmured, her eyes aimed at the floor.

"I am sorry I startled you earlier," said Dalton.

"My apologies for upsetting you," she said quietly. "Please forgive me if I made you uncomfortable."

"There is no reason to apologize," Dalton told her. "You had no way of knowing I was here."

Daanya gave a small smile, her eyes still on the ground. She bowed even lower, if that was possible, and said quietly, "Thank you."

Maajid finally got control of himself and explained to his sister, "Dalton has recently graduated from high school and is currently looking for work."

"Anything in particular?" she asked, passing him an iced tea.

"No, I just need to make some money to help my mom get settled. My father died a few months ago and we had to move. Things are tight so if I plan on going to college one day, I'll have to earn my way," Dalton responded with all of his attention on Daanya, almost forgetting her brother sat beside him.

"Thank you for the iced tea. Are you still in school?" Dalton was desperate to keep the conversation going no matter how stunted it was.

"You are welcome. I hope you enjoy it. My mother brought the recipe from Syria," she said with a smile and a quick glance at Dalton after seeing her brother was not watching her. "I have just completed high school and have yet to decide on a future field of study."

When those dark eyes rose to his, Dalton felt possessed. He needed to know more about this woman. "I too am undecided. There is so much to choose from."

Maajid tried to interject and gain control of the conversation; he said to Dalton, "I have told Daanya that most husbands favor an educated wife."

Dalton laughed, "I would think an intelligent woman would bring so much more to any relationship. I would be so lucky."

Daanya smiled and Maajid frowned, and Dalton worried he had pushed the topic too far. It was obvious Maajid was not happy being the third wheel. Dalton wondered if this was a cultural thing he had tripped over.

Daanya rose, collected the tray, and said in parting, "I am very happy to meet you, Dalton. May Allah bless you."

Dalton bowed as she left the table. He could feel Maajid's eyes on his every movement. He turned to his friend and said, "Hey, I don't want to start an argument buddy, but I think your sister is great. I understand you might have reservations, but I'd like to talk about it."

Maajid tilted his head and gazed at him for a minute before taking a deep breath.

"I guess the day was going to come eventually. With my father dead, I will speak with my mother, but it'll cost you big time," he said with a grin.

Laughing, Dalton said, "Yeah, like how much?"

"I don't know, but it'll be huge."

"I can live with that."

***

Their first date was a trip to the mall where, like most teenagers, they sat in the food courtyard and shared coffee and conversation. It didn't take long to get over the shyness as Daanya seemed as anxious to get to know him as he was to learn more about her. No subject was off limits; the afternoon screamed past them, and he was walking her up the sidewalk towards her home before he knew it. Dalton made extra sure he kept a safe distance from her, especially when they were in sight of her house.

"It's not that strict, you know," Daanya said, making a point of taking his hand.

"Well, I just don't want to screw it up. I had fun today and don't want Maajid or your mom to lose it if they think I'm disrespectful."

"I know the boundaries, so let me worry about them," she said swinging his hand as they walked. "And for the record, I don't want to screw it up either. I had fun, too."

He made an exaggerated gesture of wiping his brow which she rewarded him by rolling her eyes.

That had been a week ago.

Tonight, they were double dating at a carnival with Maajid and his girlfriend, Amena, a quiet girl who smiled continuously as if she found life hilarious. She was small with delicate features that were enhanced by a light blue hijab. The carnival was set up in one of the federal government's massive parking lots. After two bus transfers, they passed through the gates.

Dalton had been hesitant to ask Daanya to the big midway because of the cost. His mother had little enough to pay the rent and put food on the table, but once she dragged out the news about Dalton wanting to take a girl out, she wouldn't take no for an answer. She brought out a small metal box.

"It's a little mad money. You going out with a girl after all we've been through is exactly what mad money is all about," she said, pulling out a handful of bills. "Go have some fun."

Dalton didn't wait for an invitation; he grabbed Daanya's hand the minute they entered the fairgrounds, and they ran ahead towards the rides. Flashing lights, magnified music, and the screams made talking all but impossible. The tantalizing aroma of roasted peanuts and cotton candy surrounded them as they moved through the aisles.

"Which ride?" Dalton had yelled in her ear.

She pointed at the Ferris wheel, its arms all lit up against the night sky. Dalton pointed to the Ferris wheel, and Maajid and Amena ran to keep up as they dodged through the crowd.

Both couples were giggling and out of breath when they reached the line for the ride. The man took their tickets. Dalton and Daanya took the first chair, hands in the air as the safety bar was closed over their legs. Dalton leaned back into the high back chair and it rocked, causing a squeal from Daanya before she hugged his arm with both hands.

There was the usual stop and go as the chairs were loaded with the other passengers, each time the chair rocked back and forth to Dalton's delight.

"So why do you like the Ferris wheel? All you do is scream."

"Because Maajid cannot see me do this," she said placing her hand on Dalton's face and pulling him in for a soft, nervous kiss. The tentative start quickly became urgent, and they explored each other's lips. When it ended, Dalton gasped, weak and out of breath.

"Problem is, one of us has to remember where he is on the wheel," she laughed. "Right now he's below us but he will be above us in a minute."

"I'm glad you're keeping track. My brain went to mush from the first kiss."

She laughed and hugged his arm.

They gazed across the capital's cityscape, the White House ablaze in flood of light so it stood like a beacon for the world. Dalton felt good. For the first time that he could remember since his father's death, he felt contented. It may be too soon for love, but there was definitely something there. She made him happy and carefree. The fact that she was a great kisser wasn't lost on him either.

The next time the big wheel concealed them from her brother and she leaned in, Dalton whispered, "What's next? The love tunnel or the haunted house?

***

The four of them sat on top of a picnic table sipping on slushies as they waited for the bus to take them home. The night had been amazing. Dalton was still feeling the glow, but he also felt the pull of sleep. Daanya sat beside him, her head on his shoulder.

Maajid looked over at him and asked, "So what do you have planned this week?"

"My mom wants me to help out by painting a room or two this week. Her new boss had a bunch of paint left over from when he painted his restaurant and offered it to her for free."

"Nice. Free is always good."

"Tell me about it. Other than that, I have to drop some job applications around town. No one seems to be hiring, but I have to put my name out there."

Maajid jumped off the table and did a quick two-step before bowing to Dalton. All three chuckled at the strange moves, but before they could comment, Maajid looked Dalton straight in the face and said, "Thank me."

Dalton blinked. "For what?"

"I may have a job for you," he said and spun in a lopsided pirouette, almost falling.

"What do you mean? What job?"

Daanya sat up straighter beside Dalton, looking from her brother back to Dalton who looked at her. "Don't look at me," she said to Dalton. "This is all news to me."

"I made some calls and a friend of mine got back to me this afternoon. How would you like to drive school bus?"

"School bus? Don't you need a special license?"

Maajid smiled. "This company pays for the whole shot. The training period is unpaid, but the training would cost about a grand if you went to one of those driving schools. Two weeks of in-class training and then you're qualified for the September school runs which are in three weeks."

"Hell yes."

Chapter 9

After an evening with Abdullah's boys watching the Western thrill seekers skydiving and zip lining down from a skyscraper, Aazam was still bewildered at what he had witnessed. He could not understand why these people would freefall off a building. When he first saw the bodies falling down the sheer face of the building, his heart gave a lurch and he found himself holding his breath until the multicolor parachutes opened behind the figures, carrying them safely onto the soft grass of the park.

Abdullah suggested that in the godless Western culture, thrills and death-defying stunts replaced what was missing in people's lives. But if they were really looking at challenging fate, why not become a soldier and fight for a cause they believed in? At least then their lives would have meaning.

What shocked Aazam further was many of his fellow Muslims took part in these activities. Worse, Abdullah had told him that many drank alcohol, even though the Quran explicitly did not allow this

"You will see, Aazam; I will take you to one of the major clubs in the city. Both Muslims and non-Muslims go there to drink and meet single women who are not covered up in modesty as the Prophet, may he be blessed, has told us. This, too, will be part of your training, for you must look like you are used to that kind of behavior and do not condemn it."

"I want nothing to do with drinking and women," Aazam said, feeling the heat rise in his face.

"But you will do it regardless," said Abdullah his voice lower, commanding. "You will be traveling the globe and must fit in wherever you go. We invested too much into this mission to have it lost because you cannot make necessary sacrifices."

***

Aazam sat with Kalib in front of a computer looking over the profiles of some potential recruits. Kalib had organized them by nationality and then by which part of the country they lived in.

"This one fought for us for over a year, but then returned to England because his mother was diagnosed with cancer. He went back to take care of her as a good son should. He has experience with explosives. The file says he was excellent at stealth and knife attacks," Kalib explained.

Aazam nodded and said, "One more and the British team will be complete."

There were two men and one woman to consider. All three were second generation Muslims born after their parents had immigrated to England. One of the men was accosted by his white colleges and held down while a naked white girl poured alcohol down his throat while fondling him to the point of ejaculation. They then posted this on the internet as the latest conversion from the Muslim threat. This act of sacrilege screamed for revenge. The other man was treated well in school, but even though he was at the top of the class, he soon discovered that those who were less successful in their studies were able to pick up the top jobs while he was still unemployed. The unfairness of the situation ate away at him until he had nowhere to turn. Both were easy pickings for the extremist recruiters in London. Of the two men, Aazam thought both were good candidates, but the revenge motive from the sexual assault seemed to be more of an incentive than the loss of work.

The third candidate, the woman, felt her parents were not committed enough to their faith. She taught English to new immigrants and was quietly becoming a major recruiter in her own right. After much debate, it was decided that the woman was performing a specialized task. She proved vital to the continued stream of recruits ISIS required until they stabilized their borders.

"Let's wait until I have a chance to meet them. I will make the decisions after that."

Kalib nodded. "I feel good about this team."

A sudden tone from the computer interrupted the planning session. Kalib switched screens with a series of mouse clicks. He was silent for a couple of minutes as he read the message.

Looking up he said, "This you'll find interesting. The message is from Maajid in America. He says that progress has been extremely good and he is looking for confirmation for the next stage in Dalton's training." Kalib briefed Aazam on the process that had been used in the past to pull recruits tighter into the group and ensure they are willing to back up the cause.

"I like it. Simple, yet effective," Aazam said, nodding. "Give him our blessings."

Chapter 10

Abdullah led Aazam into the nightclub with a familiarity that made it clear he was a regular customer. Before the doors were opened by two muscular bouncers, Aazam could hear the heavy bass of the techno music within. As they entered, the beat assaulted his senses. Abdullah seemed unaffected as he moved deeper into the darkened room which was lit up only by the erratic strobe lights that pulsed with the music.

Pushing through the crowd, Abdullah guided them to a large booth covered in red leatherette. Lights cut through heavy smoke that drifted off the dance floor creating an otherworldly atmosphere that the party reveled through. Across the room, a disk jockey hovered over a sound system while a scantily dressed woman gyrated to the thumping beat beside him.

Aazam could not understand how these people could stand this noise. It was almost as loud as the battlefield. A woman who showed more skin and less clothing approached the table and bent forward at the waist. Aazam felt his face redden as he tried to avert his gaze from all that flesh.

Abdullah spoke, and the woman left with a smile, leaving a cloud of perfume.

"You must relax, Aazam," yelled Abdullah across the table. "If you tense up every time a woman walks by, you will stand out like a camel on a sand dune."

Aazam nodded and took a deep breath. For the memory of his friend, Najib, to whom Aazam had dedicated the success of his mission, he must succeed. When the woman came back with a couple of drinks balanced on a tray, he forced himself to show no emotions, and he even nodded to the girl as she put a glass before him.

"You are learning, but you need to assume your role," said Abdullah.

Aazam's mind raced back to the last beautiful and haunting memory of his young wife, Shasmeen. Since her death, he had been with only a few other woman. Each time left him feeling wretched. He would not be free until he avenged her.

Abdullah said, "You have not gotten over the loss of your wife, have you?"

Aazam shook his head, staring at nothing,

"Our cause demands us to make significant sacrifices, Aazam. However, you can still enjoy the sensations of the body while keeping your heart closed."

"Are you saying that Americans have clubs like this one, where sex is for sale?" Aazam asked.

"There are a lot of Westerners here tonight, and they act like it's what's they're used to."

In an attempt to get through this disgusting task, Aazam took the glass off the table and gazed into the amber liquid as if it might bite. It did. The raw alcohol burnt as it slid down his throat, and his eyes begin to tear up. He gasped, which caused a coughing fit. As the coughing subsided, he saw the napkin being offered by Abdullah and wiped the tears from his face.

"Scotch….and you sip it," Abdullah said with a gentle smile.

Once he cleared his throat, Aazam said, "Why would anyone drink this vile thing? It's terrible."

"It's an acquired taste."

Aazam nodded and took a small sip, grimacing at the taste. "I cannot drink this. Maybe something that doesn't taste like camel piss."

Abdullah ordered a variety of drinks, and before long, the table was covered with glasses of different shapes and colors. Even though Aazam only tried one sip of a number of different drinks, it did not take long before he felt the euphoric sensation the alcohol induced. He had to grab onto the table when he rose to find a washroom. For a soldier who was used to being in total control, this went against all his ingrained beliefs.

When he found his way back to the booth, he was surprised to find three half naked women sprawled across the booth, one with her hand pumping deep in Abdullah's robe.

Abdullah opened his eyes and winked, "We must fit in."

Aazam looked across at the other booths and was shocked to see similar provocative activities, some more public than others.

"I have taken the liberty of engaging these two beauties to assist you with your training."

"Abdullah…"

"Actually, I must insist. There has been a significant development, and our schedule will have to be advanced. You must be ready for any eventualities."

"What has happened?"

Abdullah looked at the women and then back at Aazam. "We will speak more tomorrow. For tonight, you must train."

One of the women snuggled close to Aazam. She handed him a drink and clinked her glass with his. The liquor no longer burned as he swallowed. Her partner molded herself to his other side and gave him a pout until he passed her a drink. In appreciation, she kissed him hard on the mouth, her tongue driving his lips apart. He could taste the alcohol on her, and his head spun. A hand traced small circles across his chest dipping over his stomach. Another hand started at his knee, moving towards his crotch. Both hands met at their intended target, and he groaned. He closed his eyes as the hands kneaded and stroked him, making him hard. He felt the pull on his belt causing the alcoholic revolving haze to clear for a moment, and he saw the laughing face of his wife.

The vision was like a splash of cold water clearing his mind. In sudden revulsion, he pushed away the hands, spilling a drink in his effort, to an indignant cry. He staggered to his feet, all the while the hands attempted to pull him back down with cooing whispers.

He had to get out of this place.

It all went against everything he believed, everything he stood for. He didn't need this to carry out his mission. He had never failed before.

He tripped on the steps as he exited the booth. Abdullah's voice was calling him back, casual at first, but them more urgent. Finally, commanding.

Ignoring the fool, Aazam made his way across the room, bouncing from one body to the next, some giving, others pushing until he fell free of the crowd and saw the front doors. He felt the sweat break out of his body as his stomach revolted. Sour bile filled his mouth making him gag, and he veered violently towards the washrooms before the entrance. Cold porcelain of the toilet pressed against his forehead as his stomach rid itself of the slow, burning poison. The sounds of his own retching caused only more retching until he dry heaved painfully.

Hours or maybe minutes passed. Large hands lifted him as easily as a child. Cold water brought him back for a moment as it splashed his face. He was pulled up, and as his head came up he saw the unsmiling features of Abdullah's bodyguard and chauffer.

Then he remembered no more.

Chapter 11

As they left the mosque, Maajid clapped Dalton on the shoulder, "Will you join us for coffee, my friend?"

"Yeah, that would be great."

With the evening prayers completed, Dalton was excited with the invitation to join a group of his fellow worshipers for a social outing. For the first time, he would be able to treat them. He had been driving school bus for a couple months now. It was the usual suspects going for coffee — Maajid, his cousin Dilawar, Parsa and Ubayd. As the group walked through the light drizzle, they discussed the massive wave of migrants flooding the European countries as they tried to escape the horrors of Syria and Iraq.

"There seems to be little talk of aid for these people," Dilawar stated. "They only seem to worry about how to stop the flood."

"You must admit no one country can deal with this issue," Dalton countered. "It's too large and too expensive." He watched the shadows grow as they entered an unfamiliar area of the city. Refuse and garbage piled the corners as if the city workers had been on strike. Many of the street lights didn't work.

"Absolutely. That is why I said the world, all the free countries, must help these people and deal with the chaos in the Middle East," Dilawar said.

Parsa said, "Don't worry, the Americans will bring their military into play. It is currently only a bombing mission, but they are just waiting for an excuse to insert more influence in the area to stop the Russian influence." A look of disgust came across the young man's face, "But you'll never see them helping the victims".

"Russia entering the mess on al-Assad's[5] side is going to escalate rather than ease the tension" Maajid predicted as he led them through this area.

Dalton saw Maajid was looking this way and that as if on guard while the others were involved with their conversation. The streets were dark and almost too quiet. Dalton scanned the building and was surprised all the windows were shuttered against the night.

Dalton listened to his friends, but he was more concerned about the area they walked through. He was interested in their views and he reminded himself now that he called himself a Muslim to start paying more attention to how his own country dealt with other Muslims because this would also affect him.

Just ahead of them, two shadows detached themselves from the alley on the right. The two men were Hispanic and wore the black bandanas that identified them as part of the Mara Salvatrucha 13 (MS-13) street gang. The group of friends slowed. Dalton was at the rear of the group and looked back the way they had come; he saw two more individuals were following behind them.

"Well, well, well. What do we have here?" said one of the men, his arms wide as he looked over the group. "Looks like a bunch of sand niggers and their pet white boy out for a stroll."

The group looked at each other blankly.

"What?" said the leader in a tone of mock astonishment. "You telling me you don't know what your Muslim pork eater friends did in Paris a couple of hours ago? Cowardly bastards killed a pile of rock fans, and I'm guessing you assholes are plotting the same."

"We don't know anything about such an attack," Maajid told his accuser, his hands held apart, palms up. "We are not plotting anything."

"Yeah right! All you fuckin' ragheads have it in for America. They should round all of you up and ship you home."

At a sign from the leader, the four men closed in on the group. Seemingly out of thin air, a baseball bat and a knife materialized. A short, heavily tattooed thug advanced with the knife held low.

"Holy fuck!" thought Dalton.

He watched as his friends put their backs to each other to face their attackers. The man with the bat took a swing at head level, but Dilawar avoided the blow by ducking and countered with a kick to the man's ribs. The brute clutched at his midsection as the bat clattered away into the shadows.

Maajid pulled off his jacket and wound it around his right arm. He watched the thug and his knife. He avoided two quick swipes of the knife, keeping his lightly shielded arm ahead for some protection.

The other two gang members tried to separate the group by grabbing at their jackets and trying to drag them out of the circle so they could attack them individually. Each helped the other fend off the advances.

The tattooed thug pulled the knife across Maajid's arm; its sharp blade cut through the jacket he used as a shield. Maajid let out a hiss of pain. Seeing blood, Dalton threw himself at the thug with an angry cry and slammed his fist into the hateful face. The blow caught his opponent off guard, and Dalton wrenched the knife out of the thug's hand and sent it clanging across the pavement. He followed through with another uppercut to the man's jaw. The man's head slammed into the pavement with a sickening crunch and he lay still.

Seeing one of their members knocked out of action drained some of the bravado out of the assailants. They were waiting for openings now, lashing out at their victims who turned in a tight circle leaving no opening.

"Not so fucking tough now are you?" Parsa chirped.

Ubayd threw a kick toward the leader. The man grabbed his leg and pulled him out of the protective circle. Ubayd's opponent pummeled his head and body with his fists, knocking any defiance from him while his friends countered any attempt of Dalton's group to rescue Ubayd. As Ubayd slumped to the ground motionless, his assailant spotted the bat and stepped away from Ubayd to retrieve his weapon.

In desperation, Dalton looked around for some kind of weapon. He saw the knife on the roadway and lunged towards it. One of the men grabbed at him, but Dalton forced his way forward, ramming his shoulder into the man's chest, spinning him towards the curb. Dalton grabbed the knife and retreated to the safety of the circle.

Ubayd lay unconscious on the street. The leader gripped the bat, striding menacingly towards his inert body. The man stood above Ubayd and raised the bat over his head.

"No!" Dalton screamed and he lunged forward.

The point of the knife disappeared into the leader's chest just as the bat began its descent. The man froze, the bat high above him. He looked down at the knife that was buried to the hilt with a confused expression before he toppled backwards, sliding off the blade which Dalton held with a death grip.

"Oh God!" thought Dalton as he stood in shock, his hands covered in blood as the body crumpled over Ubayd.

Both groups froze.

Maajid shouted to his comrades to be ready for another attack and shoved them in an attempt to wake them from their stupor. The other thug bolted, but at a sharp command from Maajid, Parsa and Dilawar grabbed the man and held him for further orders.

Dalton watched in stunned silence as Maajid slowly and gently pulled the knife out of his hand and guided him to the curb, making Dalton sit before he collapsed. Maajid crouched in front of Dalton, looking him in the eye.

"You saved Ubayd. You are a real warrior."

"But I…I killed him."

"You had no choice. It was either him or Ubayd. You saved your brother. You are a true Muslim."

Dalton looked down at his bloody hands.

"We need to get this mess cleaned up before someone else sees us here, but you need to leave right now." Maajid gestured to Dilawar, "You and Dalton have to help Ubayd get back to the mosque. Parsa and I will ensure there is no evidence left here that can be linked to us."

"What about these guys?" Dalton asked.

"I'm going to point out they will also be in deep trouble if they speak to the police. After all, they attacked us. Now hurry before someone else comes along."

Dilawar and Dalton helped Ubayd to his feet but had to guide him as he was still dazed.

Maajid waited for the trio to make their way around the street corner before turning his attention to the pair of men sitting on the pavement being guarded by Parsa, the baseball bat held ready. The third assaulter lay still on the road.

"Let me offer my congratulations, gentlemen," Maajid said. "That was a very exciting and believable display until your incompetent leader took it too far."

Both thugs remained silent, waiting to see where this was going to lead. Maajid was happy to see the fear in their expressions. He might be able to salvage the situation, but he would have to be cautious. The MS-13 had a long history of insane violence.

"But there is a positive side to this as well," he stated as he crouched low to meet their eyes. "There is more money to share between three than four if you can keep your mouths shut. What do you say?"

"Sounds good to me," answered one of the men.

"It won't take long for the police to identify your friend, and I'm sure they will find you are one of his associates if they don't know already. There will be some real pressure to find out what he might be involved in. How are you going to deal with that pressure?"Maajid asked, his eyebrows raised.

"I've been home with my wife, chilling. Don't worry, she'll vouch for me. It won't be the first time,"

"Excellent. And 'Sleeping Beauty' over there?"

"Can't speak for him. He was brought in last minute because one of our regulars got tagged. Carlos vouched for him. Miguel here is solid."

"So you don't know or care what happens to him?"

"Not at all. He's all yours.

"Contact info."

The thug recited a cell number which Maajid added to his own phone. "Once the police have finished with their investigation, call me and I will get you your money. If I give it to you now and the police find it, it will add to the pressure."

"I get that," the thug nodded. "Nice to work with a professional." He and Miguel stood and shook Maajid's hand and walked back into the gloom.

Maajid nodded to Parsa, who made sure the unconscious assaulter never woke up.

Maajid nodded to himself. Dalton would soon be ready.

Chapter 12

Even inside the penthouse, Aazam hid behind sunglasses. It was all he could do to pay attention to the briefing. His head pounded so persistently that he felt certain it would crack like an egg, and he was as dry as the desert sand. His mentor didn't look any more attentive than he did. Abdullah waved to Kalib to begin.

"Unfortunately for you, my friends, you have missed some outstanding news from our operatives in Paris," stated Kalib with a huge grin. "While you were in 'training' last night...."

"Be careful nephew," Abdullah scolded. "Do not presume to judge your superiors!"

From the look of disdain on the younger man's face, Aazam saw that Kalib didn't agree with his uncle's whoring and drinking ways either. Aazam guessed that the training was a veiled excuse to avoid following the teaching of the Quran. He felt sick and resented the older man for involving him in this behavior.

With his eyes on the floor, Kalib said, "My apologies. I spoke without thought."

"Do not forget yourself again," his uncle told him. "Get on with it."

"Our operatives in Paris struck a number of targets last night."

"Finally," Abdullah said with a grin. "What do we know? What's the tally?"

"Some of our people are still active, according to police. Some are dead from suicide attacks or police retaliation. The information on the news networks is saying that over 100 infidels are dead. France is in a state of chaos."

"Allah be praised," Abdullah sighed. He clapped Aazam on the back, almost knocking the younger man's sunglasses off his head.

"It is a victory," nodded Aazam, "however, it will make my mission that much more difficult. The Western governments will be more vigilant."

"That may be so, but Allah will see us through," said Abdullah.

Kalib nodded, "Aazam makes a valid point. We will have to plan around such obstacles."

Aazam gritted his teeth. Allah may influence the outcome, but he leaves the planning to man.

Abdullah walked over and opened the door to ensure that there was no one close to hear what he was prepared to tell Aazam and Kalib. He also turned on a radio, raising the volume to ensure that their conversation would not be overheard.

Abdullah said to Aazam, "I have heard from Abu al Meshedani and the central command, and they wish to see part of your plan advance the forward momentum."

"But the plan called for the attacks to happen all at the same time," interjected Aazam, throwing his hands up

"Aazam, you are a soldier. We must trust that the leadership knows what they are doing."

Aazam nodded, but he kept his real thoughts about the leadership to himself. Abdullah was not Najib. Aazam only trusted those who fought beside him.

"What do they propose?" asked Aazam.

Aazam could see that Abdullah was happy with the response. He would not be surprised if he was being tested right now.

"They want you to focus on Russia."

"Not America?" said Aazam, and he saw his own surprise reflected on Kalib's face.

"No," Abdullah explained, "The leadership feels that with the tensions rising between Turkey and Russia over the Russian jet being shot down, an attack inside Russia could create an escalation that could see Russia concentrate its efforts away from our forces and towards the Turks. Of course, evidence would need to be left behind that points to Turkey as the author of the attack."

Aazam realized it made sense; in fact, it was brilliant. He said, "The assault on Russia is scheduled for the spring of next year. It is imperative to the plan that the leadership agree with the date. Will they approve that date?"

"Yes," Abdullah confirmed, "But this is the only target that they have approved."

Aazam kept his facial features frozen so that none of his frustration or disgust showed. The entire plan was being cut up. The whole idea was to send a clear message to the coalition countries. He was a soldier and a strategist. The leadership was made up of politicians and clerics. What did they know? But he knew that if he showed an unwillingness to follow the dictates of the caliphate, it would be the end of him.

Chapter 13

Dalton sat on the floor in a spare room of Maajid's home, his back up against the wood paneling. Every time Dalton closed his eyes, he saw the astonished look of the man he killed and could almost feel the hot blood on his hands. The numbness and shock of killing a living being was wearing off, replaced by an emptiness that threatened to overwhelm his entire being.

"If the police find out it was me, then my life is over. And my mother, what would this do to her?"

"There is no way that they can find you out," Maajid assured him. "I explained to those other idiots who attacked us that it would be a case of self-defense. They would be in much more trouble if it came to light."

"But...what about the first guy I hit? Whatever happened to him?"

Maajid said in a quiet voice, "He never woke up. The other two killed him to create an illusion for the authorities. The bodies were arranged to look like the two fought each other."

"And they just killed their friend? What kind of people were they?"

"The worst kind," assured Maajid. "They will not be missed. You should not be troubled."

"But, I still *killed* a man," Dalton said, dropping his face into his hands.

Maajid waved his hand as dismissal. "You killed an enemy of Islam and protected your brothers. Your actions saved Ubayd from certain death. Had you hesitated, that animal would have caved in his head. You are a hero, not a killer."

"I don't feel like a hero."

"Well the others believe otherwise. I am proud to call you a friend."

A warm feeling spread through Dalton, briefly pushing some of the crushing guilt away. He replayed the fight over from the perspective of saving Ubayd, and Dalton knew his friend would more than likely be dead or severely injured if he hadn't acted when he did. The knowledge did not take away the guilt, but it did help so he might live with himself.

But why would they attack in the first place? It wasn't as if the gang members were patriotic citizens ready to rally to the flag. There had been such hatred in the leader's words and expression, especially when he made to kill Ubayd. How could anyone want to kill a complete stranger like that? He had heard the gang was vicious, but he had no idea just how murderous they could be. The fact that his friends backed him and covered for him also meant a lot. The fight and the aftermath proved that. *I'm not alone.*

***

Dalton's mother, Gail, arrived home after the late shift to find Dalton absent. He was always home when she finished work. She checked her cell phone for messages again, but there had been none. She reminded herself that he was 18 and might have spent a night at a friend's house, or even with a girl. The change was still startling. His listlessness changed back into the loving, happy son she remembered. She had attributed it to the bus driver's course, but now she wasn't so sure. A girl made sense. But she had to give him room, or she might push him away for good. She made a conscious decision not to call or text him tonight.

She picked up the leftover dishes that Dalton had left on the coffee table, making a note to remind him to pick up after himself. As she wiped the table, her eyes fell on the picture of the three of them taken only months before the accident. The faces in the photo showed real happiness. They never wanted for anything. Oh, the fun that they shared — the hockey games and tournaments in the winter and fishing trips in the summer. Of course, they had more time together back then when she didn't have to work around the clock.

"My God, we did have a lot of fun," Gail reminisced. As the rush of emotions overwhelmed her, she collapsed on the couch and cried into her hands.

The sudden show of emotions indicated just how exhausted she really was. She needed to sleep for a week. Burning the candle at both ends wasn't helping, but she saw little relief in sight until Dalton has finished college and on his own.

"On his own…"

For the first time, this idea impacted her. What did she have to look forward to when he was on his own, maybe starting a family or working and living somewhere else? What would become of her when he was gone?

"I'll be even more alone than I am now," the thought staggered her. "What will happen, when Dalton's gone?"

Exhausted as she was, sleep played no role in her night.

Chapter 14

Dalton maneuvered his 72-passenger bus through the loading route to a prestigious private school that catered to the richer kids. No matter how many times he did this, guiding the large vehicle in and around hi-end vehicles and limousines made him nervous. One mistake and Dalton was sure that he would lose his job.

He had to be at the bus yard by 6:00 A.M. to perform his daily inspection and then travel to his first pickup, 30 miles away, by 7:15 A.M. He always arrived early so that he could place his prayer mat in between the seats facing Mecca and greeting Allah prior to his run. Those few minutes were so much like the first time he allowed the sound of the prayers to move him along like flotsam on a rolling wave. It centered him and gave him purpose. Dalton found that he enjoyed the early morning with the growing light of the new day. There was a hush that was very peaceful. Of course, that ended with the first pick up.

The mornings were tame compared to the afternoon run. In the morning, the sleepy eyed children walked onto the bus like a nation of zombies with their headphones clamped tight to their heads. There were always those who chatted about sporting events or general gossip, the volume rising slowly but steadily as they grew more awake. After the high school run, he made his way through city neighborhoods picking up elementary and middle school children. The giggling and laughing made up Dalton's world.

In the afternoon, the kids were wound up after being cooped up all day. The noise level was off the charts, and Dalton would have to use the speaker, "Okay Jasmine, I know you can sing like Beyoncé, but tone it down. I can't even hear the radio."

"What!" yelled Jasmine, a 16-year-old dressed like a 20 something.

"Greg, quit picking on Tyler. And give him back his glasses. Yes, I'm talking to you! Do it now or I'm writing you up. Hey! Linda and Robert, no making out on my bus."

At first the hardest difficulty was remembering the students' names, but the honeymoon was quickly over as the kids observed the new driver to see what was beyond the limits.

After dropping the last student off, the silence was deafening. Dalton left near-exhausted because of the constant concentration. The great thing about the job was that it did not conflict with any of his prayer times.

As he shut down and locked the bus, he felt the vibration of his cell phone against his chest pocket.

"Hello," he answered.

"Dalton, my friend, how are you?"

Recognizing Maajid's resonating voice, he smiled. "Good. And you?"

"Very good. Are you coming to the mosque this evening?"

"Yes. I had planned to be there."

"Very good. We plan to go for coffee afterwards, and you are welcome to join us."

Dalton hesitated remembering what happened the last time they had tried to go for coffee. Almost as if Maajid was able to read his thoughts, his friend assured him, "What happened that night is not the normal evening out with friends."

"Of course," said Dalton. "It still weighs heavily at times."

"I would be surprised if you felt otherwise, but there have been no repercussions. The news media reported it as a drug deal gone wrong. "

"That is a relief," Dalton acknowledged.

"I told you, we always have your back."

When Dalton returned home the following night, he was unsure of how he would explain his absence to his mother. She had said nothing, though, almost as if she hadn't noticed him gone. He figured her exhaustion was the reason. Seeing her so tired, her skin so pale and bags under her eyes, made him feel guilty about getting involved in something that could hurt her. Then again, he reminded himself, he had not gone looking for trouble.

"So you'll come," Maajid said jolting him out of his thoughts.

"Yes, I'll be happy to join you."

***

Dalton spent the late morning and early afternoon cooking a spaghetti sauce for supper, filling the whole apartment with the rich smells of garlic and spices. He would leave a pot of water on the stove, a package of pasta, and a note on the table for his mother. While the sauce simmered under the low heat, he had time to wash the floor and clean the bathroom. She had refused to accept any of his pay to help out, insisting that he save it for college. He still used some money to purchase food they normally couldn't afford and had surprised her a time or two with small things, like fresh flowers or her favorite chocolates. For a while she lost that ragged, spent look. He wanted so badly to introduce her to Islam so that she could feel the same peace that he found, however, Maajid and the others warned that he stood a good chance of losing his mother due to the growing hatred of Muslims.

"She's not like that," Dalton argued.

"No, but others are. Our women cover themselves. Would she consider doing so if she converted? How would others treat her if she did? Trust me, Dalton, families split around this question. If you love your mother, and I know you do, spare her the grief of losing you to Islam. As long she doesn't know, you can continue to function as a family."

As much as Dalton wanted to share his love for Islam, he could not put it to the test. There was too much to lose.

Chapter 15

Aazam sat waiting impatiently. The planned attack on Moscow was as ready as it was going to be, and the only detail left was for Aazam to travel to Russia. Abdullah had signaled the caliphate for final approval, but the leadership wished to be briefed in person. The leaders entered the country by various routes in twos and threes so that their enemies could not track their movements or catch them all together.

The meeting was on the outskirts of the commercial district in a warehouse pushed up tight to the sand dunes. It was impossible for anyone to come close to the building, but it also made escape impossible. If Aazam had been in charge of security, there would have been a mass of resources waiting to protect the leaders.

When Aazam and Kalib arrived, they were directed to drive into a rear loading door and ushered to a specific parking spot. Six guards, hard-eyed killers, met them and searched each individual. There were at minimum four automatic weapons trained on Aazam and Kalib until they were proved unarmed. After the pat down, they were led through a metal detector followed by an upright x-ray machine. Nothing was left to chance. No weapons or recording device could survive this scrutiny. Aazam raised an eyebrow at Kalib, who sat beside him, to show his respect. He had never seen better security personnel, not even with Saddam. Aazam thought perhaps his worries were misplaced.

Abdullah met the two men on the other side of the gauntlet of security. "You have ensured our success," he announced, embracing each man. "Your hard work will make the caliphate shine. If you are successful, you can ask for anything."

"What do you mean 'if'?" Aazam said.

The air went out of Abdullah.

"Well, of course I meant 'when'..."

"Nice to know you have so much faith in us, my friend," Aazam said with contempt.

They moved deeper into the metal building, hardly feeling the movement of air even though multiple ceiling fans tried in vain to dissipate the heat. The warehouse was a vast, empty room with a bank of offices at one end. Cement k-rails divided the room, designed to stop any vehicle from entering the meeting area. A large table had been set up against one wall with a large smart board displaying a map of the Middle East. Aazam noticed that every 20 feet there were speakers faced outward with a hissing sound resounding from them. He knew these were to defeat any listening devices.

The assembled ISIS leaders stood together in groups or in pairs exchanging pleasantries and having refreshments prior to the meeting. As Aazam moved towards group of men, Abu al Meshedani made his way from his place near the table to reach out and welcome Aazam. The two men embraced, kissing both cheeks.

"You have come far, my warrior," Abu said with a nod of his head. "Your plan shows that our faith in you is well placed. You have done well."

"Thank you, Your Eminence. I am anxious to bring you a great victory."

"I am aware that you are a fighter, but you must indulge us. We look at the larger picture and have to make sure that your attack does not interfere with other plans that are in play." Abu motioned them both to a seat nearby. "Come, my friends we have much to discuss."

As the people assembled around the table, an imam came forward and gave blessings to Allah for a successful resolution to the meeting. Once done, the meeting came to order by Abu clapping his hands together.

"My friends, Allah has guided Aazam ibn Abd al-Muttalib to our cause," said Abu. "He has devised a plan to punish those who would stand against us. Although at this time, due to circumstances, we are allowing only part of his plan to move forward, we hope that he will continue with the plan in the future." Abu looked around the table, eyeing each member before continuing. "Aazam's plan is nothing less than a message to the United States and their lackeys that their influence in our affairs will not be tolerated. However, before we move on the West, we will test this plan in Moscow."

There were a few gasps which surprised Aazam. He figured that all these leaders had made the decision together.

"Yes, my brothers. We will bring the Russian bear to its knees. For all the grief they have caused us, we will take the war to them. They will pay dearly for the attacks on our state. Once Assad has been propped up, it is expected that they will turn more of their attention towards us." Abu raised and wiggled his index finger like a parent scolding a child and said, "We will not give them the chance. There is much hostility between Russia and Turkey at the moment over the downed Russian fighter. We will exploit the growing tensions between Russia and Turkey while taking the opportunity to crush this foe. All eyes will look towards Turkey rather than us for this attack. We do this so there is no indication of our future plans."

A number of shouts celebrating Allah and his blessings echoed through the room. Aazam let out the breath that he had been unaware he was holding. He looked over to Kalib and saw that the young man was smiling broadly as well.

Abu raised his hand and made a motion for Aazam to come forward. The lights dimmed, and a world map was projected onto the smartboard. The men around the table shuffled their chairs to get a better view the map.

"Brothers, I have asked Aazam to walk us all through the plan he has put together. Even though you are all aware of the need for secrecy, I must remind you that unlike the Americans, if the Russians even think that we are responsible for this coming attack, their response may well be nuclear."

Chapter 16

From his vantage point on the fourth floor, corner unit of Moscow's Four Season Hotel, Aazam could see most of Red Square with its legions of military regiments marching in formation. The annual Victory Day parade commemorating the defeat of Nazi Germany 71 years ago was in full swing. The famous square was a sea of color: the brilliant white of the Russian Navy, the dark green of the Infantry and the navy blue of the Air Force. An array of hues and textures reflected specialty branches and other Armed Forces.

Although his view of the viewing platform was partially hidden behind the State Historical Museum, thanks to the Russian media and the big screen television mounted on his hotel wall, he had a front row seat. His attention flickered back and forth for the complete picture.

Aazam was happy to see that most of the Russian leadership as well as several military marshals and foreign dignitaries were in attendance. The viewing stands which backed against the Kremlin walls were packed with representatives of the United States, Great Britain, China, and others that had fought the Germans and their Japanese allies. Veterans of that war sat proudly to either side of the podium. Putin had just arrived standing up in a convertible executive sedan. He saluted the veterans of the motherland before taking his seat and nodding to the parade master to begin the celebration. On the far side of the square, opposite the viewing stand, a military band of at least 200 faced the viewing platform and started the proceeding with the national anthem.

Putin rose and spoke, his voice echoing off the giant square, "Once again, we come together to remember the sacrifices made by the thousands of men and women from around the world who fought against the evil that was Nazi Germany. In this 71st year, we stand vigilant to similar evils which prey on the Motherland."

Aazam felt his blood rise as the speech continued. He knew better. Russian persecution of 20 million Russian Muslims was well documented. From Afghanistan to Chechnya, the Russians used any excuse to crush the perceived Muslim threat. Finding recruits for this attack had been incredibly easy. Two were veterans of the American invasion of Afghanistan who had been encouraged to leave Russia rather than face trumped up charges by the authorities. The third member of the team was a 16-year-old from the southern district of Dagestan who watched his brother beaten to death by Russian security officers as he left a mosque. All three jumped at the chance to launch a crippling blow to the super giant. The four had worked days together in a rented warehouse on the outskirts of Moscow. The preparations were designed by an explosive expert in Syria, and Aazam made sure that all steps were meticulously followed. They would only have this one opportunity.

Aazam was awed by the military might passing across his field of vision. For 20 minutes he watched regiment after regiment march by the viewing stand. Over 60,000 soldiers marched through the square followed by hundreds of tanks, personnel carriers, and missile launchers.

Unable to contain his excitement, Aazam left the hotel room after ensuring he had what he needed to escape the country. He pushed through the crowd along the street, a solid mass of humanity pressed up against the city buildings to allow the military ensemble to reach Red Square. It was slow going, but he positioned himself near one of the entrances to the subway that allowed a partial view of the viewing platform. To blend in, he held a small Russian flag and waved it as the different helicopter squadrons flew overhead. Mig-29 fighter jets flying low and slow over the crowd were cheered across the sky. All heads were raised to capture the beauty of these fantastic war machines. A trio of Tupolev Tu-95 bombers, better known as the Bear, flew in low to give the crowd a good idea of just how large these aircraft were. Each one had a wingspan that almost reached the width of Red Square.

The final fly over was a group of six Sukhoi Su-25 close support aircraft spewing red, white, and blue smoke — the colors of the Russian flag. It was also the signal for his men. His earpiece squelched twice as the team leader hit the transmit button to signal the start of their bomb run.

From his vantage point, Aazam saw the three tour buses draped with large Russian flags pull away from the curb as the last of the military traffic flowed towards the entrance of Red Square. Two police officers stepped into the roadway and raised their arms to signal the buses were not authorized. The lead bus sped up and struck the officer, his broken body falling under the wheels of the bus, while the other one dove to his right, away from the vehicle. As the surviving officer came to his feet, he pulled his radio only to be hit by the second bus. All three buses made for the square disappearing behind the Museum, out of Aazam's view.

At the view platform, Aazam could see the gathering standing, hands on chest as the Russian national anthem was played yet again. Distance made the music unrecognizable, especially after the deep roar of the aircraft and the cheering of the crowd. Aazam reached into his pocket, fingered the remote detonator, and switched it on.

As planned, his team leader signaled him when the vehicles were in position: "Allahu Akbar" echoed in his ear piece. He pressed hard on the remote button.

It took a second for the electronic signal to reach the intended targets. The explosions hurtled into the main viewing platform from three different directions like tsunamis engulfing the human lives that stood in their path. The musical band members were the first to die, if only by a microsecond.

The blast was designed to follow the route of the least resistance and was guided by the welded plates to force the blast forward rather than upward. But although most of the force was directed, the steel could not contain all of the kinetic energy from the massive explosive and it boiled outward in all directions. The blast beheaded the multi-colored, onion-shaped domes of St. Basil's Cathedral, leaving the remainder of the building in flames at the far end of the square. Aazam watched in fascinated horror as another shockwave flowed towards his position tearing flags, shattering windows, and showering glass in advance of the force. He dropped to his knees as the racing invisible hand struck the crowd, tossing bodies like leaves before a hurricane.

The wind was driven from his lungs as he was buried beneath bodies that fell like dominos. His skin began to pucker and itch and he felt a searing heat singe the air, forcing himself to resist the urge to breath, as super-heated air screamed overhead. Breathing would have burned out his lungs.

As quickly as it had come, the high-temperature blasted further down the avenue and was replaced by a different source of heat. Underneath the pile of bodies, Aazam could smell the gut-wrenching familiar smell of roasted skin and hair. In panic, he started the upward climb, pushing at unresisting limbs and the dead weight of the corpses around him. Pulling himself up from pile of splayed bodies, Aazam looked around at a world transformed. Bodies stretched in all directions around him like a field of wheat that had been crushed by driving sheets of rain except some of this crop was burning. Smoke and small fires lifted off individual bodies across the street. The pile of bodies shifted, rising and falling as those still living struggled to stand, looking like corpses rising from the grave.

Across Red Square, not one of the nine onion-shaped domes was visible; the entire building was covered by smoke and flame. Only the corners of the Kremlin wall which had imposed as an ancient fortress still stood; the center which stood in the main direction of the blast was no more, nor was the viewing platform. From his position, nothing was left. Closer, the museum was half its size with flames emerging from the broken building that had been denuded by the force of the blast. Smoke was spreading low to ground with no breeze to sweep it away.

Aazam had not even realized his hearing was impaired until snippets of cries and groans pierced the fog of his brain. It was like a hum of bees hovering over the street as more and more people began to return to their senses.

I have to move.

He moved towards the entrance to the Moscow Metro, climbing over the quacking pile of bodies. By the time he reached the stairs, he was out of breath and slick with sweat. He allowed himself to drop over the stairwell wall to the steps below to avoid climbing over more bodies.

Descending into the subterranean Metro, the gore and devastation of Red Square was replaced by the beauty of Moscow's hidden gem. The sudden change was surreal, and Aazam caught himself gawking at art deco, crystal chandeliers, and gilded mosaics.

It wasn't until the train he had boarded was howling through the tunnels did the significance of the attack hit home. He had wiped out the leadership of Russia. He had killed the Bear!

Chapter 17

Waiting in the long line to be processed by airport security, Aazam kept his head in a best seller he had picked up for this purpose. Looking at his reflection in one of the glass window of the terminal, he realized that Abdullah had been right about his light skin. By shaving when he had, it had given him the time to naturally tan the rest of his face so there was no pale skin where his beard once stood. He turned the pages every few minutes to make it seem like he was engrossed. In less than 30 minutes he was through metal detectors and x-ray devices having only his travel bag. Twenty minutes later, they were airborne and he was able to relax. He gambled that it would take some time for the security to be increased, especially when most of the hierarchy was dead.

For three days, Aazam meandered through the ancient city of Rome in awe. The art and architecture that had survived through the ages was stunning. After the stress of the last mission, it was a welcome reprieve, and he sat on the balcony every night after Isha prayer to enjoy the city lights.

He checked in with Kalib through a cellular phone equipped with heavy encryption. Within seconds, he found himself in a three way conversation with Abdullah and Kalib talking over each other in their excitement. Abdullah was beside himself with the success of the mission, calling Aazam the "sword of Allah."

"When should we expect you back?" Abdullah asked.

Aazam explained, "I want to visit the other target countries and meet with the brothers we have chosen to talk about logistics.

"We need to lead these attacks from a command post, not on the ground. We can't risk having you picked up by Interpol or by one of the other intelligence agencies," said Abdullah.

"The soldiers we have chosen will be doing the attack, like in Russia," Aazam explained. "I am going there for a planning session and to get a look and feel for the targets so I am better able to guide and support the individual teams." He paused to allow that to sink in. "My documentation is iron clad. The papers that were used to enter and leave Russia have been destroyed, and the new identity is completely clean. "

In the end, Abdullah finally agreed knowing the Aazam had proven himself in Moscow.

Aazam asked, "Kalib, is there a way for me to get the information that we pulled together on the teams? I need phone numbers, addresses, where they work, and other facts we have on them and the targets. I don't like to chance sending this through the phone, just in case."

"I should be able to put something together and ship it to a location for you to pick up. What is your first destination?"

"Germany."

"Okay, I'll contact you with the details," Kalib said.

The following morning, after checking out of his hotel, Aazam stopped at a travel office and purchased a Eurail global pass that would allow him to travel practically anywhere in Europe. He also was able to pick up a book on traveling in Europe. At a computer store, he purchased a high-end laptop, case, and cordless mouse.

Rome was such a magnet for tourism that it attracted people the world over. He was tempted to lose himself in this beautiful city. Relaxed and at peace with himself for the first time in years, he would have if not for his promise to Najib. Aazam was tired of war. The more he saw of the leadership and their hypocrisy, the more disillusioned he became. He sat quietly in his rail coach watching the stars, thinking that Shasmeen would have loved a trip like this. God, how he missed her.

***

By lunch the following day, Aazam entered the apartment and surveyed the rustic space. It boasted a window seat overlooking the Oktoberfest grounds that were empty of tents and crowds at this time of year. Although aged, the room had obviously been remodeled and boasted all the modern conveniences like Wi-Fi.

Aazam took a quick shower and changed his clothes before calling Kalib.

"What do you have for me?" Aazam asked.

"The package was sent out by an air courier yesterday and should be in place by 10 o'clock this evening."

"The package is in a storage locker at the Metro station that you arrived at. You can pick up the key for the locker from a friend of our people who runs a newspaper stand just outside the station. Ask for last month's issue of 'Time Out Dubai' magazine. The key will be taped to the inside cover."

"You're going to make me into a regular spy, Kalib," Aazam said.

Chapter 18

The door opened to Dalton's knock. Daanya's eyes widened as she recognized him, and he was tempted to reach out and kiss her. Of course, neither her mother, nor Maajid would appreciate the open display of affection.

"Dalton, I didn't know you were coming over," Daanya said, her hand going to her face as if he had caught her before she had a chance to clean the sleep from her eyes.

"I figured you would have known about the trip," Dalton said, confused for a moment.

"Trip? What are you talking about?"

The look of surprise seemed to morph into one of concern which Dalton found unsettling. He was about to answer when Maajid came up behind his sister.

"Dalton. All set for the trip?" he said throwing the door open wider.

"Yeah, got everything packed," Dalton said, dipping his shoulder to indicate the rucksack on his back. "I have to admit, I'm excited. I haven't gone camping since before my dad's accident. He and my mother use to take me on tons of trips."

"Maajid," Daanya said, her eyes narrowed, "why haven't you mentioned this trip? You're stealing my boyfriend away and you haven't even told me."

"I don't know what you're going on about," Maajid said with a shrug. "We've been talking about this for weeks. Now that school is finished and Dalton has time off work, we've decided to take a trip to West Virginia. Even Mother knows about it."

Daanya glared at her brother which Dalton found strange. Usually, they got along. This was the first time he had ever seen any friction between the siblings. It was only natural, he assumed, but he hoped it didn't affect his relationship with either.

Throughout the better part of the year, Dalton and Daanya had gotten closer. He now had spending money that allowed him to take her out on dates. They spent time with each other during the walks to and from the mosque for prayers. She explained and guided him through the new principles of Muslim life, and together they grew comfortable with each other.

His friendship with Maajid and the others grew stronger as well. They talked late in the night about every topic under the sun, debating any issue but always returning to politics and the issues that affected Muslims worldwide. Some of those discussions would get heated, especially when Parsa's temper got the best of him. Only Maajid's stern voice could calm the young man, although he would sulk for the remainder of the evening.

"Say your goodbyes, but make it quick," Maajid told his sister. "We still have to pick up the others." He stepped back to allow them a little privacy, but was close enough to ensure Dalton and his sister practiced some discretion.

Dalton pulled her into a hug, feeling her tenseness. "Hey, is it that big of a deal? We'll only be gone a few nights. I thought for sure that Maajid had told you."

She lifted her hand and cupped his cheek, her hand so warm and comforting. "I'm not upset with you, my love."

Love? It was the first time she used the word, and it felt so natural. Dalton looked into those large, brown eyes and felt such happiness that he felt himself ready to burst. He kissed her, not caring if Maajid saw or not. She cut it short and hugged him hard, her mouth close to his ear.

"Listen to me," she whispered urgently, catching him off guard as her fingers pressed firmly into back. "Be careful. Maajid and his friends are not who you think they are."

Before he could question her, she kissed him hard on the mouth, almost desperately. He was shocked at the intensity of her words and her kiss, not understanding what was happening.

She cut it off just as quick and turned away from him abruptly, saying, "Have a good time and promise to call me."

She started walking away and stopped at the doorway of the living room. "Brother, a word. Now!" she snarled, and marched down the hallway.

Dalton could only watch her retreating back, totally confused. Maajid came out of the room, looked at Dalton, and shrugged before following his sister deeper into the house.

***

As Maajid entered the kitchen, Daanya swung with all her might. As fast as she was, Maajid was quicker, grabbing her wrist and twisting it outward. She cried with pain as he glared at her with murder in his eyes.

"You would dare, Sister?"

"I'll do more," she spat, trying to rake his eyes with the nails of her other hand.

He grabbed her other arm and twisted her in a parody of a dance so that her back was to him, her arms crossed. He pulled her closer, her arms held tight to her heaving chest, and put his mouth to her ear.

"Don't tell me you've fallen for this weak-willed American?"

"Unlike you, I am not bent with hatred for your sick political agenda. Father was a soldier who happened to be on the wrong side of the battle. He died, and although I wish he lived, he knew that Saddam was a dictator and still he stood by him rather than escape with us."

"I am only glad that he is dead, because it would hurt him to hear his own daughter degrade what he stood for," Maajid said with such hatred that Daanya shuddered.

She pulled at his embrace trying to free herself, but he held her still. Tears of frustration blurred her visions.

"If you were going to use him, why did you ever introduce us?" she said, still struggling.

"I was just sweetening the pot, dear Sister." He lifted her clear off her feet and shuffled across the linoleum towards the basement door. "It was the least you could do for the cause."

She swung her feet, banging his shins, causing him to curse. In a rush, he pushed towards the door.

Her mother, all dressed in black as befitting a widow, came in the room and stared at her two children.

"Momma, help me. He wants to hurt Dalton," Daanya yelled.

The older lady looked at her son and then slapped Daanya hard in the face. "How dare you argue with your brother? He rules this house."

The blow knocked the fight out of her, shocked that her own mother would take the side of this craziness, regardless of the family dynamics. Her cheek stung and she groaned.

Maajid used the moment to push her down the stairs into the dark basement.

She tumbled, crashing against the railing, coming down hard on her shoulder. She heard herself cry out from a sharp blow to her cheek before she rolled again, landing on her back on the cement floor. Her head hit the solid concrete, and she knew no more.

Chapter 19

Picking up the key for the storage container posed no problems. When Aazam asked for the specific magazine, the vendor did not even look up to accept the money in exchange. As Aazam walked away, his fingers could feel the hard piece of the key under the magazine's layers.

Retrieving the package from the container also proved uneventful. The entrance to the small hallway off the depot which held the bank of lockers was not covered by any security camera. After an hour of watching the area, Aazam could not detect any type of surveillance. When he finally approached the lockers, he was in and out in under a minute. Another hour of walking the streets proved that he was not followed.

Back in his room, Aazam connected with Kalib in Dubai via Wi-Fi. Kalib began configuring the computer so that it would be completely safe from being intercepted or traced. He would also set up the information that Aazam required while in Europe. Because it would take some time, Aazam decided to get something to eat.

He left the apartment and walked through the streets until he came to a Lebanese restaurant, its neon sign flashing Sababa. After a very satisfying halāl[6] meal of lamb tagine with fennel, he headed back to the apartment only to find that he was being followed. As he turned to look for traffic before crossing the street, the sound of footsteps sliding to a quick halt behind him alerted him. His heart rate jumped, but he controlled his reaction. He would let out a little more line before landing his prize.

Aazam began a slow turn away from his apartment so that it wasn't apparent to the follower where he was headed. No sense leading them to his base of operations if they had just picked him up. After 10 minutes of walking, he stepped into a dark alleyway. Once around the corner and out of sight, he jumped into one of three dumpsters that hugged the alley's wall. The cloying smells of rotten food nearly overwhelmed him as he crouched low and became part of the refuse. He heard the quick steps of his pursuer at the entrance of the alley. Tentative steps sounded as the individual moved down the laneway expecting Aazam to jump out from behind the dumpsters. When that didn't happen, the tail ran to the end of the alley hoping to catch sight of him again.

Using that moment, Aazam quietly climbed out of the dumpster and lowered himself on the side away from his pursuer. He crouched low to watch the man at the other end of the alley. When the man moved down the street, Aazam followed silently. At the corner, he eased himself slowly forward. He caught a glimpse of the man standing at the next corner. He was looking up both sides of the road, searching for some sign of his quarry. When the man glanced back the way he had come, Aazam ducked quickly.

After a second, Aazam chanced a look and was able to get a partial look at the man's face under the light of the street lamp. The sight signaled a memory. He allowed the memory to surface on its own. A soda can danced across the street, being kicked by the man in his frustration at losing track of Aazam. Hands thrust into the pockets of his jacket, he stamped off in a different direction. Staying just out of sight, Aazam kept up with his stalker on a straight course that led back to the restaurant.

From the shadows of an entrance way, directly across the street from the eatery, he watched the man exchange his jacket for an apron and disappear into the rear of the business.

That brief encounter in the full light of the room allowed Aazam to see the man plainly, and he remembered Zain Hadid's insane laughter as he rushed an Iraqi security detail, his rifle leading the charge. Aazam and another were on their knees, their hands tied with plastic ties behind their backs. Zain had been able to get close undetected because the soldiers were busy tormenting their captives. Not one of the soldiers had survived the attack. Aazam owed his life to the German Muslim. He would have Kalib could find out more about the man and why he was here.

Even though he was relatively confident that his apartment was safe, he took no chances and spent the rest of the night finding and securing another.

***

"Zain Hadid," Kalib announced, "served for two years and fought in the battles for Ramadi and Mosul. When word reached us that his father had died, he requested a leave to take care of his mother. It was granted after Abu Bakr al-Baghdadi created ISIS."

They were speaking through a secure, encrypted Skype account. Aazam preferred this to the phone. He liked to read his friend's body language which sometimes said more than his words.

"Anything since?"

"He's done a few favors and run some low level errands for us, but that's it. He works as a busboy and dishwasher at the Sababa restaurant. We've managed to infiltrate government health information and found that his mother is living with him, recuperating from a stroke. I'm guessing he recognized you. For what reason other than because he served with you, only he could tell."

"Okay, we'll leave it at that for now. Is the laptop safe to use now?" Aazam asked.

Kalib nodded, "Yes. There is no way anyone will be able to track you through the internet. I have set it up so that your IP address is bounced continuously and kept hidden. As for the contact files, I have downloaded them, but you may want to hold off approaching your contacts."

"Why?

"We're not sure," Kalib admitted, a worried look on his face that surprised Aazam. Kalib was usually so confident.

"One of our people, Abu Hamed, defected to the West with some of our files. These have been made public through the European media."

"And?"

"Yes, well, some of those contacts were on that file," said Kalib. "We're not sure if they're in hiding or if they have been picked up, but we've been unable to contact two of your contacts in Germany. As we agreed, we gave them no advance notice that you would be meeting them."

Aazam close his eyes, trying to contain his rage. "And the third?"

"He was not on the list and is unknown to either of the other two. He is young and has been recently recruited by our people here at the center."

"So, he is another homegrown recruit?" Aazam watched for any sign that his friend was holding back information from him.

"Yes. Not known to anyone but his recruiters," said Kalib.

Aazam sighed, "But this operation needs more people if we are to have the effect that was planned."

"There is a way, but there is an element of risk," Kalib said. "You know that Salah Abdeslam, who organized the Paris attack, was captured in Brussels? The cowardly bastard was supposed to use the suicide vest. Instead, he fled and was captured and is cooperating with officials," Kalib said, his anger evident.

"Brussels announced after the follow up attacks in Europe that they know of our specialized troops trained to attack European and Russian targets. The problem is that Salah and his people made up one of the cells and trained with the others. He can't know all 400 soldiers, but he knew quite a few. We do not know who he has betrayed."

Aazam understood. "We don't know who has been compromised."

"Right."

Aazam thought for a moment and said, "Organize a meet with your homegrown candidate for tomorrow afternoon. We'll see if he has any friends that he can trust," Aazam finally said as a plan formed in his mind.

"Any friend he has will not be vetted —"

"I understand, but this will be a two prong attack," Aazam replied. "I want you organize a meeting for me.

Chapter 20

The first part of the trip was consumed by the same back and forth political debate that Dalton had become used to with his friends. The discussion was lively with laughter and friendly banter until Parsa once again lost his temper, this time over the plight of the Syrian refugees who were fleeing the violence of their homeland. The oppressing atmosphere that followed Maajid's bitter censure of Parsa's anger made a quiet ride for the remainder of the trip. The quiet gave Dalton time to reflect on Daanya's hurried warning.

What could she have been implying when she said that they were not who he thought they were? How could they be anything else? He had been friends with Maajid the longest, and it had been over a year since they met. Maajid had done nothing but help Dalton starting with his conversion and then getting the bus job. Hell, he even introduced Dalton to Daanya. No matter which way Dalton turned the question, he could not understand what it might be nor why she would bring it up. The fact that she was upset about the trip was obvious, but nothing he knew about her would indicate that kind of spite. He would just have to wait until he saw her again.

The countryside was all rolling hills covered with hardwoods for as far as the eye could see. As they crested one hill, they saw numerous more waiting for them. Farms were scattered across the landscape, some in the low, wide valleys while others had been hacked out of the flat topped mountains. Some of these homesteads had been here since before the American Revolution. The beauty was not lost on Dalton as the van crept deeper into the Blue Mountains.

At the hamlet of Dryfork, named after the convergence of Red Creek and the Dry Fork Cheat River, they left the Appalachian Highway and took a side road until they came to an old gate with an "NRA" sign on one side and a larger sign that said "You Can't Fix Stupid, But You Can Vote Them Out" on the other. The wooden gate was built with rough lumber and balanced on a rock. It was hinged on a bent metal spike and a ring hammered into a fence post. Dalton looked at the others with a furrowed brow.

"You'll get to know Adham and his political views very quickly. He is quite the character," Maajid assured Dalton.

Ubayd jumped out of the car, opened the gate to allow them onto the property, and then closed the gate behind them. The car followed the road through the dense forest which opened to a large field where both sheep and cattle grazed. The road followed the base of the mountain until the valley ended in a box canyon where a grouping of buildings straddled both sides of the road. As the van came to a stop, all the doors opened and the group disembarked with moans and groans as stiff muscles protested the two hour ride from Washington, D.C.

The homestead looked like it had been built a hundred years ago. The sun felt wonderful, warming Dalton's shoulders even as the breeze tousled his sandy hair. He thought it was peaceful.

The feeling was ripped to pieces as automatic rifle fire tore through the air around the group while a piercing scream descended from above. A few of the others dove for the possible safety of the vehicle, but Dalton and Ubayd stood frozen in place, at the mercy of the invisible hornets that buzzed overhead. As the screaming whistle reached its crescendo, there was a massive explosion over their heads that threatened to loosen bowels and shatter clenched jaws. The noise alone shocked the two to the ground as if a huge hand had slapped at them with no thought. Dalton felt the gravel grind into his cheek as he hit the rough roadway, bullets ripping the air apart over his head. He tried to make himself as small a target as possible by curling into a ball, and he would have burrowed under the dirt if he could.

It took a moment to realize that the silence had returned to the canyon, his tortured ears humming from the blast. Dalton looked around the valley with its swaying grass and trees and, seeing nothing, looked back at his friends. Ubayd had a scared, bewildered look that might have mirrored Dalton's own. The others were lying under, in, or around the shelter of the van. Maajid was the first to stir as he lifted himself from a prone position beside the vehicle to sit with his back to the door, knees bent up to his chest. He shook his head as if to clear it from the onslaught of noise. Dalton was surprised to see his friend chuckling to himself.

Maajid's laughter echoed back from across the valley, and Dalton looked up to see a massive black man step through the trees and approach the group whose members were still struggling to their feet.

"You're all dead."

Chapter 21

"Aren't you afraid of drawing every police officer in the state with all that noise?" Ubayd asked the massive, muscle bound black man that Maajid had introduced as Adham.

Adham smiled and said, "I have a weapons range here on the farm. They know about me and that my permits are always up to date. I've never caused them any issues, so they leave me alone."

Over a plate of southern fried chicken and garlic potatoes, Adham said. "Before I found Allah, I was Dandre Brackstorm and I was on my second tour of Iraq with the 13th Marine Expeditionary Unit in 2007. We were involved with an operation called Operation Phantom Thunder clearing Shiite militiamen, al-Qaida soldiers, and Sunni extremists out of Baghdad's northern and southern flanks. It was a big operation. There had been a huge surge of American troops sent in to gain stability, and we were working with Iraqi forces to boot."

He ripped some flesh from a chicken leg before continuing. "To make a long story short, everything was going according to plan when we came upon some contractors that had a group of women and children contained in a school and were interrogating one of the women."

"What do you mean by 'contractors'?" asked Dalton, clearly confused.

"Military contractors. Man, you are young," Adham said as if seeing Dalton for the first time. "The U.S. was hiring mercenaries. They hid under the term 'contractors.' They were untouchable. Didn't answer to anyone in the military chain of command. They caused all kinds of trouble that we had to clean up," Adham said.

Adham shoveled a pile of potatoes into his mouth, and after washing them down with a pull on a bottle of water, continued. "It got real tense until we were ordered to move and forget we ever saw these guys. We had just started to march away when a shot rang out. I doubled back and saw that the head contractor had shot a kid point blank, like it didn't matter." Adham's eyes were glazed, and Dalton could see that the big black man was there, in Iraq, watching the event play out. "I lost it then and there. I wasted three of them assholes before my own guys were able to pull me down. Then it was a Mexican standoff because the other contractors wanted payback. My boys were not going to allow that."

Dalton watched as Adham came back to reality, "After that, I was arrested, but I wasn't put in the stockade. They locked me up in Gitmo[7] with all the Iraqi prisoners. After six months, the administration wanted everything to go away. I had to accept a dishonorable discharge."

"But what about the child that was murdered?" Dalton blurted.

"Swept away."

There was a long silence among the group as each person tried to understand the implications of what they had just heard.

Adham broke the silence, "In that prison, I learned about Allah and saw what they were fighting for. I made a lot of friends in that hellhole. I changed my name and performed my shahada with my fellow prisoners as witnesses. After my release, I used my combat pay to buy this land, and I have never left."

"What do you do for money?" Ubayd asked.

"I write for magazines as a freelancer under my old name and run this gun range for different groups. It pays the bills and allows me to live in peace."

Maajid, sitting at the end of the table asked, "What do you have planned for us tomorrow, my friend?"

"Basic weapons training, and in the afternoon we get to play on the range."

Dalton looked around the group to see if he was the only one who thought this was strange. The others had big smiles and anxious expressions, as if they couldn't wait.

***

Dalton moved slowly through the bunkhouse so that he would not disturb his sleeping friends. So used to getting up before dawn to check his bus, he was unable to sleep. He got dressed, pulled his prayer blanket out of his bag, and made his way outside.

The sky was showing light over the edge of the mountain, and the stars were fading quickly as he made his way to the clearing. From the main house, he saw Adham leave the porch; Dalton made his way to him.

"Good morning, my young friend," Adham welcomed him. "You slept well?"

"Yes, thank you."

Seeing his prayer blanket, the giant asked, "May I join you in greeting Allah?"

"Please."

Adham pulled the water bucket from the well, and both men washed themselves before beginning. Dalton spread out his prayer rug. His partner obviously planned on using the natural green grass. Together they began, "Allahu Akbar." They followed two prescribed rak'a and together said the Tashahhud, or testimony of faith. Finally, they both greeted the other, "Peace be upon you and God's blessings."

"Thank you, Dalton, for the opportunity to share Fajr[8] with you."

"I, too, enjoy it. I do not have the opportunity at home," he said suddenly wondering how his mother's night had been.

"While the others start moving, would you help me with breakfast? I need a couple cups of coffee before I can do anything."

"I'd be happy to help."

***

Dalton aimed the rifle downrange and remembered to squeeze the trigger. The rifle kicked back into his shoulder, and he was rewarded by seeing the jug of water explode. Even with the ear protectors on, he could hear his friends cheering the shot. He aimed at the next jug and repeated the shot, watching water flash up and out of the vessel.

"Take your time on the next target because it is smaller and farther away," Adham coached him.

The next two targets were juice cans at 100 feet. Dalton closed one eye and concentrated on aligning the target with the iron sights. Taking a steady breath, he allowed half of it out while squeezing the trigger. The first can jumped off the dirt and fell back among the underbrush; the crack of the rifle bounced off the sides of the mountains. He aimed at the second can and squeezed off another round, but the can sat there stubbornly, mocking him.

"Clear your firearm," Adham said.

Dalton released the clip and opened the action, locking into place for inspection as he had been taught. "Clear."

"Clear," Adham repeated after checking the chamber.

Dalton rose and placed the empty rifle on the table and looked at his teacher.

"Good shooting," said Adham.

"Except for the last one. I didn't even see where it hit," replied Dalton.

The big man smiled and said, "Let's go see."

Together, they walked up to the targets. Both jugs were partially empty of water now, but the point of impact was dead center. "That's good shooting," said Adham.

Dalton felt a sense of pride that grew even greater as they approached the second can. The bullet hole was again, dead center. "Why didn't it move?"

"The bullet went clean through without hitting any imperfections or dents. You're a fast learner, my friend," Adham said, clapping Dalton on the shoulder.

"Think you're ready for an automatic weapon?"

"Do you mean a machine gun?" Dalton asked.

"Hollywood and salesmen call them machine guns. The pros call them automatic weapons," Adham explained. "Tomorrow, I'll introduce you."

Chapter 22

Aazam watched the young teen shuffle nervously from foot to foot under the corner street lamp. The kid was of average height, his slim body wrapped in a blue windbreaker. *Every cop in the world would have his eyes glued to kid.*

While this kid may be as dedicated to the cause as the killer he had met this afternoon, the soldier behaved with calm professionalism. He was quiet and relaxed on the outside, but his eyes were constantly roaming, taking in all activity around him, analyzing, assessing and looking for opportunities and escape avenues. Aazam recognized the same characteristics. He had seen many times on the battlefield. Like a desert lion, the seemingly relaxed state could explode into violent force that could kill without thought or hesitation.

The soldier had taken the thumb drive and he left after it was clear that he and his team were to work off the grid.

Watching Kalib's home-grown candidate, Aazam knew he would have to take the time and walk the kid through the material. The candidate might have met the criteria and jumped through all of Kalib's tests to prove his worth, but it was obvious he had no training. Aazam wondered if he was wasting both the boy's life and his time.

Aazam saw a movement in the alleyway behind the boy. He crouched deeper into the shadow of the building he was up against as the specter eased out to watch the young recruit. After a moment, the figure pulled out a cell phone and made a call.

This is a trap, Aazam realized.

Aazam left the cover of the shadows and walked unhurriedly away from his contact. Turning around the corner of the building, Aazam glanced back but saw no other movement. Crossing the street, he ducked behind the next building where a row of electric motor scooters stood chained to a bike stand. He chose a dark color Vespa. For an extra 10 Euros, he was able to don a dark helmet that covered his face.

Driving in a large loop, Aazam was able to enter and follow the street where his contact waited, and Aazam was just in time to witness the take-down from two blocks away. There was a sudden squeal of brakes, and then a door opened and the man in the shadows rose and shoved the recruit into the back; he followed the kid as the vehicle pulled away from the curb.

Using the traffic to avoid detection, he kept the vehicle, a Mercedes cargo van, in view. The streets were filled with similar bikes like the one Aazam drove. It made the perfect cover. Whenever possible, he would take parallel streets to further avoid being seen in case there was a second vehicle watching for a tail. The vehicle continued south, and Aazam had to fall further back as the traffic thinned out.

The van finally turned off into an industrial area and pulled up beside a small building that sat next to a massive, triple stacked, cogeneration plant. Aazam continued past the facility and out of sight of the complex. Coasting to a stop, he shut the bike off so there was no headlight or brake light showing. He pushed the bike behind a couple of overflowing dumpsters and picked his way towards the property.

His main worry was the kid would break quickly and divulge he was meeting an operative for ISIS. That in itself would send up red flags to both law or intelligence forces. It would definitely put the plan at risk. Aazam knew he stood no chance of infiltrating the building, alone and unarmed.

He need help. There was no way of knowing if the group he met this afternoon had been compromised. He reviewed all the facts he studied about Germany before leaving Dubai. Pulling out his phone, he spoke quickly to Kalib.

"It might be coincidence, or someone might have some inside information," Aazam warned.

"I'll do a sweep of our computer system to see if anyone has infiltrated us."

"Might want to check internally as well."

"Do you mean....?"

"Do you really want to leave it to chance?" Aazam asked.

When there was no reply, Aazam told Kalib what he needed. Now, all Aazam could do was wait what felt like hours but was in reality only 45 minutes. He had used the time to find the lone sentry watching from the plant's roof. The fool had tried to hide his cigarette, but the red glow of his inhalations revealed himself to the patient watcher. Aazam counted three cigarettes in the time it took for his backup to arrive. The guard would alternately check the exterior roadway and then return to observe the courtyard.

A small dark Saab drove past and parked around the corner. Within a few minutes, a lone male stood at the garbage bins, a large duffle bag on the ground beside him. Aazam circled around so he came up to the individual from behind. Assured he was alone, Aazam reached out locking his arm around the man's throat.

"Who are you and what do you want here?" Aazam asked in a hush, tense voice.

"Aazam?" blurted the man. The man tried to move until the arm squeezed harder in his throat and then froze.

"Answer the questions," Aazam said harshly.

"Hadid, Zain Hadid," he replied hesitantly. "Kalib told me my old friend Aazam needed help."

Aazam released his hold of the man and told him to turn around.

"It is you," Hadid said. "You scared the hell out of me. I had thought I had seen you the other night, at the restaurant…"

"Enough," Aazam scolded him. "Were you able to bring any weapons?"

"Yes," Hadid said, kicking the duffle bag at his feet.

"Excellent. Are you with us, or have you gone soft?"

"I was planning on returning to Iraq as soon as my mother passed, which should be any day now," Hadid said his eyes lowered. "It is a son's duty, as Muhammad, peace be upon him taught us."

"Good, now listen…"

Chapter 23

Aazam led Hadid to the spot he used earlier, keeping low and to the shadows. Hadid had an impressive cache. The weapons were silenced Heckler & Koch VP9 9mm pistols fitted with Trijicon night sights. They also had a pair of black bladed fighting knives. Hadid also brought a couple of assault rifles and shotguns in the bag, but Aazam didn't want to attract attention. Without a quick, decisive attack, the boy was as good as dead anyways.

Dark clouds drifted across the sky as the wind picked up. The wind would make everyone's movements more obscure. Aazam pointed the sentry out to Hadid, and Aazam signaled he would take care of the sentry himself. Leaving the shelter of the deep shadows, Aazam followed the chain linked fence and crawled under it where a dip in the ground left an opening. He lay in the depression until the guard moved away from the roof edge towards the exterior of the complex. He knew he had three to four minutes before the sentry returned.

Rising to a crouch, Aazam moved quickly across the edge of the parking lot, staying in the shadows of the huge, four story plant. He avoided the light coming from the other building where the kidnappers had disappeared. The building had two service doors and a single man door with no windows showing from the front. As Aazam moved, he was able to see a glow of light escaping from a side window. It might allow him a view of the interior or even an access point.

First the sentry.

Aazam glanced back at the way he had come and was satisfied that the guard could not to see him or Hadid. Pressed against the building, Aazam moved to the rear where he had spied an exterior roof access ladder. He waited for Hadid's signal.

A stone fell into the center of the yard and skipped towards Aazam's position. He heard the soft sound, but he knew the sentry above would not, having moved further away from the ledge. Aazam climbed the ladder two rungs at a time as soon as he saw two quick flashes from a flashlight. He covered 40 feet in less than 20 seconds. His heart racing, Aazam slid over the roof's parapet. Solar panels blocked his view of the guard, but Aazam knew from his surveillance the path that the guard would take. Cautiously, Aazam made his way across the roof, thanking Allah the roof was covered with silent vinyl. He crouched near the last row of solar panels, knife at the ready.

Aazam heard the slow step of the guard as he came closer and tensed, ready to spring forward. Before Aazam could attack, the steps stopped. For a moment, he thought he had been seen; he was relieved when he saw a flare of light followed by the acrid smell of the man's cigarette.

Poor disipline.

None of Aazam's soldiers would ever tempt fate by smoking while on guard duty. If the enemy didn't get them, Aazam would.

After lighting the smoke, the man moved again. In one fluid movement, Aazam pulled the man's chin upwards and jabbed the knife into the base of the man's skull. The blade entered between the third and fourth vertebrae, severed the spinal cord, and the guard collapsed into Aazam's arms like a puppet with his strings cut. Aazam eased the body to the ground, and then he severed the man's throat before he could scream out.

Aazam returned to the ground and met Hadid. Hadid signaled there was no other door or window in the rear. That left the two service doors and the main door in the front and the side office window. Aazam crab walked through the shadows to the window on the side of the smaller building, and with his body pressed against the wall he eased himself forward to peek into the room. He saw the room was an empty office.

Aazam found that window locked, but it took only a few minutes to flip the latch with his knife. He pointed and then splayed his fingers. Hadid nodded and snuck towards the front door.

Moving with exaggerated slowness, Aazam opened the window as far as it would go and reached down inside the room, his hands feeling around in the darkness before finding a garbage can directly beneath the window. He pulled it outside and laid it aside. No sense taking a chance of knocking it over and making a noise. Pushing his wide shoulders through the window, he allowed himself to lie across the window sill. He placed his hands on the floor and slowly wormed his way into the room. As his feet cleared the frame, he eased each foot down, feeling the burn to his stomach muscles as they took the strain.

Aazam crept to the office door and turned the knob, easing it open enough to peek into the room. A wide shouldered brute, his face hidden by the shadows of the room, stood over the recruit and methodically worked the kid's face with leather covered gloves. The recruit's face was a mess of blood and bruising. From the front of the building, another person asked a question in German which prompted the grunt with the fists to stop his assault and check the victim. He lifted the kid's head by the hair and moved it back and forth. Getting no response, he reached over and grabbed a bottle of water which he emptied down the throat of his captive. Most of the water ran down his chin and face. This brought the kid back to consciousness as he coughed and hacked the water from his throat and lungs. His eyes were wide with panic.

The unseen voice asked another question, this time to the captive.

The kid mumbled an incoherent answer.

The voice asked again, harsher this time, and the brute stepped closer to the boy who cowered as far as his restraints would allow. He spat a glob of blood to the floor and tried to form the words from his ruined mouth.

Aazam crouched at the door, his silenced pistol ready, waiting for Hadid to make his move. The wait seemed to take forever, but it was only a few moments. When Hadid's distraction came, it was anticlimactic.

Hadid knocked on the exterior door. The brute's head swiveled away from the prisoner towards the front of the building. Aazam eased the office door open wider, the 9mm leading the way. Scanning the room, he picked up two other assailants that had been hidden. All were Middle Eastern. A tall, thin man with a traditional beard stood in front of one of the bay doors. Another approached the entrance, his hand buried in his coat. Aazam guessed it was for a gun. He could see no other weapons, but didn't count on their absence.

While all the attention was on the entrance, Aazam duck-walked across the floor and grabbed the brute by the neck, driving the pistol's barrel under his throat. The man froze, realizing immediately that to move was to die.

The kidnapper closest to the door leaned forward and turned the knob, pushing the door with a shove. Before he could react, a gun with a long silencer came up and pushed up against his head. A flash of flame snapped the man's head backwards in a spray of crimson.

The bearded man jumped at the sight. He went to move, but at that moment saw Aazam for the first time and froze. Aazam watched smoldering anger creep across the bearded man's face, but when Aazam clubbed the brute across the back of the head with the pistol butt, rendering him unconscious, the anger turned to fear.

The bearded man said something in German, but Aazam only stared at him, not giving anything away. The silence lengthened until Aazam took a step towards the man, who startled at the move.

In Arabic, Aazam said, "We will ask the questions now," Aazam gestured with his gun that the man should sit on a tall shop stool. The man slowly moved and sat, his eyes never leaving Aazam's.

"Why grab the boy?"

The only answer he got was a defiant glare.

Aazam sighed, and without warning, he shot the brute in the head, killing him instantly. "You're next. But I promise you it'll take a lot longer," he said in a flat tone. "If you are stalling, hoping the sentry on top of the plant will help you, you can forget it. He's with Allah now."

The expression on the man's face went from shock to anger. "You ISIS butchers may kill me, but your entire nation is going to burn. You have turned the entire world against you. You have threatened both our groups with your bloodlust."

Aazam smiled. The kidnappers were al-Qaida.

"You may be right, but that is for Allah to decide. How quickly and easily you meet him is what we are discussing."

The man tried to spit at Aazam, but the fear had dried his mouth and nothing came out.

Aazam gave a slight nod, and Hadid pulled his knife and drew it across their prisoner's right ear. The man cried out, cupping the side of head as he saw his ear lying beside him on the garage floor. The bearded man refused to speak, his lips pressed tight together as he stared at Aazam in defiance.

Aazam shook his head. It was going to be a long night.

Chapter 24

"The M2A2 is a belt-fed, air-cooled, heavy machine gun that can deliver a hell of a lot of firepower to any target. The beauty is it can be fired from the ground or mounted on a vehicle," explained Adham.

Dalton gawked at the menacing weapon, a little apprehensive. He had seen all the Rambo movies and knew the devastation a weapon like this could create. Although Maajid and the others had stood by their story they came here to shoot because it was fun, Dalton felt he was being tested once again, but for what he wasn't entirely sure. He knew his friends were political and wondered just how far they would go to defend Islam.

Was this what Daanya wanted to warn me about?

He watched and listened as the giant ex-Marine explained how to load and arm the weapon and, when it was Dalton's turn, he smoothly and confidently mimicked the same actions. Adham smiled with obvious pride on his face.

"Very good, my friend," Adham said as Dalton put the safety on, having loaded and cocked the weapon. "Now for the fun part."

Dalton watched the big man check to see that the range flags were visible and everyone was behind the shooting line. He pulled on his ear protectors and repositioned his shooting glasses, announcing in a loud voice, "The range is hot. I repeat, the range is hot."

Then Adham said to Dalton, "Fire as you will."

Dalton aimed down range at a number of targets that had been set up across a low berm rising four feet before the base of the hill. Water- and sand-filled jugs and cans were stretched across the rise as targets. He squeezed the trigger; the gun bucked against his shoulder and he felt the vibrations throughout his whole body. Down range, he saw the impact of the bullets strike the ground below the targets and adjusted to bring the shells on target, squeezing short bursts so the barrel wouldn't rise too much from the recoil. Jugs and cans were decimated as the .50 caliber shells ripped them apart.

Holy fuck.

Dalton could not believe the power as he fought to keep the bouncing gun on target. Behind the targets, three- and four-inch trees were ripped apart and a number fell as if struck by an invisible axe. Before he knew it, the last of the chain-linked shells had fed through the breach and the gun locked in the open and empty position. The sound of the weapon continued to reverberate through his brain as his arms trembled from the ragged pounding of the kickback. He cleared the weapon, rose, and stood behind it.

"Well?" asked Adham.

"That…that was fucking awesome," Dalton said, unable to wipe the grin off his face. He was shaking, but he didn't think it was from the gun's vibrations.

Adham smiled as he yelled, "The range is clear!"

Maajid and the others ran forward from their observation station behind the firing line, all shouting praises and fist pumping each other about Dalton's shooting results.

He felt proud when Adham told him, "You are a born soldier, Dalton," putting his big hand on Dalton's shoulder. Dad use to clap him on the shoulder in the same way, and for a moment, he pretended it was his father. It felt good.

"A soldier of Allah!" yelled Ubayd, breaking the mood. His friends kept cheering as they walked down range to see the damage.

***

In the afternoon, Adham introduced the group to plastic explosives and detonators. As exciting as this was, explosives were a different animal. Dalton could understand why his friends would want to come to a gun range. It was exciting and incredibly cool. But explosives?

"Without the detonator, the thing won't go boom," Adham explained, "It's not like dynamite which can be detonated by fire or even old age. Plastic explosives like C4 can be molded, slapped, and even ignited with an open flame without worrying about it exploding in your face."

Seeing the doubt in Ubayd's face, Adham pulled off a small amount from the brick he held and set it on the bench in front of him. From a pocket, he pulled out a silver Zippo lighter adorned with the eagle, anchor, and globe emblem of the United States Marine Corps. Snapping the cap and igniting the lighter, he pushed the blue/orange flame onto the surface of the small sample of C4. After a couple seconds, the C4 glazed over as if it was melting and produced its own flame. "Marines have used this to cook their MREs[9] since Vietnam. It is perfectly stable."

"Modern explosives are very safe unless they have a blasting cap in them. Of course, for the blasting cap to be dangerous, it has to be hooked up to a power source."

"Do you mean," Dilawar asked, motioning to the brick of C4, "that you can have the blasting cap set in the plastic, and it's still safe as long as it's not hooked up?"

Adham smiled. "Exactly."

Dalton listened attentively, but he was wondering why Adham would even bother teaching them about explosives. Dalton then looked around, and all the others were paying strict attention to the lesson. This was getting weirder by the second.

Pulling up a bundle of blasting caps that had multi-color fuses attached, Adham tossed it at Ubayd. Ubayd tripped over his own feet and, in horror, watched the tangle of wires and blasting caps fall and land between his outstretched legs.

"What the fuck!" Ubayd squealed.

The entire group exploded with laughter. Ubayd's look of fear gave way to resentment. "Blasting caps need to be hooked up to a power source," he quoted.

With tears in his eyes, Adham extended his hand to help Ubayd to his feet. "Man, the look on your face..."

"Glad I could be of service." Ubayd said, clearly not happy.

Adham took back the bundle and said, "There are two types of blasting caps — either electrical or nonelectrical. The electrical is the fastest, although you can put in time delays so your blasts are organized like when they bring down a building for demolition. As the name explains, it needs an electrical pulse to fire." He raised another cap. "The non-electrical uses a substance similar to black power and is much slower. You need to know the speed the fuse will burn at. Much easier to deal with electrical," he said passing the cap around for everyone to look at.

On the workbench in front of him, Adham pushed forward three different items and told the group, "And these are different types of igniters, but they all do the same thing. They create an electrical charge that is sent down the wire to ignite the blasting cap, which ignites the C4." He shrugged his shoulders, "That's it."

"Is it BOOMBOOM time?" asked Dilawar.

Smiling a mischievous grin, Adham said, "Oh yeah. Definitely BOOMBOOM time."

"What?" thought Dalton.

"All right!" said Dliawar.

Chapter 25

"Man, did you see how I cut through the course? It was unreal!" Dalton said, his chest rising and falling from exertion.

The group had just finished room to room clearing training on the building behind Adham's barn. The building was designed so the walls were moveable, so each time they entered, they were faced with a different maze which they had to storm through, eliminating pop-up enemies while safeguarding allies.

A large hand slammed into his shoulder, almost knocking Dalton to his knees. He looked up to see Adham's smiling face. *I would hate to have Adham grab me if he was pissed.*

Adham's laughter bellowed in the clearing behind the barn. "Time's a little slow for a pro, but your shots were all kills. I run cops through this maze all the time and some of them might do it faster, but a lot of them miss their targets."

With the exception of Parsa who sat by himself, glaring, the others were bouncing with excitement. It was almost like hockey.

Damn it feels good!

A fire pit in front of the barn cracked and popped. The group dropped into chairs around the fire, still sweaty from negotiating the course.

"Good," said Maajid, "Because we're going to need people that don't hesitate."

The sudden hardness grabbed everyone's attention.

"You do like being part of this, don't you, Dalton?" Maajid said.

Dalton froze. All eyes were on him. Maajid's eyes were intense, while Parsa watched with open hostility. The others all watched with quiet expectation.

"Yes. Why would you think otherwise?"

Maajid looked around the circle and took a deep breath. "We need to know you are with us." He paused for effect, then added, "Completely with us."

"What the…what the hell have I done to make you question my loyalty? I've killed to protect —"

"That was in the moment," Maajid said. "I'm talking about doing something planned."

Dalton was speechless.

"I need, *we* need, to know if you are really one of us." Maajid stood, grabbed a chunk of hardwood, and placed it over the fire's center, sparks rising upwards. "I told you that the Muslim culture was a closed one. We don't squeal on each other. We don't talk to the cops."

"Yeah, but…" Dalton couldn't understand why he was being singled out. *Have the others gone through this?*

"If you are one of us and the police come around asking about the thug you killed, we don't know anything," Maajid continued, "If you're not one of us…."

Dalton's stomach dropped at the unspoken threat. It was like a slap in the face.

Maajid reached over and place a hand on Dalton's shoulder and said, "You and Daanya seem to be getting along. Would you like that to continue?"

The turn in the conversation spun Dalton around, and he sputtered.

"You would make a fine husband for my sister. You are honest, not afraid to work for a living, a good Muslim, and someone who is willing to protect those he loves," Maajid said with a soft smile. "After all, that is part of why you and I have become such good friends."

Maajid walked back to his seat and was quiet for a while.

Panic rose in Dalton. He could not concentrate. He felt his heart beating, and he had trouble gaining his breath. *This is crazy. Allah, help me!*

As if he hadn't noticed the reaction his words had on Dalton, Maajid continued, "Both here in the United States and in Europe, the Muslim community is being attacked. Since 9/11, it has been growing non-stop. Groups like PEGIDA[10] and the American Freedom Defense Initiative are openly calling for all kinds of sanctions against our people. They attack our mosques and people with growing impunity."

"But the law —" Dalton began.

"Does nothing against white, American-born Christians," interrupted Maajid.

Dalton kept quiet, letting his friend speak his mind. *He's fucking crazy!*

"It's not just Muslims being attacked," Maajid continued, "Mexicans and blacks are constantly oppressed and treated like second class people in their own country." He threw another chunk of wood on the fire as if to accent his point. The stick threw up another wave of sparks.

"A bunch of white guys armed to the teeth hold off the federal government and get acquitted, yet at the Standing Rock Dakota pipeline protests, when a bunch of Native Americans set up a peaceful blockade to protest an oil pipe across their own lands, they are met with an army of police who attacked them viciously. We will not stand by while these racist, white supremacists attack our mosques and our people. *Your* people," Maajid said, pointing his finger at Dalton. "The anti-Muslim rhetoric in this country keeps growing and painting us all with the same brush. We're sick of it."

None of the others were saying at thing.

"You enjoyed shooting and blowing shit up today, didn't you, Dalton? Made you feel good. Made you feel powerful. And you heard Adham and the others — you are a born soldier. Come with us. Be a soldier of Allah and fight for your people. We need you, Dalton, as much as you need us." Maajid said, his voice rising as he spoke. "So I need to know, are you one of us?"

Dalton watched the sparks fly until they disappeared and were replaced by the early evening stars winking through the leaves above. Overwhelmed, he reached to the heavens. *Allah help me!*

"No!" Dalton said with conviction as he stood up. "You're out of your mind if you think I would be part of something like this." He looked around the fire but saw only hostility. Only Adham would not look at him.

"Adham, you can't be part of this. You know where this will end up," Dalton pleaded.

The ex-Marine raised his head and said, "Maybe. All I know is that my government turned its back on me and left me to rot. Would have been different if I was white."

"Dammit, Adham, you've seen how many innocent people have been killed by those radicals in Europe. Do you want to be part of something like that?" Dalton asked in desperation. He was sweating heavily, trying to push down the panic so he could think straight.

Dalton stepped back and Parsa pulled out a knife, a wicked grin on his face. "If he ain't with us, then he's a liability."

"Put that away, idiot," Maajid said with disgust. "Dalton will join us regardless of his fears."

"How do you figure that?" Dalton demanded.

"Well, I hoped I would never have to use this, but you leave me no choice," Maajid said, pulling out his phone. He manipulated the screen and then passed the phone to Dalton.

Dalton hesitantly accepted the cell, not knowing what to expect. Looking down he saw a video app was open with a large arrow centered on the screen. He looked up, confused.

"Go ahead. Press it," Maajid said.

Dalton did, and the video came to life. The shot seemed to bounce in the low light but then zoomed to a figure lying on a floor. *Daayna!* She looked like she was asleep except for a trickle of blood coming from her nose.

He looked up at Maajid. "What did you do?" he stammered in horror.

"She decided to argue with her big brother. Don't worry, she'll be all right," Maajid said, but then he added harshly, "For now."

Dalton swung his fist with no conscious thought and felt the satisfying shock of hitting Maajid's jaw, causing the man to stagger away. Before Dalton could launch another attack, numerous hands grabbed him, holding him secure.

"You coward! You bastard!" Dalton spat.

Maajid slowly turned, wiping blood from his mouth. He smiled, blood on his teeth, making him look demented.

"But you haven't seen the best yet," Maajid said spitting crimson saliva into the dirt. He reached down and picked up the phone. He swiped at the screen and turned it towards Dalton's face.

On the screen, a woman was walking on the street. The shot zoomed in and he went cold as he realized the woman was his mother. Behind her walked another man, his hands in his pockets.

"Do you recognize your mother's shadow?"

Dalton squinted to center on the man's face and in horror realized who the man was. It was one of the Mara Salvatrucha 13 gang that had attacked them. Almost as if the man knew Dalton was watching, he pulled a knife out from his jacket and grinned at the camera. Dalton went ballistic fighting at the hands that held him, but they held him secure.

Maajid leaned in, just out of reach. "You'll do exactly as I say or you'll lose both of them. If I make the call, they're dead. And if I don't check in at least once a day, they're dead."

Chapter 26

Gail could hear the phone ringing as she climbed the stairs to the apartment. Cursing under her breath, she knew she would never get there in time to answer it. *That's what answering machines are for.* Fighting to keep the grocery bags from falling back down the stairs, she pulled out the key and almost fell into the apartment. She had forgotten how much work this was. Dalton had taken over this chore since graduation — something she had not appreciated until today.

Thinking about Dalton, Gail smiled. His first road trip. She and her late husband Tom had gone on a lot of trips before Dalton was born. She recalled the sense of freedom and the thrill of experiencing new places. *Maybe it's time to move on, for both of us.*

Once she got the perishable groceries put away, Gail turned her attention to the phone to check the message. *Dalton's cell.* Pulling her hand through her hair, she sat down and pressed play:

"Hi Mom. Sorry I missed you. The guys and I are having a great time. We've decided to extend the holiday. Adham has some friends in San Francisco who are willing to put us up for a week. We've decided to drive cross country, as none of us have been west before. I'll give you a call in a day or two to let you know where I am. Hope you're okay with this. You told me to get out and live life, so I'm taking your advice. Love you."

San Francisco? Gail looked at the phone cradled in her hand as if it was a strange object. She shook her head, stood, and began putting the remaining groceries away as her mind replayed the message again and again. *He sounded happy.*

Part of her was glad he was enjoying himself, but another side of her was…well, jealous. She was working two jobs, trying to keep them above the poverty line, and to top it all off, she was alone. *Stop feeling sorry for yourself, Gail. You're just nervous about being on your own.* She took a deep breath and wondered if she would have to do the online dating thing the girls at work talked about. It sounded a little intimidating throwing yourself out there for the whole world to see just how desperate you were. Of course, those who responded were in the same boat.

Gail moved down the hallway and turned on the shower to let it warm up. She and Tom had been high school sweethearts, so dating was not something she had a lot of experience with. *What the heck do people do on dates these days?* The thought of being intimate with another man was both frightening and exciting. She had only ever been with Tom, so she knew this was going to be a big hurdle in and of itself. Gail stripped and looked at herself in the mirror. Trying not to be too critical, she pulled her shoulders back and gave herself a sexy leer, muttering, "More than mortal man can handle." She laughed out loud and startled herself. *Christ, I sound like a 17-year-old.* However, she had to admit she had been lucky. Her hips were a little wider, but thanks to a fast metabolism, she was not over weight. *At least my chest hasn't fallen prey to gravity. Yet.* After drying off, she sat on the couch. No matter which TV channel she landed on, it featured some reality shows or series she knew nothing about. There had to be more to life.

***

"Need a club, easy on the mayo, with a side chicken noodle with extra crackers. Also a pastrami on rye, double mustard and dill with the beef barely," Gail yelled towards the kitchen, reaching for the coffee pot. The supper hour was hopping, and the place was packed with hungry customers. As crazy as it got, this was Gail's favorite time because her mind was filled with orders, light social interaction with the patrons, and the antics of the staff.

"I'm telling you, hun, with a little makeup and a touch of color, we can make you a killer profile that will have the boys busting your inbox," Jen said.

"That's not the only box they'll be busting," said Gloria.

"Gloria!" Gail said in shocked horror, looking around to see who else had heard the comment. To her embarrassment, most of the customers were paying close attention to the trio as if they were at a theater dinner and the waitresses were a comedy skit.

"Gail, don't you be paying any attention to her. She's just upset because her last hunk wouldn't call after the first date. Of course, she gave him desert before they got to the restaurant, so there was nothing left on the menu for him to try," said Jen.

"Well, this guy was ripped, and it had been a while. You'd have done it too," said Gloria.

"Ladies, I'm trying to run a family establishment here," Sam said, coming out of the kitchen, wiping his hands on his apron.

"Hell, Sam, let them be," said an old timer at a window booth. "This is the most action I've gotten in 10 years."

Gail smiled to herself as she grabbed a tray of steaming food. She glided around the arguing coworkers with the grace of a dancer. It was like this every night. Only the topics changed.

"Sorry for the noise, folks," she said as she laid the platters in front the two businessmen sitting at a booth.

"No need to be sorry. This is funnier than the reruns of 'Cheers,'" said one of the men.

She turned from the table and headed for the kitchen, shaking her head and chuckling to herself. As Gail passed the counter near the front entrance, she saw a young Muslim girl in a pale yellow head dress standing just inside the restaurant doors, looking at her. The girl held a small black laptop case in front of her. Even with her head covered, Gail could see the woman was stunningly beautiful with deep, dark eyes and full, sensuous lips. She reminded Gail of a Bollywood heroine. The only blemish was a vicious cut on her left cheek that extended to the base of her jaw. It was still an angry red, but it was healed over.

"Are you waiting for someone?" Gail asked her

"I am looking for Mrs. Westree," the woman responded.

Surprised, Gail moved towards the woman hesitantly and said, "I am Gail Westree."

The girl's dark eyes softened as she studied Gail's face. "He has your eyes," the stranger told her.

"Who are you?" Gail asked suddenly nervous.

"My name is Daanya Nasry. I am a friend of Dalton's, and I need your help." She reached out, and grabbed Gail's hand ferociously, "I believe Dalton is in terrible danger."

Chapter 27

"Dalton…?" Gail staggered back as if slapped, her hand slipping from the other's grasp. The young girl reached out to keep Gail from falling.

Sam and the girls who had watched from the encounter with curiosity came running forward; Gloria and Jen grabbed Gail's arms and pulled her back while Sam stood defensively in between Gail and the girl.

"What the hell did you say to her?" Sam said.

"I...," she began.

Gail pulled back and reached out to the young woman. The strength in her grasp surprised Gail. Sorrow and fear were reflected on that beautiful face, but the eyes poured genuine concern towards Gail.

"Sam. Please. She's a friend of Dalton's." Her quiet tone of voice calmed him, and he backed away from the girl.

Gail sat on one of the counter turn stools and motioned the woman to sit beside her. "I'm sorry for my reaction. When I heard you say that Dalton was danger, I overreacted." Gail's voice trembled with emotion as she spoke. "Please forgive me."

"There's nothing to forgive. I'm worried sick about him, too," the girl said.

"You said you're a friend of Dalton's?" Gail asked with a smile. "And your name is Dan….?"

"Daanya Nasry. And yes, I am a friend of Dalton's. Is there somewhere we can talk?"

Gail squeezed the girl's hand in a silent gesture before turning to Gloria and Jen. "Can you girls finish without me?"

"Definitely," Jen said, answering for both of them. "You call us if you need anything, sweetheart. Let me know everything is okay. Promise?"

"I promise," Gail said.

"Gail," Sam said. "Anything you need, you call." He eyed Daanya suspiciously. "Anything. Understand?"

"Thanks Sam, it's all right. She's here to warn me that Dalton is in trouble. She's here to help." Gail hugged him and whispered, "If I need your help, I will call. Okay?"

"You'd better," he replied in a menacing voice, not taking his eyes off Daanya.

To Daanya, Gail said, "Let me grab my jacket and purse. We'll talk outside."

She left Daanya sitting there as she went to the back office, hearing Sam tell the girls, "Okay, which tables need cover up?

Could it have something to do with his trip? The change in plans?

As the door to the restaurant closed behind them, Gail began to walk slowly, fearing what news this young woman had brought her.

"Okay, so start from the beginning," Gail said.

The young lady was silent for moment and then, with a serious expression asked, "How well do you know your son?"

"What?" laughed Gail. This was beginning to sound like a worn out movie scene.

"Are you aware he has performed his shahada and is a follower of Islam?"

Gail stopped in her tracks and stared at the girl with her mouth open. "His what? Is this some kind of joke?"

"I thought as much," Daanya said.

"I don't know what kind of game you're playing …."

"Please. I know this must be a shock, but I can prove it," Daanya said softly, looking like she was ready to cry.

"Really! This had better be good." Fear laced through her. *Oh Dalton!*

"Let me know if this sounds right," Daanya said to Gail as she continued to follow the sidewalk. "Dalton became very depressed after the death of his father, pulling away from all his friends at school. He spent all his time online searching for something to fill the hole his father's death had left. But about a year ago, something changed, and he became more like himself. He became happy, filled with a sense of purpose and energy." She looked over at Gail and said, "Am I close?"

"Yes," Gail whispered.

"He found Allah," she stated. "Somehow, he tapped into the teachings of Islam and found a world of peace and brotherhood that soothed his troubled heart. But he also found my brother and his friends, and that is where the trouble started."

"What trouble?"

"It goes back to 2003 and the second invasion of Iraq by the United States. My family was living in Baghdad at the time, and my father was a colonel with the Praetorian Guard. Weeks before the invasion, my father had the family immigrate here to the States. We were just kids at the time and didn't understand why we had to leave our homeland. As it happened, my father was killed in one of the air strikes on the capital."

"As we grew, my brothers learned how our father died and became very bitter at the Americans. When he became old enough, my eldest brother, Umar, journeyed to Iraq and was killed in the fighting for the formation of the Islamic State."

Gail stopped walking and closed her eyes as her mind took in this information, and she started to look ahead to its inevitable conclusion. "Are you saying...?"

"My brother works for ISIS as a recruiter."

From her bag, Daanya pulled out a file folder and opened it to a photo. In it, Dalton was wearing a prayer shawl and a skull cap inside a mosque. He was surrounded by an imam and a youthful, handsome man.

Pointing to the young man next to Dalton, Daanya said, "I tried to warn Dalton about Maajid, but there has been no opportunity to do so safely."

"This is crazy," Gail said, beginning to walk again as if she could leave this all behind her. The young Muslim almost had to run to catch up.

Dalton a Muslim? There's no way. But the photograph...

Gail stopped abruptly, causing Daanya to almost run into her.

"I need to think," Gail said out loud. Turning to the girl, she told her. "Please don't say anything else. I need time to...."

Daanya just nodded.

If I don't sit down, I'm going to faint again. Home. Home was safe. Gail could take her time and make sense of all this once she was home.

"Will you come to my home? To finish your story?"

"I have nowhere else to go," Daanya said. "When I left, I took my brother's laptop. I think — no, I hope — that it will expose his plans for Dalton." She shuddered in fear. "When he finds out that I have it, I am as good as dead."

***

Twenty minutes later, the two sat across from each other in Gail's kitchen, Daanya in Dalton's usual chair. Gail had put the kettle on for tea and was waiting for it to boil in the uncomfortable silence.

Where are you Dalton? What are you doing right now?

"Tell me how you two met?" Gail finally asked.

Daanya explained how she had met Dalton at the mosque and again at her home and the circumstances of him seeing her without her hijab. "Then he jumped up to hold the door for me and stood up for me against my brother, something no one else had ever dared. The way he looked at me," she said, a soft smile on her lips, "I was the only girl in the world, and I was all his."

Gail could see Dalton meant something to this young woman, and she had risked everything to sound the alarm.

Rising to pour the water for the tea, Gail smiled and said, "His father did the same thing for me. We met in high school; the first time he saw me, I was covered with paint, but he treated me as if I was the perfect princess. I was his from that moment on."

"Exactly," Daanya said blushing. "We've been going out for almost a year now."

"And he hasn't brought you to meet his mother," Gail said a little hurt.

"I think my brother may have had something to do about that." Her expression changed, going dark. "When I found out about this camping trip Maajid had planned, I suspected my brother was up to no good. There have been signs in the past that he is involved with people from Syria. I confronted my brother, but he threw me down the basement stairs where I hit my head and passed out. That's where I got this," she said, indicating the cut on the side of her face. The door was locked and my mother would not cross my brother by opening the door. I was down there for two days."

"How did you get away?" Gail asked.

"I managed to climb up a laundry chute that we have in the house. I waited until my mother left for prayers and made my escape, stopping only for my brother's laptop in case it had information on where he might have taken Dalton."

"Then I came to find you," Daanya said, reaching for Gail's hand with tears in her eyes. "We need to help Dalton. Please tell me what to do."

"We need to call the police," Gail said without hesitation.

"But won't Dalton be arrested as a terrorist?"

"I'd rather him in prison than dead."

Chapter 28

Aazam praised Allah for the moving walkway that took him through the terminal to the entrance of Dubai's International Airport. Three months of travel wore heavily on him, and he hoped to rest a couple of days in his apartment before dealing with Abdullah and Kalib. Seeing the sign for the monorail station that would take him into the city, he headed that way.

He had been meeting with the other teams, going over attack plans, and visiting target sites across the globe. There had been no other incidents since Germany, but he didn't let down his guard. Nevertheless, the stress of potential capture took its toll.

I prefer the heat of battle to all this cloak and dagger maneuvering.

Before he entered the doors to the station, he heard the pseudonym he was using paged over the airport's public announcement system.

"Would Mr. Karim El-Amin please meet his party at the Ahlan Service Desk."

Aazam wondered if it was a trap. He had just flown in from the last target country, Australia. *If I had been compromised, they would never have allowed me to leave. Could it be a Western intelligence agency? No, they have little power here.*

He considered his choices and made for an airport phone. The number for Ahlan was conveniently posted above the phone.

"Good morning, this is Karim El-Amin. I heard my name being paged."

"Yes sir, Mr. Abdullah Ali al-Anbari has arranged a limousine for you with his compliments."

You've got to be kidding me.

Aazam's temper was ready to explode at the presumption of his superior. The man was an incompetent fool. "Thank you. That is very generous. Where might I find the limousine?"

"As you leave the terminal building, there is a pool of limousines to the right of the doors. The driver will be waiting with a sign bearing your name."

"Thank you for assistance."

Within the hour, he was standing in Abdullah's penthouse, watching the marina below as his superior went on about how great a soldier Aazam was and how ISIS would never be beaten.

"In fact, did I not tell you, Abu al Meshedani himself has recommended your name to our leader to head the Western forces once your full mission is completed? The enemy will run once they realize who they face."

Or ram a drone up my ass.

"Speaking about my mission, how long do you think it will take to get the final approval?" Aazam said, turning from the window.

He was extremely tired and did not have the patience for back slapping. The Russian attack had been beneficial to the Islamic State. Russia had been pulling its troops out because of the peace talks between Assad and the Syrian rebels. After the attack, the headless Russian bear had turned turtle, pulling all military, economic, and diplomatic influence out of the area. In reality, it was off of the world's stage. It had collapsed into itself as it attempted to regain some sense of governance. Until such time, Russia's military pressure was no longer a threat to ISIS. Aazam knew instinctively the other attacks could reap similar results if the leaders of ISIS would only give the word.

"There has been no word," Abdullah said quietly.

"Well, if they hold me in such regard, why don't they take my advice?" Aazam asked, his voice strained and tight. His control was slipping. "The targets have been identified, the people are in place, the strategies finalized, and the plans are in the final stages. We just need the word."

Abdullah glared at him and stood, his hands bunched into fists.

“Who do you think you are?” Abdullah hissed. “So you were successful. So what? We have had a lot of success over the past two years, most of which was accomplished by others who knew better than to question the leadership!” his voice rose as he strode toward Aazam.

“You live and breathe by the decree of the cliphate! Do you understand?” Abdullah shouted, his face inches from Aazam, spittle spraying the soldier’s cheek.

Without warning, Aazam’s hands flashed upward, one grabbing his superior by the throat, the other behind his neck, pulling the man towards Aazam; he glared into Abdullah’s eyes and watched the shock turn into terror as he squeezed Abdullah’s throat.

“Goat’s dung. That is what you are,” Aazam said. “I don’t answer to fools who have ignored the teachings of Allah, fornicating and drinking spirits for pleasure. While you live like an American whore, others are dying every day. If it was for Allah’s sake, I wouldn’t care, but the more I see of so-called leaders like you, the more I see it is for your own power and privilege.”

He threw Abdullah away from him and the man tumbled across the floor, landing in a tangled heap with his dishdasha garment pulled over his rump, exposing his under garments.

“These fools who call themselves leaders change the law of Muhammad to suit their own needs. Where in the Quran does it endorse rape? Or killing innocent people?” Aazam shouted. “But the leadership allows these acts to attract animals like yourself to the cause. I’ve turned a blind eye to all the horrors they’ve decreed and encouraged, knowing America would not stand by. Knowing I would once again get the chance to attack them.”

“You are a dead man,” Abdullah shouted as he stood, his face a mask of rage. “You’ll not see another sunrise.”

“Not before you,” Aazam said as he grabbed the man’s garment and, using the leverage, swung Abdullah towards the wall-to-ceiling window. The thick glass vibrated heavily but didn’t break as Abdullah bounced off the sheet and landed on the floor.

Frustrated, Aazam grabbed the man by the belt and the cuff of his dishdasha and swung him like a battering ram, head first into the window. Again the glass refused to break. In a near psychotic rage, Aazam dropped the semi-conscious man and went to the office desk, looking for something to shatter the window. He tore through the drawers noting bundles of cash before finding a .45 Desert

Eagle gun. It was a show piece finished with a bright stainless steel, but it was loaded. Pocketing two spare clips, Aazam moved back to the window and fired two shots through the glass at waist level, the report deafening in the enclosed area.

Aazam heard a choir of screams from further in the unit. He had to hurry. Ensuring the safety was engaged, he shoved the pistol into the small of his back. Grabbing Abdullah once again, he swung the man back at the window. This time, with the solidity compromised, the glass ruptured outward, taking Abdullah with it.

As Aazam's temper cooled, his analytical side kicked in. He began contemplating his next move. Aazam returned to the desk and pulled out the wads of money. There were so many that he ended putting them in his carry-on. He went through the remaining drawers but found nothing useful. He cursed his loss of control and blamed it on the heavy fatigue, but that was just an excuse. It was a mistake, plain and simple. But part of him wasn't sorry. The dream of an Islamic State that truly followed Muhammad's teachings had died long ago. All he had left was his revenge. If it was meant to be, Allah would provide.

I have to get word to the teams. Once they're loose, there's no calling them back.

One of the back doors opened and Abdullah's son, Salim, eased his face around the door, braving the violence that erupted in the penthouse.

Seeing Aazam, who he knew, he took a step into the room, taking in the broken window and the wind that stirred the room.

"Father?" he asked.

"He is with Allah, Salim."

The boy's lip began to tremble and he swiped at the moisture building behind his eyes, trying to be brave. "But we had planned to watch the zip liners tonight."

"I am sorry," Aazam as the guilt hit him. Not for killing Abdullah, but for the pain he caused the boy and the rest of the family.

"I am sorry," he repeated as he left the apartment and closed the door.

Chapter 29

Abdullah's chauffeur/bodyguard did not hesitate when Aazam asked him to drive him to the facility. *Thank Allah Abdullah's penthouse faced the opposite street.* He knew the man had an arsenal in the trunk of the limousine. He just needed convincing to open it up.

"Did Abdullah or Kalib tell you we believe there is a mole in our organization?" Aazam asked through the window separator of the vehicle.

The big man, Israfil, nodded his head as he glanced in the rear view mirror.

"During my travels, Kalib and I were able to lay a couple of small traps to help us identify the traitor, and Abdullah has given me the green light to eradicate this vermin," Aazam said to the man." But first, we need to know who he is working for. Abdullah told me you would know what to do."

Israfil nodded and smiled with pleasure, but Aazam was uncertain if it was due to hearing of Abdullah's confidence in his skills or to the pleasure he anticipated in torturing the traitor. Aazam had used pain as a means of extracting information in the past, like in Germany, but he certainly didn't gain any personal pleasure from the act. It was merely an unfortunate tool that had to be used. Aazam reminded himself not to underestimate the big bodyguard.

"He may be armed, so can you arrange for some fire power?" Aazam asked.

"We have everything in the back," Israfil said. "We have a little something for every occasion."

Aazam nodded and shifted back in his seat, not in satisfaction, but to relieve the pain from the pistol that was jabbing the side of his butt.

As they neared the industrial sector, Aazam asked, "Is there a way to approach the building so we remain out of view of the cameras?"

Israfil thought about the layout of the compound and nodded, "I think we can arrive without notice."

"Good."

Israfil pulled into the property before the facility and drove to the rear of the windowless buildings, tucking the limousine out of sight. He eased the vehicle towards the far rear corner building, the hard packed sand slowing their progress. Both men exited the vehicle and walked to the trunk. Israfil opened it and stepped back so Aazam could view the weapon cache. Aazam was surprised — there was enough there to start a small war.

"How accurately can you fire a silenced pistol?" Israfil asked.

"I've had some practice, but it's dependent on the distance. Handguns aren't very accurate after 25 meters. And the silencer can also affect the shot."

"Around the corner is the corner post of the facility's fence. Atop that is a video feed that rotates 240 degrees. If I remember right, it's about 20 meters from this corner."

"Won't someone come to check the camera once I take out?"

"No," Israfil said shaking his head. "Because of the sand, they have one or two go down weekly."

"That's a hell of a security hole,"Aazam said.

The big man just shrugged and moved back so Aazam could choose and load his weapon.

Aazam picked up a Beretta 92F model and the accompanying XM-9 snap-on suppressor and checked the action. "Very nice," he said to himself. Taking a 15-round clip from the foam lined box, he rammed it into the pistol's handle and chambered a shell. Without warning, he turned and fired a shot point blank into Israfil's opened mouth. The big man's head snapped back and crumpled into the sand. Killing the bodyguard gave Aazam no pleasure.

Aazam transferred a number of plastic explosives blocks and blasting caps from the vehicle's trunk to his travel bag. Finally he chose an assault rifle, an Israeli IWI X95 9mm submachine gun with a quick-detachable sound suppressor. *Very impressive.* The irony that an Arab would arm himself with a Jewish weapon was not lost on Aazam. He walked over to the corner of the building and slowly peeked around its edge. As described, the camera stood above the corner post of the fence. He pulled back as the camera made its circuit. Watching the sand in front of him, Aazam was able to keep track of the camera's shadow in the sand. He waited until the device was pointed towards its furthest arc away from him and then leaned out and took careful aim at it. One shot shattered the small camera, pieces of plastic and lens littering the ground.

Aazam pulled back and waited patiently to see if anyone from the building would come out to investigate the feed. While he waited, he ran through the layout of the building in his head, remembering where the security teams were positioned. After 20 minutes with no one approaching the fence, Aazam concluded that Israfil had been correct. This would never have happened with the summit team Aazam knew. *Nor on my own watch.*

It took a second for him to vault the fence. Keeping his bag facing the neighboring property and the long submachine gun held along his leg, he made his way uncontested to the facility's rear corner. There was a camera over the entrance, but it was pointed toward the drive. He was able to walk under it without concern. Readying himself, he punched in his password and opened the door to the entrance. The two guards were caught with no warning, both sitting behind the desk. Aazam double tapped both men in the head before either could rise, let alone clear their weapons.

Making his way around the counter, he checked the surveillance monitors. Cycling through the different feeds, he saw no indication of alarm. The rear entrance of the building was showing one of the guards lighting a cigarette just outside the door. The fact the guard was relaxed told Aazam that his entry into the building had so far been unnoticed. There was one technician working on the internet servers near the building's center. These threats would have to be neutralized.

He saw most of the cyber container rooms were occupied, so detection was minimal. Kalib was not visible but the light to his container burned bright, so Aazam was confident he would find the man there. First, he had to eliminate anyone that might raise an alarm.

After a last look at the monitor, Aazam used the fingerprint and retinal scanner to enter the main building. He followed the central row of containers. Aazam kept an eye on the upper walkways. Spying the technician ahead of him, Aazam kept his rifle trained on the man's back. At the corner of the row of class C containers, he paused to check for any threats. Seeing none, he shouldered the rifle and pulled out the Beretta. The pistol spat one shot that ended the man's existence without warning. He crumpled to floor.

Beyond the servers was the rear entrance, a mirror of the front. A simple knock on the door and two rapid shots took out the one guard at the desk. Knowing the other guard was outside smoking, he waited to one side, his pistol aimed at the door. When the man entered, Aazam dispatched him before the guard even was aware he was there.

Before making his way to Kalib's container, Aazam planted the blocks of plastic explosive charges within the three network servers. These were tied together with blasting caps to a single radio detonator. He left the remote detonator in the duffle bag with the remaining ammunition.

Before Kalib's room, Aazam pressed the call button. Within a minute Kalib, opened the door. His eyes opened with surprise but then changed to shock as he focused on the ugly gun muzzle aimed at his forehead.

"Very slowly and very carefully, Kalib," warned Aazam, "back into the room."

"What is this, my friend?" Kalib asked, a sudden sheen of perspiration on his forehead.

"The leadership is getting cold feet. I'm going to hold them to the fire."

"They'll kill you," Kalib pleaded.

"Not before I get my revenge on the Americans."

Aazam watched as Kalib looked around for anything that might help him. Both knew Kalib carried no weapon. His weapon had always been his intellect and his powers of manipulation. Aazam watched as the hope faded from Kalib's eyes.

"Bring up the attack plan, Kalib," Aazam said softly. "If you betray me, I promise I will hurt you in ways you never thought possible. I will do the same to your girlfriend Jazlaan."

"No. Please, I will do anything. Jazlaan knows nothing about what I do."

"I want to send a message to all teams. Bring up the encrypted email program." Aazam watched the monitor and the young man at the same time.

As Kalib maneuvered through multiple windows, Aazam tried to keep up, but his computer skills were lacking. He worried Kalib might set off an alarm with a couple hidden key strokes.

"Slow it down," Aazam growled, pressing the barrel of the pistol against Kalib's skull. "If I even think you are sending out an alarm, you and Jazlaan will die."

"Please, Aazam. I will not put her at risk. I'll do as you say."

The window screens were navigated at an exaggerated slowness that even Aazam could follow. Kalib pulled up the email software, opened a new email and filled the "to" field with the addresses from a list titled International Team. Aazam recognized a few of the addresses, including Hadid's, and knew this was the correct list.

"What is your message?"

"October target confirmed. Eliminate all communication as per briefing," Aazam dictated.

"What briefing? Why eliminate their option for security updates? It doesn't make sense."

"Press the 'send' button, Kalib," Aazam said, again in the soft, but deadly voice.

Kalib looked up once more at Aazam, his eyes pleading. Aazam just nodded. Kalib moved the cursor over the "send" button and hesitated. Aazam rested his hand on the young man's shoulder and whispered, "For Jazlaan."

Kalib pressed the button and the email disappeared. He neither heard nor felt the 9mm slug enter the back of his skull. His brilliant mind painted the computer screen.

Aazam left the facility as he had entered. He crossed the grounds and hopped the fence as before. Moving Israfil's body out of the way of the limousine was heavy work because of his size; under the desert sky, even Aazam broke into a sweat. Careful not to get stuck in the sand, Aazam backed the huge vehicle from behind the building and made for the main road. From his pocket, he retrieved the remote detonator, casually released the safety, and pressed the fire button. He was rewarded by a dull thump as the servers exploded.

The die was cast. Now he had to find a way to America with all sides hunting him.

Chapter 30

Rubbing what felt like a handful of sand from her eyes, Gail wondered how much longer she could hold up. She and Daanya had been separated almost from the beginning while first the police and then agents of the Federal Bureau of the Investigation (FBI) went over their stories. The questions and the sessions were repeated over and over again until she found she was answering without thinking.

"When did you find out your son was a Muslim?" asked one agent.

"Today."

"And you never suspected? You must have seen him praying. They have to pray five times a day."

"No, I never saw him praying. I work two jobs, so I'm gone most of the day."

"How did you meet Daanya Nasry?"

She knew they were trying to trip her up, and at first she was resentful, but after hours of interrogation, she answered with the first thing that came into her head so they would just get it over with. Her image in the mirror of the interrogation room depicted dark bags under her eyes and disheveled hair which she had run her hands through a hundred times. Part of her wondered if the mirror was two-way like in all the movies.

Dalton, where are you?

As worried as she was, she was having trouble wrapping her head around the idea of the secret life Dalton had obviously been living. *He didn't trust me enough to share this with me.* When the idea of him being a Muslim finally set in, she understood her fear of the religion was in part due to her ignorance of it. Since 9/11, the media shocked the world with vivid violence perpetrated in the name of Allah. With that kind of image, Gail thought she understood why Dalton might hide it from her. *It still hurts.*

The door to the room opened, and the agent she had been dealing with entered the room followed by another individual. The new arrival didn't have the same look as the other officer. He moved with grace like a dancer, effortless yet tightly controlled. Sandy, shoulder length hair framed a face that was darkened by sun and wind. Although he was of average height and build, there was an aura of danger about him. She looked away from the man and back at the mirror where she was once again greeted by her reflection. This time, her tired eyes and disheveled hair made her feel vulnerable.

"Mrs. Westree, this is —" started the agent.

"I'm Hawkins. Pete Hawkins. I'm with Homeland Security," interrupted the stranger in a friendly voice, stepping forward and offering Gail his hand. The handshake was firm but not oppressive.

To the agent, he said, "I have it from here, fellows. Are Mrs. Westree and Miss Nasry free to leave after this?"

The agent sighed and nodded. "As long as both keep us informed if they plan on leaving town."

Hawkins asked Gail," You okay with that?"

She nodded.

Turning back to the officers, he said, "Thanks for the great work; I'll be in touch later today."

The door closed behind them, and Hawkins said to Gail, "I know you're tired and probably hungry as well, so why don't we grab Daanya and get out of here. We can talk while we eat."

***

The trio entered the restaurant and placed their orders, and the two women practically dove into their coffees.

"God, that's good," Gail said. "How can those cops call that crap they serve coffee?"

"They don't. That's the crap they give to the criminals until they confess," Hawkins said with a smile. The smile extended to his eyes, lighting them up.

Daanya was just as tired, but she showed it a lot better than Gail.

"For the record," he said, "I am a counter-terrorist agent and I work for Homeland Security as a consultant," he passed his ID folder across to Gail who sat next to him.

Looking at Daanya, he said, "We've known about your brother and have been monitoring him for awhile. You did a very brave thing coming forward. That had to have been an extremely hard thing to do."

Daanya nodded but kept quiet.

He turned his grey eyes towards Gail and said, "We've only found out about your son recently, but we didn't know just how he fit in with this group. Thanks to you, we have a better picture. We were not aware of this road trip, as you called it."

"What has Dalton gotten himself into? Can you tell me anything?" Gail asked.

"What we know at the moment is that Maajid was a recruiter for ISIS. He's recruited a number of individuals from across the country and assisted them with travel arrangements to the Middle East."

"So why haven't you done anything about it?" Gail asked, suddenly angry.

"Because, we need to find out who else they deal with. If we grab Maajid, we might be missing a lot more who are out there that we do not know about."

He paused while the waitress served their plates and refilled their coffee. When she left, he said, "Maajid and his friends have never, to our knowledge, performed any terrorist acts except for the recruiting. This may have changed with their little road trip, but we have nothing concrete."

Hawkins pulled out a photo and slid it across the table so both women could see it. "Have either of you seen this man?"

Both shook their heads after studying the black and white mug shot of a Middle Eastern man. "Who is he?" Gail asked.

"His name is Aazamibn ibn Abd al-Muttalib. He is a commander for the Islamic State, and we believe he was responsible for the attack in Moscow. We know he has been traveling across the globe, but we don't know why. I'm tracking down any lead I can find, in case he's attached to the other end."

"The Moscow attack...do you think Dalton is mixed up with him?" Gail said, her voice cracking. Daanya gripped her hand and squeezed it.

"No. No. There's no evidence that points to that. I'm grasping at straws, but I can't afford not to overlook a single clue," said Hawkins.

"So what can you do for us? For Dalton?"

"We have to wait until he and his friends surface. I've issued a federal bulletin to all law enforcement agencies to be on the watch for Dalton and the group he is traveling with."

"But won't that put him in danger from the police?"

"The bulletin is to identify and locate, not to arrest. We want to find them and explore what they may be up to."

Gail was having trouble gathering her thoughts. She should have a thousand questions, but putting a few words together was an effort. Gail raised her eyes from her plate of poached eggs and fixed Hawkins in her sights. "Maajid's laptop? Did it reveal anything?"

Hawkins smiled back at her and then at Daanya. "Wondering when that might dawn on you."

"Don't patronize me." Gail said, unable to keep the anger out of her voice. "What else are you keeping from us until we happen to remember to ask?"

Hands up, Hawkins said, "Whoa. I was not patronizing you. It's very clear both of you are drained, and I didn't want to overload you until you were ready." Looking around the restaurant, he turned his attention back to Gail and Daanya, "I'm on your side here. You came to us, the authorities, to help you get Dalton out of a spot which he may or may not have wanted to be involved in."

He held up his hand when both women started to challenge his assumption. "Let me finish. If I'm going to be any help to either one of you, I need you to be able think rationally at all times. One seemingly insignificant fact could help me find Dalton."

He laid his hands on the table and, in a softer voice said, "But you have to understand, my first loyalty is to this country. I give you my promise I will do my very best to extricate him out of this situation, but he may end up being the enemy. You need to know that before we go forward."

Gail covered her face with her hands. *God, please. Where are you, baby?* She could feel her eyes start to fill. Beside her, Daanya took her hand.

Chapter 31

Gail's mouth felt like it was full of stale cotton balls. The sun burned her eyes as it streamed into the room through a misaligned window blind. Raking her tongue across the roof of her mouth, she tried to gather enough saliva to swallow.

Where the hell's the clock? Lifting her head, she spied it across the room on the floor, unsure how it ended up there. Pressured by her bladder, Gail threw back the covers and staggered to the bathroom. As the pressure was released in a blessed stream, she began to arrange her thoughts.

Hawkins had dropped them off after the restaurant with a promise of checking in on them if he heard anything. The laptop was evidence but there was very little found in the initial scan.

She peeked into Dalton's room and saw Daanya was still asleep. *Poor kid. She's as lost as I am.*

Although it was late afternoon, Gail put on a pot of coffee. While she waited for the pot to perk, she fired up her tablet. Pulling up Google, she typed ISIS recruiters and it gave thousands of hits. One web page stood out after a few pages of scrolling: Mothers of ISIS. Clicking on it, she read about other mothers who had lost their children to the turmoil in the Middle East. Gail wondered why she was doing this to herself, but she was unable to close the page. These children had been radicalized and spirited away to the fighting in Syria or Iraq, and they were killed fighting other Muslims in the name of Allah. She blinked to ward off more tears and pushed the tablet away from herself with disgust. *Dalton is still alive. So get a grip.*

When she heard the bedsprings groan in the other room she knew Daanya was getting up; Gail poured a second cup and placed it across the kitchen table from her. The bedroom door opened and the girl nodded to her shyly before she ducked into the bathroom.

"Any news?" Daanya asked when she came out of the bathroom.

"No, nothing yet. You feeling any better?" She was surprised the young woman wasn't wearing her hijab, her dark brown hair flowing like a deep river down one shoulder.

"Yes, just groggy."

"Maybe the coffee will help."

"Thank you."

"You are very beautiful without the hijab, Daanya," Gail told her as she watched the color rise in the woman's face. "I'm not sure of the rules, but I'm guessing it has to do with men?"

"It comes from the Quran, where Muhammad warned both men and women to show modesty in public. Among family and other women, I do not have to wear it unless I prefer. It is also a sign of my belief in Islam.

"I hope you'll forgive me, but with all that's happening, why would anyone want to follow Islam? I mean, I admit I know nothing of the religion, but with all the violence, how could anyone follow such a faith?"

She saw the look of surprise on Daanya's face, but then it turned to a smile.

"The fighting and the violence has nothing to do with Islam."

"How can you say that? That's all it's about. Jihad and killing infidels," Gail said, sounding annoyed.

Daanya put her cup down. "Let me ask you this. Does Christianity preach hatred and bigotry? How about theft and murder?"

"No, of course not." *Where the hell is she going with this?*

"Then how can you explain," Daanya said, counting with her fingers, "the systematic slaughter of the Aztec people perpetrated by the Roman Catholic Church and their lust for gold, or the thousands that were persecuted during the Spanish Inquisition? What about their helping Nazi war criminals escape justice or turning a blind eye to all the child abuse by their own priests?"

"Well...," Gail found she couldn't defend those actions.

"The religion did not cause those atrocities. Men representing the religion did."

"But so many of them are fighting. And so many more are joining them. It's worldwide."

"What most people do not consider is that there are over a billion Muslims in the world. If even a hundred thousand were terrorists, they would be a drop in the bucket. They are insignificant." Daanya lowered her eyes. "The real issue is not Islam. The message of Islam is the same as Christianity and the other world religions. Pope Francis has been promoting the idea that we are all children of God and that the common belief is love. To me Islam has always been about love."

"Then why the violence?"

"Greed, power, poverty, politics. You name a reason and I'm sure you can find someone using it to control others. They warp the message of Allah to suit their needs and actions. If they were true believers, they would strive to be just as the Quran tells us: 'It may be that God will grant love (and friendship) between you and those whom ye (now) hold as enemies. For God has power (over all things), and God is oft-forgiving, most merciful. God does not forbid you, with regard to those who fight you not for (your) faith nor drive you out of your homes, from dealing kindly and justly with them for God loves those who are just.'"[11]

Gail allowed the words to sink in and looking at it from different angles to see if she agreed with it, but couldn't find fault. Looking up at Daanya, she saw the young woman waiting for her, giving her the time to digest.

"Then why is it so hard to tell the world? To expose the extremist?"

"Because there are Western groups who are equally extreme and attack Islam at every chance."

"Yeah, people like Sam," thought Gail. Then she asked, "So how do we get the word out?"

Both were startled by the phone before Daanya could answer.

Gail reached for her cell phone. Looking Daanya in the eye, she answered, "Hello."

"Gail, it's Hawkins. We have a lead. Are the two of you interested in a road trip?"

Chapter 32

"What's the plan, Mr. Hawkins?" Gail asked.

"We got lucky with a traffic cam. Plates match a van owned by Dilawar Maloof," Hawkins said.

"My cousin," said Daanya, riding shotgun in the government sedan.

Hawkins nodded, "We also picked up a GPS signal from two of their phones in West Virginia. We're heading there now."

"Just so you know, this is usually against protocol, but I've managed to convince my superiors that having the two of you with me would be serving double duty. First, you'll be with me to help me get into Dalton's head — how he thinks and what he might do, depending what we find. Secondly, I can keep an eye on the both of you in case Maajid decides he needs some extra leverage to get Dalton to comply with his plans."

"Sounds like something my brother might consider," said Daanya.

"Where in West Virginia are we headed, Mr. Hawkins?" Gail asked from the rear seat.

"Little crossing, called Dryfork. And it's Hawkins. My dad was Mr. Hawkins."

"Never heard Dryfork, Hawkins," Gail said with a smile. She allowed her gaze to move away from the mirror and towards the approaching hills.

"Not surprising. It took map coordinates to get our satellite people to find the place."

"Sounds like it's in the middle of nowhere," Daanya said.

"No better place for a fugitive to hide," Hawkins said, "Or a place to plan an attack."

His comment sent a shiver up Gail's spine.

"Anyways, both signals went offline earlier this morning," he added.

"What's that mean?" asked Gail.

"I'm guessing they don't want anyone to track their movements. It also tells me we're dealing with professionals. Your average Joe wouldn't think about the GPS signal in their cell phone."

"Do you think they are still there?" asked Daanya.

"We can't be sure, but I'm guessing no. There was no van in the satellite image that I was able to get. Of course, it could be hidden in the trees or in a building," he said.

Checking the mirrors, Hawkins added, "Gail, there's a leather travel case beside you. Inside you'll find a satellite shot of the area and another of the property where the signal originated."

She found the bag and pulled both pictures out. The first image was a wide angle of the whole area, like a mega golf course with a patchwork of green fairways. Any flat area had been cultivated. The crossing of Dryfork followed the banks of Cheat River which curved in sinuous loops around the Appalachian Mountains. It was beautiful, like something out of a country living magazine.

The second photo showed a close up of a farmstead that was huddled between a mountain to the east, a forest to the north, and a river to the west. Numerous fields were laid out across the farm, and they were separated by rock fences and trees. The farmstead looked like any other American farm with a main house, barn, and a number of other outbuildings.

"Nice place," Gail said.

"Almost too nice for a terrorist training camp, right?" Hawkins said, taking his foot of the accelerator and then resumed speed.

"Is that what you think this is?"

He nodded, "It could be. There have been a number of state police reports concerning shooting on the property. The owner is a veteran of Iraq. His name was Dandre Brackstorm but he changed it to Adham al-Wahab when he converted to Islam. He owns a rifle range and writes for a number of shooting magazines. According to the report, he has all the proper paperwork and licenses, so he is well within his rights."

"So why do you think it's a terrorist training camp? That's a stretch, isn't it, Hawkins?" Gail asked.

"Yeah, it would be, except that when I searched the owner's background, I found some interesting stuff."

He again looked up into the rear-view mirror and Gail saw that his focus was not on her, but on a point behind her. She started to turn.

"Don't," he said.

She froze.

"Sorry. Didn't mean to come across so hard," he said. "I'm used to working alone. I don't want the person following us to know I've made him."

She noticed his grey eyes were full of mischief. Her anxiety dropped a notch, but she wasn't sure if he was laughing at them.

"Are you mocking us, Mr. Hawkins?" Gail snapped.

Daanya also was rigid in her seat.

"Hell no! I'm looking at having some fun with our friend back there," he said with a grin. "I'm guessing you have a makeup mirror in your purse? Either one of you?"

Daanya had one; she pulled out a small compact and looked at him for an explanation.

"I need you to put on some makeup, or rather, look like you're putting on some makeup. What I really want you to do is use that mirror and get the license plate of the black car behind us. I've tried, but we're liable to end up in the ditch or worse. This way, we can hopefully find out who he is before we decide what to do with him."

Within seconds, she had the plate number, which Gail recorded.

Hawkins handed a cell phone to Daanya. "Speed dial #002 and put it on speaker." He gave her a wink for encouragement.

"Homeland Security, how may I direct your call?"

"Situation Room, clearance AFR153HG," Hawkins said loud enough so the receptionist could hear over the traffic.

"One minute, Mr. Hawkins."

"Hawkins, what's your situation?" asked a woman's voice.

"Steph, I have you on speaker phone. We've picked up a tail, and I'm hoping you can call in some favors and grab our friend before he can contact his people."

"Let me set it up and I'll call you with an update. What details do you have?"

***

The operations center had them take an alternate route to gain time to stage the pickup. After about an hour of secondary highways and back tracking, they were funneled into the staging area. As they approached the road work ahead, a signal man flagged them to stop. A backhoe moved gravel from a pile heaped up on the side of the roadway and spread it over a section of broken pavement. Gail looked for a sign of police presence, but saw nothing to indicate they were there.

Hawkins slowed the vehicle to a stop, waiting for the flagman. Gail resisted the urge to turn and check out the vehicle behind them. As their car moved past the backhoe, she heard a blast of a horn and involuntarily swung her head toward the sound. The excavator had pushed into the space where they had just been and dropped its main bucket on the hood of the suspect's car, crushing it almost in two and stopping the vehicle's forwards motion. The car's rear tires smoked as it tried to regain momentum, black rubber smoke issuing in protest. From beneath his reflective vest, the flagman exchanged his sign for a SIG-Sauer MPX-K submachine gun and aimed at the suspect in the car's front seat. Another construction worker came from the driver's side and rammed the butt end of his weapon through the open window and into the side of the suspect's head.

Hawkins stopped and exited the car. Both Gail and Daanya followed with no thought to the danger, but Hawkins stopped them with a raised hand. "Stay back."

Hawkins moved towards the car, and Gail watched as the man was hauled forcefully out and slammed against the rear side panel. A stream of blood erupted from his nose as his head impacted against the metal.

He cried out, "Fuck! Take it easy. I ain't done nothing wrong."

He was a Latino male in his early 20s. Jogging pants and a muscle shirt exposed arms covered in tattoos which suggested he was a gangbanger.

One agent secured the man's hands with a zip tie and turned him around to face Hawkins.

"You haven't done anything wrong, eh?" Hawkins said, "How about aiding a known terrorist?"

"Fuck you," spat the gang member.

Hawkins smiled at the man in a manner that gave even Gail a chill.

"I ain't talking 'til I see my lawyer."

"You ever hear of the National Defense Authorization Act, NDAA?" he asked the suspect. "It's a little piece of legislation that allows me to hold you without charges," he said, pausing for effect, "indefinitely." He allowed the information to sink in before saying, "You're in the big leagues now buddy. The rules are a whole lot different."

The suspect was unceremoniously shoved into a cargo van with a construction company logo pasted on the side door.

Hawkins led one of the operatives away from the vehicle and said, "We need to know what his relationship is with Maajid and the others. What orders he's following and what he hoped to gain."

"We'll open him up like a can of beer on Super Bowl Night."

Slapping him on the back, Hawkins said, "I need it before halftime Steve."

"I hear ya."

Chapter 33

By the time Hawkins got them on the road again, the sun was just setting. He suggested they take a motel room and continue in the morning.

"It'll be safer moving into that area in daylight," he said.

Gail opened her mouth to argue but then nodded and said, "Good thing we brought a change of clothes. A shower will feel good."

They stopped in Seneca Rocks, West Virginia, and Hawkins rented two rooms from a roadside motel with an attached restaurant. After dropping his bag in the room, Hawkins called the operative that was interrogating the gang member they caught.

"The suspect turned out to be Santiago Camino," the man told him, "A small time felon and member of the Mara Salvatrucha 13 street gang. He has a long but rather unimpressive arrest sheet. Assault and possession mainly."

"What would bring a Muslim extremist and junior member of a powerful street gang together?" Hawkins asked.

"Well, the story he's singing is that he and his buddies staged an attack on this Muslim group to see if one of their recruits would back their play."

"We've seen that game before. Right out of the recruitment booklet," Hawkins said.

"This time it worked better than they anticipated. Seems this Dalton kid ended up burying six inches of steel in another gang member's chest."

"Christ."

"It was classic self-defense, but you know for sure, they use it to pull the kid in deeper."

Hawkins thanked the man and hung up. There was no way he was going to drop this on Gail. Not right now, at least. It was the one thing that might tip her over.

Hawkins, Gail, and Daanya met for a quick meal an hour later. The place was busy with tourists, but they were able to find a booth near the rear of the restaurant.

"I have to admit," Gail said, "it's nice to be on this side of the diner for a change."

"I bet," Hawkins said. "How long have you been doing that?"

"Since my husband died. I was in my second year of nursing school when Tom was killed. The little insurance we had was taken up with the funeral expenses, so I had no choice but to start working."

"It must have been difficult to give up on what you wanted to do," Daanya said.

Gail shrugged, "I've been fortunate to find good people to work with." She looked at Daanya and placed her hand on her arm, "Sam's not the monster he lets everyone think he is. Deep down, he's a very caring man."

"Maybe," Daanya said, "All I know is he scared the hell out of me."

They ordered their food and Gail turned the conversation around. "Okay Hawkins, you know all about us, but we know virtually nothing about you."

He smiled, "Just your average super spy. You know, the whole 007 thing. Swoop in at the last minute, save the world, and then ride off into the sunset."

The two women laughed, and it sounded nice. So much of his world was not nice.

He shrugged, "Really, there's not much to tell. Grew up outside Denver. Got into a mess of trouble and the judge offered me time in the military or in prison. I opted for the Army and joined the Rangers. Since then, I spent time in Afghanistan and Iraq before being offered the gig with the DHS."

There was a lot more he could add, but half was classified and the other shit he was trying to forget. No sense burdening them with his sins.

"Why do you do it?" Gail asked, concerned.

"Because someone has to, and I'm very good at my job," he said. "Besides, I get off on the spy stuff."

"Okay, macho man," Gail said, with a soft smile.

They finished up their meals and agreed to meet for breakfast early the next morning before the quick trip to where Dalton's phone last pinged its GPS signal.

***

Hawkins checked the GPS unit next to him in the passenger seat. It indicated he was across the river from the homestead. He found a break in the trees to pull off the road and shut off the engine. Headlights extinguished, he waited until his eyes adjusted to the night. He hadn't told Gail or Daanya about this late night excursion.

Hawkins pulled on a headset and turned on the radio holstered on his hip. "Hawk to Mother, how do you read?"

"Five by five, Hawk. We have you lit up. Target is still clear."

"Roger. Moving in."

He scooped the Heckler & Koch MP5 submachine gun with its Osprey silencer off the rear floor and exited the vehicle. The pistol holstered on his right hip carried a similar noise suppressor in a breakaway holster. Thanks to Hollywood, many people thought silencers made no noise at all; but in reality, they only suppress the noise. If he had to use the weapon, the sound would not carry to the small crossroad community three quarters of mile away.

Once squared away, he donned a set of night vision gear, making sure the headset wasn't compromised. Switching the goggles on turned the world around him a green tinge. He stepped into the shadows leaving his car behind and moved towards the homestead. The adrenalin coursed through him. He could feel his heart rate jump. His hearing seemed to catch every whisper in the night as if magnified, and he could tell by the soft splash that beyond the trees was a stream or creek with quick moving water.

God I love this.

He had been hesitant to leave the military because he was scared to lose this part of the job, but a friend who had put his name forward for the posting reassured him he would have plenty of wet work.

Hawkins broke through the trees and slid down an embankment into the shallow river. Keeping low, he crossed quickly; the splashing and gurgling of the water masked his noise. On the far side of the river, he eased himself up the embankment and surveyed the open farmland before him. He took his time, right to left, checking for anything out of place.

In his headphones he heard, “Still clear, Hawk.”

He double tapped the transmission button to acknowledge. The command center watched both him and the property via thermal imaging satellite overhead. He might not pick up a hidden foe, but there was no hiding from the eye in the sky. He climbed over the bank and moved toward the farm buildings, utilizing trees and bushes to hide his movements. He would have to cross the open area of plowed field, but nothing showed through his goggles.

He was just about to leave cover when his headphones broke silence again. “Hawk, we’re marking an irregular pattern of indentations in the field directly in front of your position. Possible anti-personnel mines.”

Christ! That got the blood flowing.

Hawkins removed a telescopic rod from a pant leg pocket, unwrapped a length of loose wire from the rod, and then expanded the pole to its four foot limit. It almost looked like an old fashioned fishing pole. He pushed the rod ahead of him, wire trailing as he inched forward. He was about to pass between the last two trees before the field when the wire fell across a tripwire, warning him. He started to circle around the trap, only to find two more. He was boxed in.

Brackstorm knew his trade. Too bad he went rogue.

To avoid the traps, Hawkins had to back out the way he entered. He didn’t know what the traps were armed with, but the fact they was here in such close proximity to a possible minefield told him Brackstorm had something to hide or was completely paranoid. Having read his file, Hawkins thought it might be a combination of both.

Although it was slow going, Hawkins finally made it to the farm yard, avoiding the field all together. Between the warm night and the stress of walking around potential death traps, he was soaked with perspiration. The cool breeze through the valley invigorated him.

Going from building to building, he found and disarmed a number of cleverly hidden claymore mines. His respect for the ex-Marine grew. Hawkins followed the lane that serviced the farm, finding three different IEDs that would have wiped out any unwelcome guests. The devices were placed to take out three or more law enforcement vehicles as they entered the property in column. The fact the gate itself had no trap proved he dealt with a real professional. This had been done to make the property look safe.

"Hawk to Mother, entrance and main grounds clear."

"Roger. Find anything?"

"The suspect's vehicle is in the barn. Find out what Brackstorm drives. Check out his alias as well."

"Will do. What's next."

"Now I have to break the news to the mother that her son is already gone."

Chapter 34

"Why would you go there without us?" Gail demanded once Hawkins had told the two women about his late night excursion; they were nursing a morning coffee.

"Because we're dealing with a very well-trained individual," he said, putting the coffee cup down on the table. He looked like he had been up all night with bags hanging loosely under his eyes.

Gail had slept fitfully and had risen before the sun. When she left the shower, Daanya was in the process of praying, her prayer mat stretched between the beds. The poor girl froze like a thief caught in the act. Gail hugged her and told her to continue.

"Then why are you dragging both of us across the country if you're going to take off and do your own thing?" She could feel her face heating up, but she didn't care.

"You're here to talk some sense into your son or," he indicated Daanya, "your boyfriend, if we get the chance." He rubbed his tired eyes before adding, "It's not going to help Dalton if I get his mom or girlfriend killed before that."

Gail realized he was right and tried to calm down. She asked, "So what did you find?"

"Enough booby traps to kill off half a regiment," he said, draining his coffee and raising the cup towards the waitress for a refill. "The place was empty, however we'll go through it in case either of you spot something Dalton may have left behind. Daanya, your cousin's car was in the barn, so they have an alternative mode of transportation. I'm guessing an R.V. or bus from the size of the tracks."

“How about the cell phones you were tracking?” Daanya asked, her head covered with a mauve hijab that enhanced her eyes.

“I didn’t have time for more than a cursory search. There is a team going over the entire place as we speak.” Picking up the menu, he added, “The sooner we eat, the sooner we can get there and see if they found anything.”

***

Through the trees, Gail could see sunlight reflected off a hidden creek before the hillside blocked it off and the forest opened up to reveal cultivated fields. She had a hard time believing a violent terrorist could be part of this tranquil setting. A state trooper guarded the main gate to the property and moved his car out of the way once Hawkins’ presence had been authorized over the radio. Hawkins eased the car forward, and Gail suppressed a shiver as the car entered a tunnel of overhanging tree branches that blocked the light. She tried to think what it had been like for Hawkins last night in the complete darkness, searching for explosives left behind. She couldn’t fathom anyone actually wanting to do that kind of work.

The car left the gloom and had them all squinting. Hawkins pulled beside another state cruiser and stepped out. A tall, casually dressed man, assumedly one of his team members, met Hawkins. He pulled Hawkins aside and spoke quickly to him. Hawkins nodded and walked back.

“The team has some information for us. We’ll do the grand tour in a few minutes, but first, this is Tommy Chen; everyone calls him ‘Gunnie.’”

Gunnie nodded to both women and then waved over another state trooper who had been leaning up against his cruiser. “What can you tell us, Officer?” Hawkins asked.

“Not much to tell. He came across as a nice guy. Kept to himself. Stirred up a ton of attention when he first moved in years ago and started blasting away with his guns, but his range is licensed and once the townspeople accepted that, they left him alone. This,” he indicated the DHS vehicles, “came as a complete surprise.”

“I’m sure it did. Thanks for your help,” Hawkins said, handing him a card. “Drop me a note if you remember anything else.”

They followed Tommy into the main house, and Gail stopped and gazed at all the activity inside. As she looked around, she saw at least 15 people spread out over the large kitchen/living room. There were computers lying on every flat surface, and the din of voices and computers was numbing after the serenity of the barnyard. To Gail, it looked like chaos.

She noticed Hawkins diving into the maelstrom like a fish returning to water. People started fielding facts and data to him, and others threw questions. Hawkins was in his element, moving from one person to the next, sharing a joke, answering a question, or giving an order.

After a few minutes, he looked up

"Okay people. I need it quiet!" he shouted.

The noise subsided immediately, and Gail wondered if the sudden compliance was from their military training. She felt Daanya stand close, almost as if she was looking for cover. Those beautiful dark eyes darted nervously across the room, so Gail gave Daanya's hand a squeeze and smiled at her.

"This is Gail Westree and Daanya Nasry. What news do we have?"

A tall willow of a girl, her hair hidden beneath a hijab, raised her hand, "I'll start."

Gail felt her jaw drop at seeing a Muslim on Hawkins' team.

"Gail, Daanya, this is Amena. She's my second in command, and I trust her with my life," Hawkins said.

Amena acknowledged Hawkins's compliment and said, "Dalton was definitely here. We found his phone and wallet inside the barn, which was used as a bunk house."

Gail nodded her thanks. *We're on the right trail.*

Another agent, a young man who looked like he was still in his teens, spoke next. "We've collected DNA samples from all the bunks and should have clear samples isolated in a few hours for future reference."

"What's that for?" Daanya asked.

"It will be helpful if we find similar DNA samples in other locations," Hawkins said before the young agent could respond.

Gail thought, "He's talking about identification of a dead person. Oh my God!" Without realizing it, her nails dug into

Daanya's hand. When the young girl flinched, she relaxed her grip and mouthed the word, "Sorry."

Gunnie looked up from a computer monitor and announced, "Brackstorm owned a 2002 Ford pickup, parked in the yard. There is no other vehicle listed in his or his alias' name. The tire tracks suggest a larger vehicle — a bus, R.V. or a semi."

"We're almost done here, Gail," Hawkins said. "Let me finish up and we'll go out and check the barn. Dalton might have left something there."

She nodded.

"Gunnie, make sure you get a demolition crew out here to disarm the mines and trip wires. I've marked the ones I found on the map, but there may be more," Hawkins ordered. He looked around the room, his eyes holding on Gail's. "Anyone else?"

One hand rose at a corner table. The fellow was partially surrounded by computer monitors so only the top of his head showed. "The team did a sweep of the property and found there had been some recent action on the range. We have a ton of fresh empty shells of different calibers as well as evidence of explosives."

"Thanks, everyone. Great work."

Hawkins led Gail and Daanya from the farm house and guided them to the barn. Gail realized both Hawkins and Daanya had positioned themselves on either side of her. Entering, Gail saw the cots were set up outside a row of stalls, the ground covered with rough lumber. There was the smell of damp hay and a faint scent of old manure. The loft had bales of hay stacked neatly in piles, but from the black covering of mold, she didn't think it was used for animals. She recognized the wallet sitting on one of the cot as Dalton's; she bought it for him last year for Christmas. Sitting down on the bed, she picked it up and flipped through it, seeing his bus license and other documentation. She found the picture of the three of them, an old picture with Tom and her surrounding Dalton in his hockey equipment. They were all smiling. Tears burned her eyes. Before realizing it, her loud wail filled the barn as her misery overwhelmed her.

Chapter 35

Dalton and the group made the long trip to Cheyenne, Wyoming, at Adham's insistence.

"It's called ANFO — ammonium nitrate and fuel oil," Adham explained to them before they left his farm. They were just finishing breakfast after having packed the old mobile home in the barn.

"So, what's the big deal?" asked Maajid.

"It would take us weeks of purifying the ammonium nitrate and mixing it to an exact ratio with the fuel oil. That's after we steal a shipment of it," Adham said. "But this ANFO is pre-mixed for the mining sector, so it's perfect for us."

Dalton listened to the banter, understanding only parts of it. Maajid was not forthcoming and refused to spell out what exactly he planned, but the fact they were talking about explosives made him more uneasy. Dalton knew he had no real choice, though. He kept playing the video over and over in his head. If he refused to participate, he stood to lose both his mom and Daanya.

"So other than the mixing, why is this so much better than what we discussed earlier?" Maajid demanded, his tone harsh enough that Dalton looked up.

Adham leaned over Maajid in a threatening manner and said in a quiet voice, "Because I've forgotten more about explosives than you know."

Dalton almost laughed out loud at the fear in Maajid's face as he tried to backpedal away from Adham.

"Okay. Okay," Maajid said in a rush. "Explain it to me."

"It's dry," Adham said, "which means we can pack it into any container we want and direct the blast anywhere we want it to go."

By taking turns driving and stopping only to eat and pray, the trip took three days. Maajid was able to secure a small warehouse in an industrial park on the south side of the town. A trip to a camping store outfitted themselves with cots, blankets, and a couple propane stoves. Adham left them and showed up a couple hours later with a blue van he picked up at a used car lot up the road.

That night, Dalton and Parsa were driven south of the explosive plant with Maajid. They took a dirt road off the highway; Maajid parked the van behind an outcrop of rocks.

"You two will enter the plant undetected and will document any shift in movement, guards, and shipments in and out of the place," Maajid said handing them note pads and pens. He also passed each a Midland GXT two-way radio with an ear bud.

"Dalton, there are two large fuel tanks on the west side of the facility. You will choose one and watch from there. Parsa, there is a raised walkway between the processing plant and the loading station for the rail line; you will watch from there. I will be watching you with this," he held up a night vision monocle, "and will radio if there is any danger."

"What if we're caught?" Dalton asked.

"Then I make a phone call," Maajid said, the threat hanging between them.

Dalton gritted his teeth and fought to control himself. He wanted to throttle Maajid, but it wouldn't do any good. He would bide his time. From his vantage point high up on the massive diesel tank, Dalton watched the technician close up the top loading caps on top of the transport's cargo trailer. The bright lights illuminated the entire procedure including the placement of the hazardous material placards. He saw some of the shipments contained wet slurry that splashed into the tanks. The techs would take extra care, cleaning the product from the vehicle's white paint before allowing it to leave. Other loads were made up of a dry powder, the dust of which floated in the air around the roof hatches. The trucks with the dry explosive were moved to a parking area behind the administration building until the early mornings when the drivers arrived. The truck's placards were folded close to indicate they were empty, but that was just a ploy to deter theft. Even with the powerful lights, the shadows here could hide an army. Dalton laid on top of the super tank some 50 feet off the ground and recorded all movement. For an instant he thought to falsify the movements, but he knew Maajid was somewhere out in the dark watching him. He was probably keeping his own notes to compare. Chemicals arrived around the clock to feed the hoppers and vats, some by truck and some by rail, and Dalton recorded them all. Business must have been booming because three separate shifts of workers kept the plant running day and night. The night stretched, and Dalton's thoughts kept returning to his mother and Daanya. His mom must be worried sick. He had promised to call, but Maajid would not allow it, saying he would not chance having the call traced. Dalton guessed Maajid feared he would say something that might lead the authorities to them.

The radio crackled in his ear. "Dalton, you have a visitor coming up the stairs. Do not allow him to raise alarm."

Dalton's head turned towards the stairs. *What? How the hell do I do that?*

He pushed back from the ledge and moved as quietly as he could towards the metal stairwell. He peered down and saw a worker trudging up the stairwell. He ran to the other side of the huge tank and saw nothing but welded steel loops spaced every 10 feet around the side of the tank. He snapped a glance back towards the staircase while he tried to push the panic away as his mind scrambled for a way out. *Even if I push the guy off, he's liable to scream. I don't want to kill anyone else.*

The loops. He pulled off his belt and dropped to his stomach. He reached over the edge of the tank and pushed the tongue of the belt through the loop. He then fed it through the buckle and pulled it tight. Wrapping the leather around his fist as tight as he could, he eased his legs and then his stomach over the edge. Anyone on the ground looking up would see him instantly. When the man's head crested the tank, Dalton lowered himself fully, his arms accepting his weight. If the man walked towards his position, Dalton would allow himself to drop to the length of the belt.

The tank was so vast Dalton couldn't hear the man's footsteps. After a moment, he pulled himself until he could see over the edge. There. At the top of the stairs, his back towards Dalton, the man was lost in a cloud of thick smoke.

A joint? The idiot is smoking a joint on top of a fuel tank?

Dalton lowered himself and closed his eyes, expecting the world to turn to flames.

But it didn't.

His arms began to shake as he neared the end of his endurance. Dalton pulled himself up knowing he would be caught if the man was still there, but he had no choice. It was all he could do to pull himself to the point where he could get his elbows over the edge and relieve the pressure on his arms.

The man was gone.

It took all of Dalton's strength to pull himself onto the roof, and he collapsed with fatigue.

"Killing him would have been easier," said Maajid through the radio, the contempt in his voice obvious.

The rest of the night was uneventful. After more than six hours on the tank, the cold coming from the mountains had taken its toll, but it was Parsa that complained first.

That was a small victory.

***

"What I want to do is create a huge distraction," Adham said when they returned to the warehouse. "So when we hijack the shipment, no one will miss it until we are long gone."

"What are you planning?" Maajid asked.

"Once we are sure of the regular movements of the workers, Dalton or Parsa can guide us into the plant. I need to see the layout up close so I can come up with a plan for the distraction."

Two nights later they went out again, this time with Adham and Dilawar. While Dalton took his regular post on top of the fuel tank, the others moved through the property to get a closer look at the equipment and pump stations. As in the past, they made the approach from the south of the plant which had only dirt roads and rail lines as access. Maajid pointed out the different landmarks of the plant to Adham so he was able to align the map he had memorized with the actual layout. They climbed up the rise and slowly made their way down to a small, dried out creek. With their eyes adjusted to the night, they were able to follow the group's old tracks in sand and stone creek bed.

Adham pointed to the track and whispered, "We better hope no one sees this. You've packed down one hell of a trail with your coming and going."

"It's only like this until it turns away from the plant," Maajid said. "After that, it's all stone and there's no trail."

"Maybe, but anyone who finds it will wonder," Adham said. "And once we do this, they will be looking."

The rear of the property was littered with old pressure tanks and 45-gallon barrels which helped them stay in cover. Across a service room was a large building identified as the main processing building. Some employees were taking a break, the glow of their cigarettes and the murmur of their conversation marking their position.

Once the workers paraded back into the building, Maajid and his group waited five minutes to ensure all the workers had returned to work before he whispered to Dilawar and Adham, "You should be clear for an hour or so except for some trucks moving between the loading station and the lot, plus the security guard. He makes a circuit every hour on the hour. I'll radio if I see anything."

"It should only take me half that time to find what kind of setup they have," Adham whispered back. To Dalton, he said, "Will you be able to see us if we leave from this location?"

"I can see pretty much everything," Dalton said.

"Okay, when you see us back here, you follow us out. Just make sure you follow a different way out. Don't retrace your path."

Dalton nodded realizing the only reason he was there was so they could keep him in sight.

With a final look across the compound, Adham and Dilawar left the cover and crossed the service road. Dalton watched them move off towards the processing building until they disappeared. He then carefully made his way to the top of the tank and resumed his vigil.

The guard at the main gate came out on the hour to drive around the complex. Dalton watched the truck make its way across the plant; it didn't even slow down until it arrived at what Dalton assumed was a cafeteria. A few minutes later, the guard returned with a coffee cup to his vehicle, and the truck returned to the security hut at the entrance to the plant. Dalton released a sigh of relief. The others had not been sighted. Part of him wanted them to be seen or captured, but he worried what Maajid would do to the women back home.

Twenty minutes later, Dalton made his way back to the rendezvous, having seen Adham and Dilawar slipping through the shadows towards the back of the property. Both men carried a small bush that had been pulled out of the ground by the roots. Dalton had no time to question them as they took off into the night. Before long, the four men crouched by the riverbed and Dalton understood what Adham was doing with the bushes. Adham smoothed the worse of the footsteps in the sand with his hands, then used the brush to obliterate any man-made marks.

***

"We need to do this tonight," Adham said. They were gathered back at their warehouse around a table covered with maps, a scattering of coffee cups, and fast food containers.

"What's the rush?" asked Maajid.

"We came across surveillance cameras outside the main processing building. Right now they are not hooked up, but I figure come Monday, the installers might be back to finish their job. If we wait, it will be another risk."

"I didn't notice anything," Dalton said.

"You didn't know what to look for," said Adham.

"There were a number of those dome lenses mounted on the building's wall and a couple of revolving cameras situated on tall steel posts," Dilawar added. "The wires haven't been connected yet.

Maajid looked at Adham, "Can we be ready by then?"

"The weekend does have a reduced workforce at the plant, so that will decrease the risk," Dalton said. *Less people to get hurt.*

Adham thought for a minute before nodding, "Nothing really changes except I have to build some charges for the distraction. We can go over the plan once more before we move out this evening."

Maajid looked to each person to ensure there were no other issues or hesitation before nodding, "Okay, let's get those charges put together and then get some shut eye. It'll be a long night."

***

The wind had picked up from the east, and Dalton was glad for his windbreaker; there was a definite coolness to the late summer air that had scattered the cloud cover. Once in place on top of the fuel tank, he signaled Adham by depressing the transmit button twice on the two-way radio. Now that Dalton had been informed of the security system, Dalton was surprised he hadn't recognized the installations before. He was able to find six of them along the path to the diesel tank that had been his post for the past week. He had to pass two of the cameras just to mount the staircase on the tank. *Wonder what the pothead is going to do once the cameras went online.*

They timed their arrival so the guard had just completed his rounds and the evening coffee break for the employees was over. Adham had just under an hour to plant the explosive charges that were assembled earlier to create the distraction.

Forty minutes later, Dalton heard his radio crackle twice, signaling that Adham and Ubayd were at the base of the tank. After checking the surrounding area, Dalton made his way down the staircase, diving into the shadows of the large bank of pipes which led away from the reservoir.

Once Dalton made it to their position, Adham and Ubayd began moving in a crouch and followed the shadows of the railcars. They moved towards the west side of the complex where the administration building lay. In the last spot of cover, they crouched in the dry grass and waited for the guard to start his rounds. Across the roadway in the lot behind the building, three trucks stood ready for the morning drivers. These were the same trucks Dalton had seen loaded with the ANFO.

The lone figure left the building and lit up a smoke, inhaling deeply. He stretched his back and legs while he finished his slow poison. After firing up the truck, he did a slow turn of the parking lot. The truck's headlights lit up the locked gate beside the security hut before the truck moved slowly down the service road. Country music wailed from the open windows, fading as it moved on.

One by one, the three crossed the road and followed the low ditch parallel to the administration building. Dalton kept looking back to check for the guard's return run. When they reached the end of the ditch, they took shelter behind a large electrical junction box mounted on a cement pad.

Ubayd ran to the first of three transports and ensured it was fully loaded with the proper explosive. From the driver's door, he pulled out the manifest and checked the load and corresponding

Department of Transportation (DOT) numbers. There were no keys in the ignition or in the cab.

He ran back and whispered, “All set. We need the keys for truck E209.”

Adham nodded.

The headlights of the approaching guard truck came into sight. The three kept out of sight behind the electrical junction as the truck’s lights flashed across the lot. The truck door slammed. Dalton peeked around and saw the guard had lit another cigarette while looking toward the distant highway. After a minute, the man flicked the butt across the dirt parking lot and entered the building.

Adham pulled a small box out from his backpack and lifted and expanded the collapsible antenna. He nodded to his co-conspirators and armed the remote detonator. He pressed the central button.

A muffled blast was all Dalton heard. He wondered if something had gone wrong, expecting a larger explosion. Adham changed the frequency and repeated the process. This time the sound rolled across the plant like thunder. A blinding fireball pushed back the night. The third blast sent another fireball skyward from a different direction. The fire swept through the unburned areas as flammable liquid spread across the ground

Dalton squinted as the night became day, ducking involuntarily at each eruption. Adham wore a huge grin which made Dalton shiver. Ubayd had a stunned, scared look which Dalton thought might match his own.

The security guard ran out of the building, wide-eyed with his mouth open. He stood dumbfounded until a particular explosion shook him out of his stupor. He ran back into the office. Seconds later, the gate motor engaged and started pulling the chain linked panels open. The office door banged open and the guard threw himself at his truck. With a squawk of rubber, the truck started toward the fire taking the backroad around the inferno.

“At least we didn’t have to kill him,” thought Dalton.

Adham let the night swallow the man. He gave the sign and moved forward in a crouched run. All three entered the building with Dalton watching from the door. Ubayd located the large key rack and grabbed the key. With the coast still clear, they ran back to the truck. Dalton could feel the heat off the fire even though they were over a hundred yards away. As planned, Ubayd took the driver seat and the other two jumped into the cab. Adham pushed Dalton into the console so he could squeeze his bulk in before slamming the door.

"Sorry, man!"

Crushed, Dalton tried to position himself so he could at least breathe. The engine roared to life and the truck lurched forward as the brakes were released. Ubayd shifted gears and turned toward the entrance. The truck shuddered as a wave of superheated air rushed over them. Ubayd kept his foot on the pedal. Pieces of metal flung wide by the explosions were falling all around them like meteors. The truck made the turn through the gates, leaving the fire behind them. Ubayd slowed the truck for the rail tracks that fed the plant and geared down to turn onto the main road heading in the opposite direction to avoid emergency responders. The transport's inertia pulled into the curve, giving Dalton a chance to breathe as Adham's huge frame was pushed away from him.

After a mile, the road ended. Ubayd slowed and pulled onto the highway tarmac. The highway brought them parallel with the plant. The fire continued to grow. There were still explosions going off as the fire found caches of ammonium nitrate. The entire countryside was lit like day. The firefighters would not be able to safely get close enough to make a difference.

Dalton closed his eyes. *It was supposed to be a diversion. No one is going to survive that.*

He finally managed to wiggle out from underneath Adham. The giant laughed like a fool at Dalton's curses and grunts.

"What the fuck are you laughing at?" Dalton asked, his anger masked his horror.

The big man laughed even more.

Dalton's hands were shaking as he considered what Maajid's plan might entail with this kind of weapon at hand.

"Adrenalin," Adham said mistaking his reaction.

Dalton looked at him. Adham's face was outlined only by the dim light of the truck's dashboard.

"Happens after any firefight," said Adham. "Bet you feel like a million bucks, eh? Like you could take on the world."

But Dalton felt sick and helpless.

Ubayd took the southbound ramp onto I-25 towards Denver. As they passed a Sunoco station, Adham tapped the transmit button twice on his radio. A few minutes later, a dark colored van passed them. Both the driver and passengers gave them the victory sign.

They had a bomb to build.

Chapter 36

Aazam waited at an outside cantina in the heart of Monterrey, hidden from the worst of the suns by a vine covered trellis. He attempted to relax as he sipped filtered water from a plastic bottle, but the people he had arranged to meet were incredibly dangerous and he was unsure of the reception he would receive.

The file on Alejandro Morales was extensive but fascinating reading. He was the head of one of Mexico's largest and most barbaric drug cartels, and there was no lack of stories; Aazam admitted to himself that he was nervous. Soldiers were predictable, but Morales was a different kind of animal. Aazam had been on the run for two weeks and needed Morales to enter the United States. Although Aazam was exhausted, he needed to be sharp. One wrong word or look could get him killed.

He allowed his eyes to wander casually over the few patrons who sat along the adobe building's wall. Most of the traffic had slowed due to the daily siesta; the odd tourist sped past, trying to pack every second of the day with new exotic experiences before they returned to their normal, safe, everyday lives. He started on his second bottled water when he was approached by a woman, her head covered by a delicate, white rebozo scarf.

Without waiting to be invited, she sat down and said, "My employer sends his regards. He is a very busy man and asks your forgiveness for not attending in person."

Aazam smiled his acknowledgment, "You must thank him for the opportunity to do business."

The woman did not smile back, but continued as if he hadn't spoken, "As there has been little business between us in so long, it is hoped you would be willing to extend us a favor at the same time we assist you."

"How can I help?" Aazam asked.

"My employer has arranged for you to travel up the coast in one of the rice boats to Louisiana." She slid a note with the name of the ship and it's captain. "They'll be expecting you."

"Rice boats?"

"Since the drought in California, most of Mexico's rice comes from the Gulf states. In return, Mexico sends produce. The ships run nonstop. It is one of these that will bring you north. You will be met by other business associates along the route who will transport you to shore, thereby allowing you to avoid scrutiny."

Aazam nodded, "And the favor?"

"You will carry an extra piece of luggage that you will pass to the same people who will take you to shore."

"Drugs?" Aazam asked.

"Does it matter?"

"Not at all. Please tell your employer I hope we can do business again in the future."

She nodded and stood up. "The piece of luggage will be in your cabin. I needn't say what would happen if the shipment did not reach its destination."

"No. Totally unnecessary."

***

The huge rice freighter was definitely not built for comfort. Aazam was given his own berth — a claustrophobic cubicle that had room only for a bunk, a chair, and a small fold up writing table. He was left on his own and, except for a few trips topside for fresh air, he caught up on sleep that two weeks on the run had deprived him of.

On the third night, Aazam and his luggage were lowered to a pitch black cigar boat with no running lights. Aazam sat apart from the two American men aboard who were both dressed in dark clothing and who were both dark from sun and wind. The relaxed manner in which they maneuvered the vessel spoke of a lifetime on the water. Pulling away from the ship, the boat ran north for shore. Once they crossed into the freshwater which emptied into the Gulf from the Louisiana swamps, they pulled along shore and the smaller of the two checked the bag Aazam had transported while the driver kept the boat steady in the slow current. Satisfied, the bag was stored in a watertight compartment.

Using night vision goggles and the onboard GPS, they began the slow crawl through the labyrinth that made up the Bayou Dularge. The sounds of insects and the odd splash was all Aazam could hear over the quiet four stroke outboard as the boat moved through the night. Aazam strained his eyes to pick out any landmarks, but the view was uninterrupted by trees and low hanging moss. The boat followed a slow moving current, winding back and forth as the water found the easiest route. Aazam noticed the driver kept the boat in the center of the channel, avoiding both shores. Aazam was unsure if anyone could navigate through the stygian blackness without the modern equipment. He hated that he had to trust these men so entirely.

For some time, Aazam listened to the hiss of their whispers whenever his back was turned. When he had first boarded, his two companions were relaxed, but this changed with every mile deeper into the interior they went. Aazam had seen the same stiffness before on every soldier he had ever commanded. They were trying to build up courage. Aazam wasn't sure what had set them off. The smaller of the two seemed to be the leader. The man's eyes burned with hatred as he peered at Aazam. *It doesn't make any sense. I've never see this man before.* He was just another mule who had just handed over a fortune in Mexican heroin.

Aazam's instincts screamed a warning. He waited for the inevitable.

The sudden sway of the boat gave him the sign he had been waiting for. The Driver cut the engine while the smaller man moved forward, towards Aazam.

"You ain't no Mexican. You're a fucking Arab," said the smaller smuggler. "I fought against your type in Iraq. You sneaking into America means you're probably a terrorist or something."

"You're getting paid," Aazam said watching the man's hands where a large hunting knife appeared. "What's it matter to you?"

"I might make some money moving drugs, but I ain't no traitor."

The knife came from below the man's waist, towards Aazam's unprotected stomach. Aazam stepped in towards the threat and swung his closest arm which he held rigid to block the knife. It knocked his assailant's arm off target; it also left the man unbalanced and open. Aazam pivoted so his hip stopped the man's forward movement, and Aazam used his free arm to come up under the man's jaw. His elbow connected with full force, driving through the man's throat. The man's body contracted violently, trying to force air through the collapsed airway.

The other smuggler pulled off the night vision goggles. He managed to move around the steering console before seeing his friend's quick death. He froze; shock evident in his slack expression. Without taking his eyes off the driver, Aazam bent and pried the knife out of the first man's hand.

Rising, he said aloud, "Decide carefully how you want this to end."

The tall one looked from Aazam to his friend, whose convulsions were slowing down, and then back to Aazam. Aazam stepped towards him and grabbed the man by the shoulder, spinning him around, and placing the knife blade at his throat.

"You are only useful if you can navigate this swamp. Do you understand?"

The man whimpered, but nodded.

Aazam pushed the smuggler into the driver's seat, noticing the automatic rifle mounted beside the chair. The fool hadn't even thought to pick it up. *Why have we ever feared the Americans?*

Aazam pulled the rifle, an AR-15, from its boot and pointed it at the driver.

"What other weapons do you have on board?" he asked.

The man pointed to a compartment in front of the steering console. Keeping the rifle trained on the smuggler, Aazam stepped back and opened the compartment to find a cache of weapons. There were a couple more rifles, a number of different pistols, and a canvas bag with a couple of fragmentation grenades. *With this kind of weaponry, why would the fool attack me with a knife?*

Aazam pulled out a pistol — a 9mm Browning. Dropping the clip to ensure it was loaded, he placed the rifle into the cabinet and closed the top. The pistol was better in close quarters and suited his purpose for now. In the slot beside the pistol, he found a sound suppressor and screwed it onto the pistol. He did this without taking his eyes off the driver. Aazam moved to the corpse of the first smuggler and pushed it overboard with his shoe. The body disappeared into the dark water. He pointed the gun at the other man.

"How far to the nearest town?"

"The river will take you to Patterson. It...it's about 12 miles from here," stammered the man. "Our camp is just about a mile from here."

"Probably with more of your friends waiting." It was more of a statement than a question. The fact that the smuggler failed to respond told Aazam his assumption was right.

"Listen carefully," Aazam said, the pistol pointed menacingly towards his captive, "You can live if you get me to this Patterson. But I'll kill you the minute I think you are deceiving me." He gave time for the threat to sink in and then asked, "Understand?"

The man nodded, swallowing hard.

It took over two hours of negotiating the river around fallen trees, sand bars, and multiple tributaries before the glow of the town could be seen reflected in the night sky. At Aazam's directions, the boat pulled up against a fishing shack built on stilts. Tying the boat to the floating dock, he waved the man forward with his pistol. The tall smuggler moved hesitantly towards the dock. Aazam offered his hand, and the man nodded and accepted as he stepped towards the dock.

Aazam used the motion to pull the man towards him and bury the knife deep under the man's ribcage, searching for his heart. The man stiffened in his grip and slid into the space between the dock and the boat.

Untying the boat line, Aazam allowed the boat to fall back into the current while he walked back to the console. He engaged the motor and turned the boat into a small inlet just off the river, tucked behind the fishing shack. He gunned the motor so the boat rode up the bank and wedged itself onto the mud bank. Aazam then turned off the motor and listened to the night. There were no sounds to indicate his actions had been noticed. After a few minutes, the sounds of the swamp resumed, and Aazam felt comfortable he was alone. He pulled out his phone and dialed his Mexican contact.

"The shipment has reached its destination as promised, however your associates were not accommodating. I am leaving the shipment at the following coordinates. I am sure you have others who can facilitate the pickup." He read off the coordinates off the boat's GPS.

"Please thank your employer. Hopefully we might do business in the future," Aazam said before tossing the cell phone into the water.

He might need an escape plan. It never paid to burn too many bridges.

Chapter 37

Ubayd pulled the transport truck between the open doors of the warehouse and into darkness; the only light came from the truck's headlights reflected against the opposite wall. As the doors closed behind them, he shut down the machine, eliminating all light as instructed. They sat there for a moment until Dilawar tripped the lights. Dalton squinted until his eyes adjusted and he saw a full-size school bus parked beside them.

Dalton went cold. *If he thinks I'm driving this full of kids...*

Adham opened the passenger's door and slid out, dumping Dalton off his lap. "It's been nice, but you've got a bony ass, boy." The giant laughed as he stretched, looking around at his surroundings. The building was another two-story warehouse with enough room for six transport trucks. It looked empty with only the one truck and bus.

Dalton didn't reply. He lowered himself from the truck's cab, still staggered by just how badly he'd been played. Faces flashed in his mind's eye. The faces of *his* kids. As much as he liked Adham, there was no way he could take a chance to trust the man. He didn't know his history or allegiance with Maajid, however, from Adham's story, Dalton felt certain the big ex-Marine would never stand by and allow Maajid to kill innocent children. At least that was something he might be able to exploit if Maajid's plan turned in that direction.

His thoughts were interrupted as Maajid and the others came around the dark side of the truck.

"You did it! We could see the entire sky light up. What did you blow up?" Maajid grabbed Adham and hugged him while the others high-fived each other. Dalton concentrated on keeping the smile pasted on his face.

Maajid asked, “How did the fire get so large?”

“I don’t know. Shit luck,” Adham said. There was no way I could have planned that big of a distraction.”

“The radio said none of the employees are accounted for yet. The fools haven’t even noticed one of their trucks are missing.” Maajid said.

Dalton almost lost his composure when he heard this. *My God, there must have been 20 to 30 people who worked there. *

“Death to the infidels!” Parsa yelled.

“Quiet, you fool,” Maajid said, his anger and attention directed away from Dalton. “We don’t need someone walking past the building to hear that.”

“Sorry,” Parsa said, his head hung

“I understand the thrill of it, but always be on guard. This night’s work is only one step in our journey.”

“I don’t know about the rest of you, but I’m starving. Is there food in that fridge?” Dalton said, indicating the large appliance pushed up against a stove. It was the one way he could extricate himself from the conversation.

“Now that you mention it, I could eat a horse,” Adham said.

“I can tell you that you are the size of a horse,” Dalton said, trying to hide his panicked thoughts.

Adham laughed and flexed his muscles. “You want to be big, you have to eat big.”

Dalton found a number of ingredients and started chopping vegetables for a beef stir fry for the entire group. He used the preparations to hide the emotions that were screaming at him to run. A pair of tables were shoved together near the fridges. One was set up with two propane stoves and a five-gallon container of water while the other was used for eating. A third was set aside as a planning desk.

After being up most of the night, it didn’t take long for everyone to fall into a deep slumber after eating. It was midday when Dalton woke to find most of the others were already up. Pulling on his clothes, he grabbed an apple from the fridge and walked over to the school bus where Maajid and Adham were talking.

"Good morning, my friend," Adham said. "We need your knowledge."

Maajid said, "We got you a bus you knew. Same year and model. You can help us find the best way to hide the explosives."

"Why a bus?" Dalton asked.

"Because no one would suspect danger from something they identify with children."

Dalton nodded. He had done shopping trips for senior groups and fan trips for the Washington Redskins. No one had ever questioned his being anywhere.

"I have to admit though," Dalton said, "When I saw the school bus, I thought you might have planned on using children."

That got the reaction he was fishing for.

Adham froze and then turned to Maajid, "You wouldn't dare," said Adham in a flat voice.

"No. I would never do that to you," Maajid said his hands raised and panic in his voice. "I know all about the kids back in Iraq."

"As long as we understand each other," Adham said as he stepped close to the much smaller man.

Dalton had to bite the inside of his cheek to avoid smiling at the cowering man.

Maajid stepped back, "I know exactly where you stand on the question of children, Adham. I would never put you in that position."

Adham relaxed and said nothing more.

Turning his back on Adham, Maajid threw a glance of sheer hatred towards Dalton for bringing up the idea. It was replaced quickly by his usual trademark of measured calmness. "Dalton is the bus expert, so ask him the questions."

The atmosphere was still charged, yet all three visibly relaxed as Adham turned to Dalton. "Dalton, if the authorities boarded the vehicle, where could you hide a bomb which would not be found?" Adham asked.

"I've never considered that question before." Dalton stepped forward and toggled the switch to open the loading door. He started up the steps before turning back, "Give me some time to think about it."

He closed the door in their faces with the overhead toggle and walked the length of the bus. How could he be a part of this? If he constructed this weapon, it might be used to kill children or other innocent people. It was something he couldn't allow. He didn't for a minute believe Maajid's assurance that children wouldn't be used. Everything that came out of that guy was a lie. It was one thing to contemplate the idea of killing an individual who could end up hurting thousands, but a bomb was not a surgical weapon. It killed everything. But Dalton had to play the part, at least until the opportunity to either escape or sabotage Maajid's plan presented itself. To do anything else put him in an untenable position.

His eyes roamed haphazardly across the interior of the bus, always shifting back to the buses heater. During the bitter winter, he and his passengers endured a cold ride to school because of a broken heater. The cold he could dress for, but the frosting of the windows compromised the visibility. It was the main reason one of the company's mechanics came out to fix the issue. The old man had taken the unit apart with deft fingers, and Dalton had gotten a look at the simple unit. The heat from the engine was pushed through the bus by fans and, in this case, it was the front fan that wasn't working. The mechanic had installed a new sealed unit within minutes, and they were rewarded with a steady stream of warm air. The air pushed through enclosed ducts within the buses thin walls. The wall was kept flush by a thin layer of sheet metal. Except for the ductwork that allowed the passage of air, the rest of the space was not used at all.

"It's just so the ductwork doesn't stand out by itself. The kids would either destroy it or hurt themselves on the edges," the mechanic had explained. "By covering it with a shell to the floor, we avoid entire issue."

Dalton called Adham over and showed him what he had recalled, explaining the void under the sheet metal.

"This is exactly what I need, my friend. I can take it from here."

Have I just condemned people to die? If they want me to drive this thing, maybe I can figure out how I can disarm it.

"Let me give you a hand," said Dalton.

Chapter 38

Gail swiped at a rebel strand of hair as she cleaned off her last table for the night. Sam stood in the kitchen cursing his newest employee of the restaurant when Gail pushed through the doors with her last tray of dishes. The restaurant had been closed for the evening, but the girls had ambushed Sam with a new recipe, compliments of Daanya.

"Give it a break," yelled Gail. "If you're looking for a fight, then let me tell you, Sam Freeman, I'm in a mood."

She was rewarded by the look on his face as his eyes found hers.

He obviously doesn't want any of this.

"But..."

"Stop being so bloody stubborn and give it a try. If you like it, we can put out as a Wednesday special and see how it does. If the customers don't like it, you can revert back to the old menu. And I repeat 'old,' as in boring, as in cut my throat if I have to eat this one more time, old."

He snatched the ladle from Daanya who stood by a large pot of roasted lamb in stewed vegetables which filled the kitchen with the scent of garlic, cinnamon, and allspice.

Daanya stepped back, a quiet smile on her lips as she made eye contact with Gail. Gail once again was taken back at the poise and maturity this young woman brought towards everything she did. She has been an anchor, yet Gail still knew so little about her. With the shift of thought towards her son, Gail leaned against the counter. She put a hand across her mouth, hoping no one saw the quiver of her lip as she pushed through the fear. It had been weeks since they had returned from the suspected training camp in West Virginian and, except for Hawkins' weekly phone calls, there had been no news of Dalton or the men he was traveling with. With effort, she shook herself back to the present.

"There's nothing wrong with my food. No one has ever complained," Sam said, trying to keep his pride.

"Go on and try it, you big baby," Gloria said around her ever present wad of gum, enjoying his discomfort.

Sam took a piece of the lamb, dipped it into the juices, and rammed it into his mouth. After a couple of chews, Gail could see the sour expression on his face change as the flavor washed over his pallet.

"Not bad," he said

Gail looked at Daanya and smiled, "Consider that high praise from this cantankerous old fart."

"Who the hell are you calling 'old'?" Sam asked defensively, running a hand over the thin grey hair combed over his bald spot. He looked at Daanya and asked, "How would you serve it?"

"Either on a bed of saffron rice or fresh baked bread."

Gail knew he was going to add it to the menu, but to save face, it would be on his terms. This was killing him.

When Gail and Daanya returned from the West Virginia farm, sitting and waiting in the apartment for news had driven both of them crazy. Gail knew that keeping busy was the best way to avoid sinking into despair, so she approached Sam about hiring Daanya. That had been one hell of a fight. Because of his son's injuries sustained from the war in Afghanistan, Sam saw it as a betrayal of his son.

Jen and Gloria turned the argument on a dime by bringing Sam's son, Brandon, by the restaurant to meet Daanya. Like everyone, he was enchanted with her, and they spoke quietly about his time in Afghanistan and her family's immigration to America.

"Dad," Brandon said, "it's people like Daanya I was fighting to protect. She's not Afghan, but her people are facing the same extremism we encountered. Her brother may be the enemy, but her stance on what he's doing should tell you she's not like him."

As Gail predicted, Sam couldn't argue with his son's logic, and he grudgingly began to warm to the young Muslim.

Gail heard her cell phone ring and crossed over to the hook on the wall to pick it up. *Please be Dalton.* The caller ID told her it was Hawkins

"Hi, Hawkins. Have you heard anything?"

"Well I was going to drive you home and fill you and Daanya in, but no one is answering the door to the restaurant. I can see movement in the kitchen, so figure you're having a party. Mind if I crash?"

"Hold on," she said. She hung up and moved to the double doors leading to the restaurant side of the business. She saw him there drenched in the evening downpour, looking like a drowned stray. She unlocked the door and ushered him in.

"You're soaked right through. Let me get a towel."

"I'm all right, nothing like a summer shower," he said with an anxious smile.

Reaching over the counter, she grabbed a tea towel and tossed it at him. He snatched it midair and rubbed the excess from his hair and face, hanging the towel over the back of a bench to dry as he shed his windbreaker.

"Well, don't keep me in suspense. Do you have anything?"

He looked at her and nodded, "Do you want to wait until Daanya is with us?"

"She's here." Seeing the surprised look on his face, she gave him a tight smile and said, "Sam gave her a job. In fact, would you like to be the guinea pig for her first meal?

"I guess so," Hawkins said with some reservation, not knowing if he was being set up.

Minutes later, Daanya came out with a dinner plate heaped with the lamb and vegetables and placed it before Hawkins before scooting beside Gail in the booth across from him. Sam and the girls also followed from the kitchen, and Gail knew they wanted to know if Dalton was all right. She felt her heart swell

Hawkins took one look at the plate and dove in. "Oh my God! Just as good as I remembered."

"You've had this before?" Sam said in surprise.

"Oh yeah," Hawkins nodded. "When we were on patrol in Iraq, it was either eat the local fair or K-rations[12]. Guess what we choose?" He wolfed down another mouthful before looking at Daanya, "You've done yourself proud, girl. This is fantastic."

Daanya nodded her appreciation, but from the expression on her face, Gail could see that, like her, Daanya wasn't interested in what he thought about the food.

"Dalton. What have you heard?" asked Gail. Hawkins looked at the others, and Gail knew what was coming. "Hawkins, these people are family. I trust each and every one of them."

He shook his head. "I'm sorry. This information is for you and Daanya only. For security reasons."

Sam reached over and said in an uncharacteristically soft voice, "Gail, this guy is ex-military and they do things for a reason. Usually a good one."

The old man looked over at Hawkins, "We'll wait in the kitchen. You do your job and find that boy, you hear?"

Hawkins nodded. "Thank you, Sam."

Gail was annoyed, but the need to hear anything about Dalton overrode her feelings.

Hawkins took another mouthful and seemed to gather his thoughts before saying, "A couple of weeks ago, there was a massive fire and explosion at an explosive plant in Cheyenne, Wyoming. Thirty-two killed. Do you remember seeing it on the news?"

Gail looked at Daanya. They had both watched the news surrounding that event, both praying Dalton was nowhere near that horrible disaster.

"Yes, we remember that. One of the biggest explosions in history," replied Gail.

"That's the one. At first, it was thought to be a ruptured gas line or faulty valve, but it wasn't until the fire was out that they noticed one of the explosive trucks was missing."

Gail went cold. *Explosives. Suicide bomber. No. Please, God, no.*

Hawkins reached out and placed his hand over hers and nodded.

"We found a warehouse they were using as a base. We found DNA evidence that put Dalton and the others there for a number of weeks. The place was abandoned around the same time as the fire. No one remembers seeing any activity near the warehouse. Where they are now is anyone's guess."

"Except now they have a bunch of explosives," Gail whispered.

Daanya said, "How do you hide a transport truck with explosives? There's got to be some kind of trail."

"Believe me, we've exhausted every avenue."

Gail put her head into her hands and began to cry, softly at first, but then wracking sobs that threatened to consume her. She felt Daanya's arms surround her and then pull her to her chest. Gail felt like a child helpless and frightened by a horrible dream

"Gail, I'm sorry. There's more."

She froze, waiting for the inevitable. He was going to say it — Dalton was dead. She braced herself, knowing nothing would prepare her for that final word.

"Do you remember the guy we took into custody on the way to the farm?"

She looked at him in confusion for a minute until her mind snapped back to the takedown on the highway.

"Well, he finally broke under interrogation. And we now have a clear picture of how they radicalized Dalton."

She couldn't trust herself to speak, but Daanya asked for the two of them. "What did you find?"

"This guy, Santiago, he and few of his friends were hired by Maajid to cause a fight that was meant to firm Dalton's allegiance to the group. The staged attack backfired. Dalton actually killed the leader of this group, protecting one of the others."

Gail's vision snapped back and forth, not focusing on anything. She felt herself coming unglued in a waking nightmare.

"Gail. Gail," said Hawkins, "Breath, that's right, breath. Dalton's fine. He's okay."

His words slowly sunk in, and she kept her eyes on his. Someone handed her a glass of water, and she sipped at it.

"Okay?" Hawkins asked.

She nodded, not trusting her voice. She looked to Daanya and saw her tear stained cheeks. *She's hurting, yet she's helping me.* Gail reached up and cupped the side of the girl's face, wiping away a tear with her thumb.

"We'll be okay," Gail said in a ragged whisper. Daanya nodded.

"Gail," Hawkins said, pulling her attention back to him. "You need to listen. From what we got from this guy, Dalton didn't do anything except in self-defense. But it was orchestrated by Maajid. What Dalton doesn't know is Maajid killed a second member of the gang, a member Dalton had previously knocked out."

"So my brother is controlling Dalton with the added threat of being a murderer?" Daanya said.

Hawkins nodded.

Gail saw red as the anger and frustration bubbled over. "They are systematically turning my son into a killer. First this...this charade and then that training site and gun range."

"That's exactly what they are trying to do, Gail. That's what radicalization is all about," Hawkins said gently.

"Did you find out why this Santiago was following us?" Daanya asked.

"He was following you Daanya. Your brother was keeping tabs on you. Now he knows you've teamed up with Gail and with me. He may not know what agency I work for, but he knows you've been to the police."

"How can we be sure my brother knows anything? After all, you caught Santiago."

"Because when I said we broke this guy. I wasn't exaggerating."

Gail shivered at Hawkins' implication.

"But why bother following me?" Daanya asked.

"Keeping an eye on all of the players makes sense, but you are his main focus."

Gail voiced what was not being said, "In case he needs to use Daanya to control Dalton. And if he comes for her, it might be the only chance to find them." Her bloodshot eyes bore into Hawkins, and she pointed her finger at him. In a voice that challenged him, she said, "You better be as good as you say you are!"

Chapter 39

The work on the bus progressed slowly. Dalton and Adham started at the rear of the vehicle working on their hands and knees to strip the bus of its seats, a hilarious operation for a man of Adham's size. After two days and a fair share of cursing, the bus lay empty. Once they had stripped the sheet metal panels to expose the duct work, Adham ordered everyone out as Dalton took measurements of the interior. Using masking tape, they marked where the false wall would sit and then re-measured.

"I'm not just measuring for the new wall," Adham explained, "I need to know the exact amount of explosive we're dealing with so I can gauge what size steel plate to use to direct the blast."

"Why do you need a steel plate?" Dalton asked.

"Think about a building full of smoke. What's the easiest way for the smoke to escape the building?"Adham asked.

"Through the windows and doors."

"Exactly. It will follow the route of least restriction. It's easier to go through a window than through a roof or wall." He drew a three dimensional box on a piece of paper and pointed at it. "Now if we just have a perfect box and put explosives in it, which way will the explosion go?"

Wondering if this was a trick question, Dalton hesitantly said, "Should go in all directions if the material is the same...." he stopped and smiled as the logic sunk in.

“So if you keep one wall opened, the blast will follow the path of least resistance.”

“Bingo. Simple, right?”

Dalton could only wait while Adham retreated to one of the back offices to begin the painstaking calculations that were required. Maajid, who was the only member to have access to the internet, gathered whatever specifics on the chemical components of the blasting material the ex-Marine needed. Once satisfied, Adham placed an order through Maajid. Parsa and Dilawar rented a flatbed truck to pick up the steel. With a lot of cursing and grunting, the sheets were lowered to the cement floor. Before the truck cleared the garage doors, Adham began marking the steel.

“‘Measure twice, cut once,’ my old man would preach to me when I used to work with him building furniture that he would sell alongside the road,” Adham reminisced.

The steel was assembled inside the bus and welded in place. After a week of work, the interior shell was completed. They transferred the measurements to flat stock sheet metal that would cover the steel.

Dalton knew the warehouse had been selected with care and previously been a fabrication shop that closed down after the death of the owner. Many of the tools had been sold off, but a fair number of the larger, mounted machines remained. One of the key machines was a sheet metal bender that allowed Adham to replicate the original wall to meet and join the newer, expanded wall. For Dalton, the work was interesting enough to hide his agitation. What he found ironic was since stealing the truck Adham actually seemed to think Dalton had changed his decision on being part of the plan. Dalton assumed it was because he did what he was told, didn’t argue, didn’t try to escape, and helped out. But he was only waiting for the opportunity that might help Daanya and his mother.

“You’re a better worker than some of our comrades,” Adham said, feeding the sheet metal into the bender to the measured mark.

“It’s better than sitting around waiting,” Dalton said.

"It is a mark of someone who wants to make a difference, not just talk about it."

"As long as it's the right difference," Dalton said. "The more I think about it, the more I believe we are doing the work for the opposition. This is going to escalate the issue rather than solve it." Dalton looked at the big man and shook his head. "I'm scared that it will prove America is right and that Islam is violent."

Adham didn't say anything, but his troubled look remained as he continued with the work.

Once they finished cutting and forming the sheet metal to cover the hidden chamber, Adham and Dalton waited while Parsa and Ubayd swept and washed down the floor of the garage. They would then carry all the sheet metal over to be painted.

"At least we got those two off their butts," Adham said with a chuckle.

"There will be plenty for them to do once we start to shorten the benches."

"Too true. That'll give them a real workout," Adham said with a smile. "Let's leave them to their work. It'll give us a chance to get out of here and stretch our legs. I have not seen daylight in days."

Dalton was happy to leave the building. He admitted to himself he, too, was feeling a little claustrophobic. He saw their warehouse was one of many similar sized buildings that lined the roadway which was busy with commercial vehicles. The sun felt good on their faces, and they both walked through the industrial park with renewed energy.

The two men walked quietly, each consumed with his own thoughts. Dalton was so tempted to bolt — to run as fast as he could, to find a cop and end this madness. But of course, Maajid would only make a phone call and one, if not both, people he cared about would end up dead. He was scared shitless and couldn't think about how to get out of this mess. He was watched all the time. Not openly, but rather he was never left alone.

The big man asked, "What's eating you? Ten minutes ago you were skipping. Now you're bringing me down."

"Do you...do you think about dying, Adham?"

He was quiet for a long while, and Dalton wondered if he would answer. Adham kept walking with his head down, but after a long sigh, he turned and said, "Used to. All the time."

"I mean...Maajid isn't telling us anything about the plan. Are we supposed to die? Is that his plan?"

"He hasn't told me everything either Dalton, but man, you have every right to ask."

"You don't seem to care," Dalton pointed out. "Are you ready to die?"

"It's complicated."

"Try me."

Adham stopped and closed his eyes. With another sigh, he said, "I've been waiting to die since I was in Iraq. I mean, I loved being a Marine, but after being in some of them firefights, I never thought I would see home. I watched good friends getting mowed down like so much grass. One minute you were talking to them, and the next they were gone. But I made it back. Within a couple of weeks of being home, I was missing it all. Didn't take long before I signed up for another tour. Being close to death makes you realize just how alive you can be."

He pulled his hand across his scalp and looked ahead as he started walking again. "I was halfway into my second tour when that crazy shit with the school happened, and before I knew it, I was buried in Gitmo. Even there, I thought they would just get rid of me like they had with the child. I remember waiting for it each and every night. I was waiting for it when I ate, when I went for interrogation. Hell, I was expecting it when I went for a shit."

A smile split his face, "It ended when I found Allah. I know it sounds like a cliché, but from that moment, it didn't seem to matter. Living. Dying. Either way, God would take care of me."

Dalton smiled as well, thinking how his own despair and sadness had been lifted when he had accepted Islam. He looked over at Adham and reached over to pat the man's huge back.

"When I found Allah, he showed me there was life after losing my father. I find it hard to believe he did that so I can get myself killed fighting a war that is unwinnable," Dalton said. He was skating on thin ice, but he needed to see where Adham stood.

"What I'm really having a hard time with is the difference between what the extremists are saying about killing the infidel and making war in the name of Allah and what I read in the actual Quran," Dalton said, anguish and confusion in his voice. "I've read the entire Quran and it talks about love, not hate. About mercy, not revenge. In fact, when I first accepted Islam, Maajid told me both Christianity and Islam were basically the same."

"What about all the quotes about killing the unbeliever?" Adham asked.

"Most are taken out of context. The meaning changes when you read the entire passage instead of just a line or two. It does talk about defending yourself, but only when attacked. That's why part of me can't understand the idea of a bomb. Innocent people who have never attacked Islam will be killed. That's bothering me."

"Maajid keeps telling me we would be going after one of the white supremacist groups," Adham said.

"Then why won't he tell us the target?"

Chapter 40

On the way back to the warehouse, Adham said, "Listen, you may be right. I'll force Maajid to name the target. But I better warn you, Dalton," Adham said stopping to face him, "Maajid takes his orders from someone else."

"Who?" Dalton asked, surprised.

"I'm not sure, but he follows their orders to the letter. He may not have a choice either."

Dalton thought about this revelation for the rest of the walk back, not sure what to make of it. The fact they were being controlled by a third party who may or may not have their best interests in mind was unsettling. *Who's playing who?*

When they entered the warehouse, the van was missing. A quick look around the building showed the others had finished with the floors and all the sheet metal had been moved to be painted. They sat at the table talking amongst themselves.

"Where's Maajid?" Adham asked.

"Don't know," Parsa said. "He got a phone call, then packed up his computer and told us he'd be back in a few days. We are to continue working on the bus."

Adham looked over at Dalton and gave him a look of exasperation. The ex-Marine turned back to the others, and Dalton could see from the disgust on his face that he was not happy at the turn of events.

"Did any of you think to question him?" Adham asked.

The blank stares told the tale.

"So you don't know if an informant called him to say the police were on their way to raid this building?" Adham continued.

Dalton watched as the look of horror took over the faces of the trio when Adham's words sunk in. They all stood up, heads turned to look at each other in their panic before they returned their attention to Adham.

"There's not a single brain cell between the three of you, is there?" Adham yelled as he stepped towards them.

This time the faces showed a more immediate form of fright as the mountain that was Adham towered over them, ready to erupt. All three were ready to bolt.

"Sit down!" yelled Adham.

Even Dalton cringed.

Adham's fists curled like huge hams. A vein throbbed on the side of the man's skull. The three dropped like their strings had been cut, almost falling over themselves to comply.

He continued to glare at the trio for a few moments to ensure they knew who was in charge, then relaxed. In a calm voice made more menacing for its subtlety, he said, "You're going to do exactly as I tell you or you're going to know a world of pain. Got it?"

Three heads nodded like they were on the same neck.

"Because we don't know where our beloved leader has run off to, one of you will always be on lookout duty, starting with Dilawar. Parsa will take the next watch followed by Ubayd. Use the walkie-talkies to alert us of any sign of police. I'll scout a place for you to watch from and an escape route. Dalton and I will continue the work on the bus. Any questions?"

There were none.

Dalton almost laughed as Adham had to wait impatiently before Dilawar realized he was to follow the big man outside to find a spot to watch from. Ignoring the blank looks of the remaining two, Dalton walked over to where the sheet metal had been laid out to be painted. It had to be primed first, so he began uncoiling the airlines and getting the spray gun ready. He was just stirring the paint when Adham returned to the building. He stopped and spoke to the two others, gesturing to the rear of the building before walking over to Dalton.

"If all hell breaks loose, leave by the back door. If the cops haven't covered that exit, you might be able to lose them through the rail yard that's at the end of the irrigation ditch. It's halfway filled with water, but you should be able to jump it easily enough," Adham said as he pointed to the door in the corner of the building. "Have a look when we take a break."

Dalton nodded, and the two started with the paint job.

***

Dalton was surprised at the amount of work they'd gotten done in such a short time. The steel inner walls made up six distinctive chambers along the length of the bus, three on each side. Each of the chambers had its own detonator, accessed from the under chassis of the bus. This reason for this was twofold — first, they did not have to drive around with a fully armed bomb, and second, all of the wiring was hidden below in its own conduit tube. The six individual wires met and ran to the front of the vehicle and surfaced beside the driver's seat. The driver would be able to detonate it manually.

The plans for the setup also called for a secondary, remote detonator.

"Maajid said it was in case the driver was incapacitated," Adham said.

"Unless this is what Maajid had planned from the beginning," thought Dalton.

It took three days to paint the metal and bolt it back in place over the cavity filled with explosive. During that time, whichever one of the men not standing guard or sleeping was put to work taking the upholstery apart on the bench seats. Adham shortened each bench by three inches on the outside to allow for the false wall. The benches were then re-assembled and bolted into place. Dalton couldn't even detect a major difference. The benches hugged the wall and the aisle as they normally did. The six inch difference was lost in the total width of the bus.

While Adham and Dalton worked inside, the others helped tape over all the bus components that would not be painted. Mirrors, windows, and tires were covered with newsprint taped into place to avoid spray over. When everything was complete, Adham painted over the chrome yellow fist with a primer followed by two coats of navy blue. Once dried, stencils were applied to the side of the bus and in white paint. The new signage proclaimed the bus was from George Washington University. The final touch were the wheelchair emblems located on the sides and rear of the bus.

To celebrate, Adham gave Dalton some money and told him to have enough food delivered for the five of them. Excited for the excuse to leave the building, Dalton left before anyone could argue. There were a number of restaurants when they entered the complex over a week ago, and he knew he just had to follow the main road out.

After a 15 minute walk, he stood in front of five different restaurants. He decided on a restaurant and placed an order. There was a 20 minute wait for the food, so Dalton decided to enjoy the sun. He had already spent enough time indoors, and had been so caught up with the bus.

Suddenly Dalton realized, "I could just leave."

With Maajid gone, it would give him a head start so he could warn Daanya and his mom about the danger. Except for some clothes, there was nothing of value back at the warehouse. *It may be my only chance.* Looking around, he spied an open telephone booth beside the Chinese restaurant a few doors down. He would call his mother and at least let her know he was coming home.

Now that the decision was made, he felt invigorated and ran to the pay phone. He only had the money left over from the food order, but it was mostly bills. No change.

Collect. I'll try calling collect.

He picked up the receiver and dialed for the operator. He almost slammed the phone down when he was transferred to an automated service. In agonizing frustration, he cycled through the menu to the collect call segment, then had to enter the 10 digit number and record his name at the prompt.

It was taking too long.

Finally, the phone was ringing. He almost hung up thinking his mother was at work and there was no one to accept the call when the phone was answered.

"Hello?" said a female's voice that was not his mother.

"There is a collect call from Dalton Westree," said a computerized voice. "Press # to accept or hang -"

The caller must have accepted, because suddenly he heard his name repeated by the female caller.

"Dalton!"

"Who's this?"

"It's Daanya. Where are you? Are you all right?"

"Daanya? What are you doing there? Where's my mother?"

"Your mother's at work. Are you coming home? Please say, 'Yes.'"

"Yes. That's why I'm calling. Let her know I'm coming home. I'm in Denver so it'll take a little while, but I'm heading home right now."

"Be careful of Maajid, Dalton. The police believe he's a terrorist."

"I know. He's planning an explosion."

There was silence on the other end as Daanya digested the news.

"Listen," Dalton said. "I've got to go while I can. Know I love you and my moth—"

He was slammed from behind, and his face hit the glass of the booth with bone numbing force. His head lit up with flashing lights which he had no time to observe as a pair of hands grabbed him and dragged him from the booth and threw him against a vehicle. The same hands flipped him over like he was a child, and he stared into a face devoid of human emotion. It was like the man had no facial expressions, neither anger nor pleasure. The eyes were that of a shark. Dead.

Beyond this monster, Dalton could make out Maajid as he picked up the receiver and placed it to his ear. Dalton thought he could her Daanya's horrified cries before Maajid answered her.

"Bitch. You will pay for betraying me," he said, slamming the receiver down.

Maajid, walked over to where Dalton lay, blood and snot sliding across his face. He crouched down beside him.

"I see you met my new friend," he said gesturing towards the monster who hovered over him.

"Dalton, say hello to Aazam."

Chapter 41

"Hawkins."

"Hawkins," Gail said over the phone, "he called. He's in Denver. Daanya talked with him."

He heard fear in her voice and said, "I know, Gail. I'm on top of it."

"How...are you monitoring my phone?" she asked

"Of course."

"Well, you could have told me about it."

"If you knew, you would have been hesitant in how you spoke to him. That could have tipped him off. Gail, you have to trust that my people and I know what we're doing."

"Still, it feels..."

"Like a violation?"

"Yes."

"Does it help if I say I'm sorry?"

"Were you able to find out anything?"

"We traced the call to a phone booth in Denver. There was blood traces on the glass of the phone booth that matches Dalton's." Hawkins could hear her groan and could visualize the tortured look in her eyes. "Right now, the Denver police are going door to door in the industrial park looking for any trace of Dalton and the group he's with," he said to reassure her.

Hawkins stopped her from asking more questions by saying, "Gail, let me give you a call later when I know more. This is developing fast, and I have to get back to work."

"You promise to call?"

"As soon as I can," he said before hanging up.

He turned back to the operations room with its multiple large LED screens mounted across the far wall. One featured a satellite map of the industrial complex in Denver. At a glance, Hawkins could see all avenues in and out of the park were closed by police barricades. A second screen showed a list of addresses, and those already checked were marked with a solid line through them. A third showed a lopsided view of a parking lot. Hawkins knew the camera view came from a military version of the Go-Pro camera mounted on someone's helmet. It was as close to being there as you could get when you're sitting over a thousand miles away.

"What's happening?" he asked Amena.

"Nothing yet. They are booting up the Andros and going through a pre-check. Once they have completed the check, they'll deploy it towards the warehouse highlighted in red."

She was talking about the remote controlled mechanized assault vehicle. He'd seen it deployed in Iraq for explosive ordnance disposal. It was a way to gather intelligence in hostile environments without putting lives in jeopardy. The controller was able to direct the robot's controls from the safety of a mile or more away. A similar unit had been used in Dallas to take out a sniper.

"What do we know about the owners?" Hawkins asked.

"The building is being rented. Present tenants have paid for six months like the one in Cheyenne," Amena said, looking up from her notes.

"Cash?"

"Cash," she answered. "But this time, the rental company collected the fee in person and the property manager confirmed the renter was Dilawar Maloof. He used a different name but was identified by one of our photos. And get this — the manager remembered there was a second man waiting outside in a dark van."

"That fits nicely. Any bet the other man was Maajid?" Hawkins asked. "It would fit his M.O.[13] to use his own cousin to make the deal so he isn't identified."

"Yeah, it fits everything we've compiled on him. I've added the dark colored van to the profile."

"Great," Hawkins said nodding. "Now, if only these guys are home."

Amena looked at him and said, "You don't think they're there, do you?"

"No. If I was Maajid, as soon as I found Dalton calling home I'd move my base of operations. As a precaution, if anything." He stroked the stubble on his face and reminded himself he hadn't showered in a couple days.

Haven't slept much either.

"We're online," said one of the technicians.

Hawkins and Amena turned their attention to the big screen that came alive with a wide-lens view of a street with warehouses on both sides. The picture from the Andros jumped and shook as the robot moved along the street on four rubber pneumatic wheels that maneuvered well over different types of terrain. It came with an extendable shaft for the camera and an articulating arm that powerful enough to crush bones yet delicate enough to pick up an egg.

"Have our people calculated the blast radius if the entire truck explodes?" Hawkins asked across the room.

A hand shot up and another member of the team said, "Affirmative. The command post is staged a full mile away from the building in case they've rigged it to blow. All buildings in the complex have been evacuated."

"Thank you," Hawkins said. He pointed at the screen, "This will take awhile."

Amena nodded and walked to the rear of the room. In minutes, she returned with two mugs of steaming coffee. "To keep you awake. Let's grab a couple of chairs."

No one was able to take their eyes off the screen as the viewer bumped along the empty road. After Hawkins' second cup of coffee, the robot finally swung into the target driveway and scurried towards the main entrance.

The pilot of the robot guided the vehicle towards the front of the building. Most, but not all, of the windows had the blinds drawn, so there was little choice in the matter. Hawkins and his team watched as the view changed from the building's front to a look past it's reflection to the interior of a typical office. There was very little to see in the office other than empty desks, cabinets, and tables. The lack of computers, posters, or certificates on the walls indicated it was not being used.

The machine moved across the front of the building, its progress unperturbed by the rough ground of the shrub garden that dressed up the building lot. Each and every window showed no visible movement or sign of human occupancy.

At the end of the building, the machine arched out towards the corner of the huge loading lot. There were two main doors, one leading to the offices and one leading to the garage area which boasted three bay doors. The glass office door offered another view of the lifeless interior. The machine moved to the first bay door, and the mast was raised to peek into the line of windows that crossed at chest height. The pilot turned on a high intensity LED spotlight to illuminate the darkened garage. On the screen, the light revealed a row of tables and chairs and, as the camera lens panned to the right, the back end of a large transport trailer. An orange explosives placard was mounted on the rear of the trailer.

"Bingo," Hawkins said in a whisper, almost to himself.

No other vehicle could be seen from this angle, so the pilot had no choice but to follow the row of windows and doors to view the near empty garage in its entirety. Hawkins and the team listened to some radio chatter between the pilot and his supervisors before making an attempt to enter the building with a key supplied by the owner. From their view, they saw the machine return to the garage's main door. The robot's arm, key pointed forward, extended towards the door lock. Slowly, the key was inserted and turned.

Nothing happened.

The group in the operations room let out a sigh of relief.

The robot arm moved forward again, grabbed the doorknob, and turned in a slow, controlled motion. Still nothing. Hawkins found he was holding his breath as the door swung open. The light pushed the darkness along a tunnel of its path, the edges fading into gloom. The operator of the machine maneuvered the vehicle to the right and, with the robotic arm, flicked the light switch on the wall.

The screen went black with a burst of static.

"The satellite feed!" shouted one of the technicians.

Hawkins, along with every other set of eyes, swung to the first screen and saw an expanding flash of light with the warehouse at its center. In the choppy resolution, the team watched as the eerily silent explosion pushed through the industrial park, knocking buildings down like they were made of cardboard instead of steel and brick. The initial surrounding buildings slowed the pressure wave so much that Hawkins was able to visually recognize it. The devastation pushed out in all directions. Behind the structure, a number of rail cars had been knocked of their tracks like toys under a childish tantrum.

"Oh Christ," said Hawkins.

The target building was lost to the dust and smoke, but as the wind picked up, Hawkins saw the tangled steel support beams could be seen poking out of the rubble at different angles. Multiple fires flickered in the rubble of the industrial park.

Denver's fire crews would be earning their pay tonight

Chapter 42

Hawkins ran for his car. There was no way he could do this over the phone. He only hoped he got there before the news of the explosion reached Gail and Daanya.

Good luck with social media and 24 hour news coverage. Family members were advised on Facebook and Twitter that their loved ones had been killed in a vehicle collision even before police had left the scene to advise the next of kin. Quite often, the media showed images of horrific scenes of twisted metal or bodies covered with sheets, and this is how some poor spouse or parent found out about the loss.

Hawkins circled Gail's neighborhood, checking for possible surveillance. He had contacted the two teams assigned to watch over Daanya and Gail to inform them of his arrival. He took the stairs two at a time, his soft soled shoes making very little noise. At the top, he listened carefully for any sounds inside the unit. Part of it was a standard caution so he was not walking into a volatile environment, but with the news he carried, he also listened for the sound of crying. Hearing nothing, he tapped on the door. The door cracked open, the security chain going taut as Daanya's furtive face peeked out. The scared expression changed to recognition, and the door closed and then reopened to allow him to enter.

"Hello, Mr. Hawkins. Any news?

"Is Gail here?" he asked.

The look in her eyes changed. *She must have second sight or something.*

"Please have a seat and I'll get her. I convinced her to lie down."

In minutes, she reappeared with Gail who looked like she hadn't slept.

"What's happened?" Gail asked.

"Denver police found where they were staying and entered with a robot recognizance unit because of the explosives." He picked his next words carefully. "The warehouse appeared to be empty. When the robot entered the building, it triggered a booby trap and the explosives truck detonated, destroying the entire building."

"Oh my God!" said Gail, with her hand over her mouth. She looked over to Daanya who was equally shocked.

"The robot explored the offices and the interior from outside, and there was no sign of anyone in there," he said to reintegrate the thought that Dalton was more than likely not inside. What he didn't say was the search hadn't confirmed it yet. Amena would inform him immediately if there were any remains.

"Oh, thank God!" Gail said, reaching out and hugging Daanya.

"I wanted you to hear it from me before you saw it online.

"So we still don't know where they are?" Gail stated.

"No," he said, shaking his head. "We're always one step behind."

He turned to Daanya, "I'm going to ask you to come in and spend some time with one of our people to go over that phone conversation."

"Why?" she asked, her eyes narrowed in confusion. "You heard what I heard."

"There might be nothing, but with our tech guys, they can break down the conversation so you hear background noises and voice patterns. Having you there might help."

She looked at Gail and then back at Hawkins. "If it might help, I'll try."

"Great. Do you work this afternoon?"

"No. Sam can only afford me a few hours a week."

He checked his watch and looked at Gail, "We can give you a ride into work."

"Give me a minute," she said, and she left the room.

Hawkins used the time to walk back to his vehicle, again checking for a tail. He drove to the building entrance and waited for a couple of minutes before both women came out.

After dropping Gail off at the restaurant, he and Daanya headed to the operations center in silence for a while before Daanya surprised Hawkins by saying, "Dalton may have been in the warehouse, right?"

He took a deep breath to give himself some time to form his words, but she beat him to it.

"You don't have to sugar coat it for me, Mr. Hawkins.

He glanced over at her. Nodding, he said, "You're right; he may have been in the explosion. At this point, we have nothing on which to base an answer either way."

"I understand that," she said, "And you did it to spare Gail's feelings. She is near breaking point. What I fear is how far she'll fall if he was in the building." She took in a deep breath before saying, "I think you should be preparing her for that rather than giving her blind hope."

He snorted. "How the hell does someone so young become so wise?" he said.

"I'm a realist. My love for Dalton is new, but I don't have near the investment she has in Dalton. I am able to see beyond the emotions." He watched from the corner of his eye as she turned to him, "That's not to say I'm not scared for him."

"I wouldn't think otherwise."

"Which is why I want to do more."

"Hold on. Let me pull over," he said as he signaled. He pulled in behind a delivery van that was pulling away from the curb. Shutting the vehicle off, he turned to her with all his attention.

"What are you thinking?"

"You mentioned we are always one step behind, so why don't we take the initiative?"

He saw by her eyes she was deadly serious.

"Let's hear it."

"We know Maajid may be targeting me to use as leverage against Dalton."

"That's only a guess."

"Yes, but one confirmed by the gang member."

"Go on," Hawkins said,

"Then, let him get me."

He threw his hands up. "Just like that. You think it's that easy?"

"It can be," she said with full confidence. "A trip home and the right message would have him racing to grab me if Dalton is still alive. If he's dead, then we haven't risked anything because it won't matter."

"Do you really think your brother would risk his plan to avenge your betrayal of him?"

"Maybe not, but if Dalton is alive, Maajid would need a powerful incentive to force him to play his part, especially after finding he was trying to escape. I would be that motivation."

Hawkins's admitted she was right. Maajid would not need his sister if Dalton had been left in that warehouse in Denver.

"This could get you killed."

"If we don't stop him, Maajid will end up killing me anyways. His honor demands it." He watched as she closed her eyes, her hands trembling. "If I can save him, then I am willing to risk everything."

Kid's got guts.

"Okay, so say he grabs you, what then?"

"You follow and it gives you their location and a chance at stopping this craziness. It has to stop. For Dalton and Gail's sake and for every law-abiding patriotic Muslim in this country. We cannot allow the blame for this insanity to be dumped on Islam," she said, her voice becoming more urgent. “Islam has nothing to do with terrorism, Mr. Hawkins. And you know it.”

He nodded. She continued, “The problem is the public doesn’t. If Maajid is successful, the people in this country will blame all Muslims.” Then Daanya let out a huge sigh and, in a whisper, said, “If I have to sacrifice myself to stop it and save Dalton, I’m willing to do so.”

Chapter 43

"So," said Daanya, "You're telling me this pill has a GPS locator in it? And that it'll be powered by my body chemistry?" She held the pill to the light as if she would be able to glean its secrets.

"I don't know how it works, but it does," Hawkins said.

"I still think this is sheer lunacy," Gail said.

"Gail," Daanya said, "we've gone over this. It may be the only real chance we have of getting ahead of Maajid's plan." She walked over and took Gail's hands in her own. "I've explained my reasons. Please understand why I do this. I need you to accept this and be behind my decision. Please."

"I don't have to like the plan in order to respect your decision." A lone tear fell down Gail's cheek. "I may have lost my son. I can't afford to lose you, too."

Daanya felt for the older woman. *In the past few weeks, this woman has become so important to me.* She reached out and rubbed Gail's arm. Gail closed her eyes and nodded.

Amena broke the tension by saying, "Believe it or not, this ingestible technology has already been approved by the FDA." She handed a fact sheet to Daanya and said, "MIT started using the technology to monitor body and organ functions. We've adapted it. There are two kinds on the market, one that lasts for 72 hours and the other, which we're using, lasts indefinitely by feeding off your own body. We've decided to use this one because we don't know when your brother might grab you. We also can't ensure you'll have time to ingest it when he does show up."

"How safe is it?" Daanya asked.

"Mine has been working for three years now," Hawkins said.

"You have one in you? Right this minute?" Daanya asked, surprised at this.

"All our field agents do. It's the easiest way to keep them safe."

Without hesitating, Daanya popped the pill in her mouth and swallowed it with a sip of water. She waited as it went down, wondering if she would feel anything once it began to work. She looked over at Amena who hovered over a laptop that monitored the tracking device.

"There it is," said Amena with a smile. We'll keep track of you as you return home, but the feedback says everything is working."

"That was anticlimactic. I figured there would be more to it," said Daanya.

"You'll never know it's there. Unlike other tracking options, this one is undetectable," Hawkins said. "Even a tracking chip under the skin shows up in a metal detector."

"So, we're ready then?" Daanya asked.

"Yes," Hawkins said. "Just remember, when we arrive, keep low and make yourself as small as you can. We'll be coming in hard."

***

Dalton groaned. He tried to open his eyes, but he only saw blackness. He raised his hand to his face and found he was swollen to gigantic proportions. He had to take shallow breaths as his ribs hurt every time he took a deep breath. It felt like his chest was filled with burning glass. He didn't need his sight to know he was laid out in some kind of vehicle; he could hear the tires on the pavement. From the feel of the motion, he figured they were on a highway.

He put his hand out and felt a metal bar rising from the floor bar a foot or so above. That other bar stretched across the area in front of him. It was a frame of some kind with wooden backing. He should have known what this was, but his mind wasn't working right. It felt like the time he and his friend Ben McAlister drank a stolen bottle of whiskey that night before the school dance. Someone, probably Adham, had been kind enough to lay blankets for a bed. Even so, his whole body ached from the beating and was stiff to move.

"So you're finally waking up, are ya?" said Adham's deep voice above him. "Bet you wished you hadn't, eh?"

Dalton tried to answer, but his mouth felt just as swollen as his eyes. The only sound that came out of him was a groan.

"Don't bother talking. Here, take a sip."

Dalton felt those big hands lift his neck gently, and he felt cool water rush over his lips. Most went down his shirt, but it felt delicious. After a moment, Adham poured out a little more.

"That's enough for now. Let it go down. I don't need you throwing it back up."

Dalton felt a cool, wet cloth sweep across this swollen face, and although it caused pain, it also helped to throw back the fuzziness. *Hard to believe that giant could be so gentle.*

"If you haven't figured it out, we're on the bus heading east. You've been out for almost 18 hours and missed all the fun."

He reached again for the metal frame. *This must be a bus seat. I'm on the floor at the back of the bus.* Dalton listened as Adham filled him in. The newcomer, Aazam, now seemed to be in charge. He decided it was safer for them to relocate than take the chance the authorities would be able to track them.

"From a security point of view, I had to agree with him, and it turned out he was right. The police entered the building within 12 hours. Aazam doesn't play nice. He rigged the remaining explosives to wipe out the cops, but all he got was a bloody robot. It's all over the news."

Dalton could only lay there and listen. Part of him wanted to cry, thinking he would never be able to get free.

He drifted off, waking only when the bus came to a stop. Adham, leaned over him and told him, "We've pulled into a truck stop for food. Do you think you could eat some soup? Or a sandwich?"

Dalton nodded his head. "Thirsty," he tried to say, but it came out like a dried croak.

Adham seemed to understand and put a bottle in his hands. "Water. Slow sips." And then he was gone.

Minutes later, Dalton heard footsteps walk down the center of the bus and stop over him. At first he thought it might be Adham, but then he felt a certainty this was not the big Marine.

"You're lucky I didn't kill you," Maajid said in a low growl. "Once you agreed to do this, there was no turning back. You have betrayed Allah and all of us."

Dalton waited for the final blow. He couldn't have spoken even if he wanted to. The cold compresses Adham had put over his eyes must have helped the swelling to recede because he thought he was able to see Maajid's shadow hovering over him. The only other clue he was still there was his breathing.

Finally, Maajid said, "I only wonder if your betrayal was fueled by lust for my sister or because down deep, you are nothing but a coward." After another horrifying pause, he said, "I think I'll put it to the test."

Chapter 44

Daanya walked towards the restaurant for her shift, feeling isolated and alone. Where was her courage now? *It was my idea.* She wished she had listened to Gail about the risks. She stopped and put her hand on a lamp post to steady herself. The wave of dizziness faded. The cold metal seemed to ground her and push the anxiety away. *Stop this... focus on Dalton.*

She continued down the street. She had been making this walk to and from the restaurant for nine days now, always at the same time so she built a recognized routine. She was surprised that it was becoming harder to continue rather than easier. Hawkins told her it was because the stress was accumulative. *I wish Maajid would just do it.*

She had returned to her family home and was confronted by her mother at the front door.

"You are not welcome here sarmuta," her mother yelled.

To be called a bitch by my own mother. Oh Mother, can't you see what he's doing?

"Don't worry, I'm not here to stay, Mother. I have a message for Maajid. You can tell him I no longer recognize his authority over me, and I will marry whomever I decide. And if he hurts Dalton, I will kill him myself with a shoe."

The insult was one of the worst for an Arab, and Daanya had used it purposely. The use of a shoe was considered eternally dirty and unclean. Hearing this, her mother screamed her hate, striking Daanya's face.

Daanya's head tossed back and forth as her mother shook her by the hair. Pulling away, Daanya retreated to the street, tears and blood covering her face. Her mother then took her indignation and grief out on herself, tearing at her hair and ripping the fabric of her own dress as she continued to scream in Arabic.

The physical pain and shame was nothing compared to what Daanya felt for what she put her mother through. It had been one thing to plan out the speech but another to actually say it aloud. To hurt her mother like that. *Regardless of the ideology, she is still my mother.*

"You have become an American whore! You turn your back on Allah and his teachings," her mother spat. "I am only glad your father never lived to see how low his favorite daughter has fallen."

Daanya didn't stop until she had turned the corner where Hawkins waited in his car. She threw herself into the passenger's seat and cried her pain into his shoulder, wishing he had been Dalton. Back at the apartment, Gail stayed with her until she had cried herself to sleep.

Daanya continued on, lost in her thoughts. She did not even see the man until he was almost beside her. A quick glance told her he was of Middle Eastern background, but she did not recognize him. He nodded to her as he went by, and she relaxed. A second later, though, an arm reached around her neck and cut off her breath. A second hand roughly closed over her mouth. The man dragged her towards a dark blue van and violently shoved her inside. Another person forced her to the floor of the vehicle, his weight on the back of her neck. The sliding door closed, and the van began to move.

Her face was pushed into a floor mat, the grooves pressing painfully into her cheek. The hands holding her down were replaced by a boot on her neck, causing more pain. Hands groped her entire body, and she knew they were looking for a tracking device as Hawkins had warned her. One pair of hands lingered on her breasts, and she tried to bite the arm above her, but the owner just chuckled. A blanket or tarp was covered over her, blocking out the light. She whimpered out loud. Being sightless was more horrifying than the kidnapping. One of her captors laughed at her cries. She tried to speak, but was instantly slapped across the head. She had no choice but to lay there. She shook involuntarily. The longer she lay there, the worse it got. Her captors didn't speak at all. Their very silence fed her terror. She would have preferred them screaming their hatred at her.

Eventually, the vehicle slowed and then came to a stop. A door opened and closed. Minutes later, the vehicle pulled forward and what little light came through the tarp was cut off. *We must be inside a building.* Finally, the weight of the man's boot rose from her neck as he exited the car. She was left lying there on her own with no directions. Slowly, waiting to be struck again, she began to painfully get up off the floor. She had grown stiff. Her muscles screamed in defiance as she stretched herself to a kneeling position between the seats. She blinked, trying to adjust her eyes to the sudden brightness. Squinting, she looked around through the windows of the van.

She heard the quiet murmur of voices behind her and glanced over her shoulder. Standing across the garage bay was a group of men. Maajid stood watching and waiting for her. She felt both a wave of relief as well as a bout of fear. This was only the first part. She would have little control over what followed. She put a leg outside the vehicle and pushed herself off the van's floor and into the garage's interior. It was time for her to play the outraged, undisciplined sibling.

"Were you waiting for a special invitation, dear sister?" Maajid said, his voice dripping with scorn.

"You bastard! I knew you had to be behind this. Coward!" she said, walking towards him with murder in her eyes. "First Dalton and now this. How dare you!"

Maajid did a double take. For a minute, he lost his composure and looked startled, his eyes wide. Then his face darkened in anger. He stood straight up and pointed a finger at her, "Enough!" he shouted. "Either behave, Daanya, or I shall hurt your little friend some more." He glared at her as he let the threat sink in.

"Dalton's hurt. What did you do?" She didn't have to feign the terror that was visible in her eyes. Her head swiveled around the garage.

Maajid threw his thumb towards a back room, "You have 10 minutes before he leaves. Make sure you use it well."

She ran for the room and was met by a monster of man.

"You must be Daanya," he said in a deep, gentle voice. "He's fine. Looks worse than it is." He moved to allow her into the room.

Dalton sat on the edge of a cot. His face was discolored with yellow and blue blotches. He had some swelling, but the marks on his face were days old.

"Oh Dalton! What did he do to you?"

"Maajid decided to teach me a lesson for calling home," he said softly. "Don't worry, he hits like a girl."

She laughed and put her arms around him, making him groan aloud. Pulling back, she looked at him, horrified she had hurt him.

"Unfortunately, he kicks better than he hits. I have a couple broken ribs."

"I'm so sorry," she said, tears running freely.

"Shhh...It's okay," he said. "There was no way you could have known."

Daanya gently pulled him to her, holding him lightly. "You never heard what I told you the other day."

"What did you tell me?"

"You had just told me you loved me and your mother," she said, "I told you I loved you. That was when Maajid came on the line, and I was so scared I would never get the chance to tell you."

She pulled back and looked him in the eyes, "I do love you."

He pulled her closer so his face was next to hers. In a fierce whisper, he said, "Did you get my message about the explosives?"

She nodded into his shoulder.

"They have a school bus loaded with explosives that I'm supposed to drive. They haven't said what our target is yet, only that it will happen in four days. This new guy, Aazam, is in charge. He's ISIS."

She started at the name. Hawkins had mentioned Aazam as the mastermind behind the Moscow attack. All the drivers had been killed in Moscow.

"You can't drive. Maajid and Aazam will end up killing you," she said, pulling back to look him in eye.

"That's why they grabbed you. I either drive or they'll kill you."

Her fingers dug into his arms.

"Then let me die. You can't sacrifice innocent people to save me. I would never be able to live with myself."

"But I can't just let them kill you."

"You don't know they will. Anything can happen." She kissed him to give him hope and to stop herself from telling him that Hawkins was on his way.

"Dalton, if you really love me, you won't let them win."

Chapter 45

True to his word, Maajid sent Adham to collect Dalton in 10 minutes.

"Where are we going?" Dalton asked.

"Don't know. I've been cut out of the loop. This is becoming old in a hurry," Adham said. He started to help Dalton stand but was waved off.

"I can do it. You've helped enough, my friend." Dalton slowly raised himself from the cot, grimacing from the effort.

Daanya watched as he stopped and looked at Adham. To the ex-Marine, he said, "This isn't your kind of fight Adham. You should bail if you get the chance. I think they plan on doing something you won't be able to live with. This has nothing to do with Islam."

"A Marine never leaves a man behind," Adham said. He turned to Daanya and said with a smile, "I'll look after him."

With eyes filled with tears, she reached up and kissed Adham's cheek, "Thank you,"

Adham turned and left the room.

Dalton touched Daanya's cheek, their eyes holding each other. "I love you."

"Come back to me," she whispered. "Trust in Allah."

He nodded and turned to leave.

She watched him walk across the garage floor, realizing once he left the building, the planned assault by

Hawkins' people would fail to end this. She had risked everything only to have him slip away.

Allah, please keep him safe.

For whatever reason, her brother, or maybe Aazam, was splitting their force. Maajid, Adham, Dalton, and Aazam loaded into the van and pulled out of the garage. That left her guarded by Dilawar, Ubayd, and Parsa. Maybe she could use her time to find out more. It might help Hawkins later on.

Standing alone outside the back room, she saw they were working on something on top of a table. With her arms wrapped around herself, she slowly made her way towards them. As she approached, she saw them look at her, guilt evident in their expressions. She had grown up with them and their families, prayed at the same Mosque. She stumbled to a stop as she realized what they were working on.

Suicide vests!

"Are you mad?" she said, horror in her expression.

"Mind yourself, Daanya," Dilawar growled.

"You're not my father, Cousin. You hold no authority over me," she said.

Her relative turned his gaze from her, suddenly focused on the vest in his hands. The other two were equally unnerved.

"I only see two vests. Who gets to wear them? I bet my brother doesn't. Why should he? You three have always done exactly what he's told you. Bloody sheep."

"Go to the back room, Daanya. There's nothing for you here," Parsa told her.

"Oh the big man has a voice," she taunted. "Did you tell your mother goodbye? For all your talk of acting on behalf of Allah, you forgot his message concerning mothers. Do you think she would want this?"

He lowered his eyes and would not look at her.

"And what is written about killing a believer? Aazam is ISIS and ISIS has killed thousands of believers. Do you want to be included in God's punishment? The Quran spells it out clearly. Dalton is a believer. He called you 'friend,' yet you sat by and allowed Maajid to beat him for calling his mother."

"You don't know what you're talking about. Dalton was going to expose us," Parsa said, trying to sound like the victim.

"I was on the other end of the phone, Parsa. He just wanted to come home. He saw where this was headed and saw it was going to hurt every Muslim in the West."

That got their attention. Parsa and Ubayd exchanged a glance.

"For one minute, forget about Maajid. Think for yourselves. When they find out a Muslim group has killed innocent American civilians, what will follow? The authorities have tied you with the explosives plant in Wyoming. Please," Daanya said, "think it through."

All three avoided her eyes, trying to resist her argument.

"Aazam was behind the attack in Moscow," she said in desperation.

All three seemed to jump as if they had all grabbed the same electric wire.

"What?" she asked. "Maajid didn't tell you? Aazam pulled the same plan there. All his followers died, yet he is here today, alive and planning to send more sheep to their deaths for ISIS. "

"How do you know this?" Parsa asked.

"Homeland Security has been tracking him," she said.

Daanya tried to show them the fear she felt in her heart, "For Allah's sake, please think this through. Stop being led by the nose. If Maajid and Aazam really believe this is the true course, they would not turn down the chance to wear that vest," she said, pointing at the deadly garment.

Daanya didn't know just how much she had accomplished, but she caught the look of uncertainty on Ubayd.

What cost would be too high for him?

She lay on the cot and could still smell Dalton on the pillow. It was a comforting, light scent, and she imagined him lying beside her. It was with this fantasy she fell into a troubled asleep.

She woke at the sound of someone walking towards her room. Staying still, she cracked her eyes open to see Ubayd framed in the doorway. At first she thought he was checking on her, but he seemed to hesitate like he was trying to make up his mind.

She sat up and swung her legs off the cot, "What is it Ubayd?"

"He saved my life," he blurted.

"Who did?"

"Dalton. Dalton saved my life. There was a fight. A guy was going to crush my head with a baseball bat. Dalton stopped him," he said in a rush.

"He killed the man with a knife," Daanya finished for him.

A look of shock and horror filled the young man's face. "You know about that? How?"

"Ubayd, the police picked up one of the men who was part of that group and he confessed to his part in the setup."

A look of confusion filled the man's eyes and he asked, "Setup?"

"He told the police he and his friend were hired by Maajid to stage the attack to solidify Dalton to the group. It was part of his indoctrination…" She saw the surprise on his face. "Oh my God! You didn't know...He, the guy they interrogated, said there had been a second person hurt, but he had been alive when he left so one of you must have killed him."

She could see him mulling over the events of that night. Finally he said, "I was hurt. Dilawar and Dalton took me home for help, so it must be Parsa or Maajid."

"Why would they kill him?" she asked.

It was at that moment the lights in the building went out. She heard Ubayd turn and run back to the others. Remembering Hawkins' warning, she lay back down and curled into a ball. She heard multiple doors being breached followed by a metallic clinking, like a tin can dancing across a street.

Bam!

An explosion assaulted her ears. It was loud even though it came from the garage area. The noise echoed through the open space.

Bam!

This one right on top of the other. Closer. Louder. The pain in her head magnified. Her teeth slammed together, making her jaw ache.

Bam!

This one at the entrance to her room. The flashes attacked Daanya's eyes, and she felt an urge to vomit. One hand on her head, the other at her stomach. No! She squeezed the muscles in her rectum as she felt the urge to defecate. Warm wetness seeped between her thighs as her bladder released itself. Shame filled her even as her mind tried to grasp what was happening around her. There was pandemonium, cries and forceful shouts, but she couldn't make out the words due to the ringing. She was blind. Strobe lights stuttered across the back of her eyes, deep into her skull. The world spun.

A hand touched her shoulder and she flinched as a voice shouted, "Stay still!" as if from afar. Behind that one, another announced, "The package is secure," in a muffled voice. As her hearing slowly returned, she heard phantom voices say, "Clear!" from farther away.

Finally, the lights came back on. Squinting, she was able to make out three heavily armed figures, all dressed in black, facing the door, sheltering her with their bodies.

One of the figures pulled off the heavy one-eyed attachment with its array of straps and gave her a stunning smile.

It was Hawkins.

Chapter 46

To Gail, the news of Daanya's rescue was bittersweet. That they missed Dalton by mere hours was devastating.

When would this nightmare end?

She lay in her hotel bed. Hawkins had just called and, after filling her in, told her he would send someone by to bring her home. The stress was wearing on her. One look at the mirror showed the physical evidence. Her hair didn't have its regular bounce, and there were dark circles under her eyes that sleep couldn't erase. It was like she had aged 10 years in a matter of weeks. She had even lost weight which should have been a blessing, but it came from the lack of appetite rather than physical activity. Her face had taken on the sunken look of a refugee who has lost everything dear and waited for death. She began to cry again with the need to see Dalton, touch him, and hold him. He was her life, her reason for being. She would die for him.

I would kill for him.

The violent thought shook her to her core. She had never agreed with violence. She had seen it in the news and in school and always thought of the waste and the uselessness of it. It didn't solve anything. If anything, it generated more of the same. But the thought lingered. In the long night, with her mind reeling with horrible scenarios that pushed back the healing slumber, it festered.

Long before the sun showed itself, she made a decision. She had a phone call to make and a favor to ask.

***

Gail met Brandon Freeman the next day outside a building that had originally been a neighborhood clothing store until it fell victim to the shopping mall down the street. The cinder brick building was now a gun shop with a front of worn barn boards as if depicting the Wild West. "Melvin's Gunshop" had been in the neighborhood since Gail moved into the area, but she had never entered.

She had originally entertained the idea of dodging her watch dogs, the two federal agents in the tan sedan Hawkins had assigned her for protection, but she didn't fool herself with the idea that their training hadn't prepared them to follow those who didn't want to be followed.

"Good morning, Mrs. Westree."

"Good morning, Brandon. How many times must I tell you, we're family, so call me 'Gail,'" she said with a smile. "Thank you for taking the time to help me this morning."

"Time is what I have a lot of. I was intrigued by your request."

"Well, I'm sure your father has kept you abreast of what's happened to Dalton and Daanya," she said. "I think it's only wise to protect myself."

"Have you shot before?" he asked as he maneuvered his wheelchair through the door she held open.

"Years ago with my husband. We sold the gun when Dalton was a toddler, for safety reasons."

Brandon nodded.

"What can I do for ya today?" asked Melvin, the store owner.

"The lady is looking for something for self-protection," said Brandon.

The store owner looked at Brandon and his wheelchair and asked, "Veteran?"

"Iraq, 2004. 3rd Battalion, 5th Marine."

"Twenty percent off anything in the store. We support our veterans here," the shop owner said proudly, shaking Brandon's hand. "I was involved with the assault on Granada, but it was all over when I came ashore. Goddamn Marines didn't leave us anything."

Melvin looked over at Gail and said, "Let's get you over to the counter and size up your hand to find what's comfortable." Seeing her confused look, he said, "No sense selling you something you can't even wrap your hand around. I'm guessing you want it to fit in your purse?"

Over the next half hour, they went through a number of guns until Gail settled for a 9mm Walther CCP. The pistol fit snugly in her hand and was not overly heavy on her wrist. The gas-delayed blowback system meant reduced recoil that helped keep the gun on target. Using the indoor range at the back of the store, Melvin showed her how to load and shoot as well as how to clean it.

"I'll send this paperwork out this morning. Usually hear back inside of three days, but sometimes earlier. I'll call you when you can pick it up."

With that, she spent what little savings she had put away.

For Dalton. What else was it good for?

***

Hawkins was sitting on the steps outside her apartment when she returned home. She wasn't surprised to see him. She had figured with the phone being monitored and the surveillance team, word of her shopping trip would have reached him.

"If you wanted a gun, you could've asked," he said.

"You hadn't offered, so I decided to do it myself," she returned, her tone neutral.

"Sorry, I should have asked. I took the liberty of having the paperwork rushed through. You'll have it later this afternoon."

He laughed at the look on her face. "Gail, you're a grown up. I couldn't stop you if I tried. I just want you to promise me you'll use some common sense when you carry it. You can sometimes get more done if you don't pull it out. Last resort only."

She nodded and sat on the step beside him.

"Were you able to find out anything else from Daanya's debriefing?"

"Actually, quite a lot.

"Dalton confirmed they're using a school bus as a car bomb in four days, so it narrows things down. We just need to figure what's happening in four days." He looked at her out of the corner of his eye. "When we do, we'll move in."

Gail held his gaze, not allowing any expression to show. *So will I.*

Chapter 47

"How the hell could they have tracked her?" Maajid said to Aazam. "You were there. You saw we searched her thoroughly. We even ditched her purse to be safe."

Dalton sat on an old couch that had been rescued from a street curb, it's broken springs digging into his back. The collage of scents of stale alcohol and vomit percolated up from the faded fabric with every shift in weight, causing his empty stomach to heave. They were holed up in a small abandoned gas station, the bus barely fitting in the single bay that smelled of grease, oil, and tires.

The drive to their new home had been done in a tense silence. Dalton felt sick with worry for Daanya. Maajid would not, in the end, harm his sister, but he felt no assurance for Aazam.

He scares the fuck out of me.

Adham's winks of encouragement didn't lessen the strain. The news of the raid on their recently vacated hideout came from an all-news channel that nattered nonstop from a pawnshop radio.

"Satellite," Aazam said, in a matter-of-fact manner. "At home, we schedule all our movements around the cycles of the satellites. I did not think they would be watching their own citizens. The fault is mine."

Just like that, the admission stopped any further discussion. He saw Maajid deflate, probably scared this ISIS killer was going to blame him. Looking at Adham, he was unable to read his thoughts but would not have been surprised if he had thought the same. For a moment, the four remaining members exchanged glances.

Who's in? Who's out? Who lives? Who dies?

Dalton caught the slightest of tilts to Maajid's head, and he and Aazam walked across the bay floor before talking in whispers. *They must be discussing what to do about me. Without Daanya, they had no leverage to force me to drive.*

He hoped.

He felt a tap on his hip. Looking around, he saw Adham had poked him with a small, black rectangular box Dalton recognized as a radio receiver detonator. This was similar to the one they had wired into the driver's console of the bus.

"Remember how we wired this?" Adham whispered, his face turned away so the other didn't know they were talking.

Dalton nodded.

"Cut these two wires to disrupt the signal," he said flipping the two wires at the end of the box, keeping his hands low. "Cut the antenna wire we strung to the bus radio antenna if you can, but these are the important ones." He stood and stretched, glancing towards the other two to ensure they were still out of hearing range. "The first two will disengage the manual detonator as well."

"Right." Dalton looked down and saw Adham had left the detonator on the couch beside him. Dalton glanced over to where Aazam and Maajid stood. He slowly moved his hand over it, shoving it into the front pocket of his jeans.

Dalton looked up at the ex-Marine. There was an annoyed, impatient expression on the man's face. He noticed the muscles in the man's jaw and neck tighten and release and wondered what was about to happen. Adham looked ready to explode.

Fists clenched, he turned towards Maajid and Aazam and, in a loud, harsh voice, said, "It's over!"

The two swung in surprise and stared at Adham.

"Wha…What?" Maajid stammered.

"I said, it's over."

"I'll tell you when it's over," Maajid said, his face flushing in anger. "You're not in charge. I am."

As he spoke, he walked, almost marched, towards Adham. Dalton almost laughed. Compared to Adham, Maajid looked like a child having a tantrum. He stood, hands on his hips, inches from Adham, looking straight up. But Adham could crush him with one hand.

"No, you're not, idiot," Adham said, his eyes on Aazam who stood quietly, his weight leaning on one leg, his hands behind his back. With his chin, the big man nodded toward Aazam and said, "He is."

Maajid looked behind him but said nothing.

As the tension rose, Dalton slowly rose to stand beside his friend.

"You're a soldier. You can read the battlefield," Adham said to Aazam. "You've lost half your force. You've lost the element of surprise. And by now the authorities will know about your plan."

"You don't know that. My friends would never talk." Maajid said, his voice rising in the empty space of the garage.

Adham ignored him. To Aazam, he said, "You know I'm right, don't ya?" It was more a statement than a question.

Dalton watched as the Iraqi nodded.

Maajid looked from one soldier to the other, a look of disbelief on his face. "You would just give up on the others? Believe they would betray us?"

Without taking his eyes of Aazam, Adham said, "Kid, you're out of your league. If they haven't talked yet, they'll be pumped up with sodium thiopental or some other cocktail, and they'll be telling their life story to whoever asks."

The calm certainty of Adham's attitude and the fact Aazam did not argue with him stopped all other protests.

Adham said to Aazam, "It is time for a tactical withdrawal. Fight another day when they are not expecting it."

"We cannot," Aazam said, finally breaking his silence. "This is bigger than all of us. Plans are in place to attack all the coalition countries. We are the spark that will ignite the world."

Dalton and the others were shocked by his words. Adham had been right. This was way beyond them.

And I allowed myself to be part of this?

"Are you out of your fucking mind!?" Dalton blurted out. "What do you hope it'll accomplish? You'll turn the whole world against Islam. And for what, so a bunch of psychopaths can stay in power poisoning the purity of Islam?"

As he spoke, he was walking straight at Aazam. Dalton was shaking in both anger and condemnation. Adham put out a hand on his shoulder and tried to rein him in, but he shrugged it off.

"No, my friend. You and I have talked about it. This is exactly what we feared," he said to Adham. He turned to Aazam. "Don't you see? This will vindicate everything the Christian right has been proclaiming and predicting. If you attack, the American public will demand that Muslims be persecuted. So will the rest of the world."

"Yes," Aazam said, his dead eyes finally showing some life. "And when they do, the Muslim people will flock to the flag of the Islamic State. Once united, we will have a force that will be strong enough to crush the Americans and the sheep that make up the coalition."

"You're an idiot!" Dalton said, oblivious of the quiet rage that walked across Aazam's features. "ISIS has killed more Muslims in their fight for power than the Americans ever did."

"America and their lackeys bomb my people with impunity. They have no right to be in Iraq or Syria. They are only there for their own interests. The oil is all they care about," Aazam said in a quiet, dangerous tone, his blazing eyes the true indicator of his fanatical zeal. "Well, I am here to bring the war to them. To bomb them as they do us.

It is so easy to fight an enemy that is on the other side of the world, risking nothing of your own. Now they will learn what it is to lose their love ones."

"Did you not learn anything from 9/11? By attacking America, you will bring the full weight of its military on your people," Adham said, "ISIS will cease to exist, and the rest of the Islamic people will be blamed for your actions. Dalton is right. The American people will demand it."

Aazam stood there quietly watch the two of them. Dalton could not believe how passionately the Iraqi spoke, yet his body language was so relaxed. It was like the reaction of two different people within the same body. Even as Dalton watched, Aazam's eyes calmed and became dead; they reminded Dalton of a cobra swaying rhythmically in a hypnotic, calming manner before striking.

"It doesn't matter," Adham said. "There's no way we'll be able to reach the target now. It's over." He looked at Dalton. "We're out of here."

Dalton nodded to his friend and started to turn with him when the cobra struck.

From the corner of Dalton's eye, he saw Aazam's arm came around his body and level a pistol towards them, firing off two shots in close succession. Even with the noise suppressor, it created an echo in the closed space, blending the two together.

He missed. Relief filled Dalton's mind as the smell of gunfire registered in his senses.

But he hadn't. Dalton's mind could not comprehend what his eyes saw. The two shots had carved a trench in the back of Adham's head, throwing him forward to land in a bloody heap on the concrete floor. Before Dalton could react, Aazam had him by the neck and pushed him down towards the gore that had been his friend. With no equilibrium, Dalton could not alter his path until his hands struck the floor, straddled on either side of that bloody mess, and he was able to push back. Even then, his face was inches from what was left of Adham, with Aazam pushing against him. He could feel the warm wetness coming off Adham's body.

"Look at him," Aazam said harshly, pushing hard. "Look at him."

Dalton kept his eyes closed, sure he would pass out if he looked deep into the destroyed face of his friend. He felt a hard, hot pressure pushing on his temple and realized Aazam held the muzzle of his pistol against his head.

I'm dead. I'm next.

"I said look at him!"

The command rather than the sound of the expected shot surprised him; his eyes flew open, revealing the shattered skull of a man he thought was near invincible. Blood, bone, and brains filled his vision until they started to swirl and twist, a toneless whistle rising to overwhelm his consciousness.

The world went black. It came back with a dull pain. Then the pain became sharper.

As Dalton's eyes opened, Aazam slapped him again. Dalton raised his hands to ward off the blows but found his hands were pinned at his side. Blinking to focus, he could only look at those black, dead eyes.

"Are you listening?" said that maddeningly calm voice.

He nodded.

"You understand what happened to your friend Adham?

Another nod to which Aazam replied with his own.

"You girlfriend and mother will receive the same if you ever go against me again."

Dalton went cold.

"I will hunt them down myself."

Chapter 48

The briefing room was standing room only, over-heated, and rancid with the clammy, pungent smell of stale sweat made worse by the body armor most of the soldiers wore. Gail took shallow breaths to avoid the stench. Beside her, Daanya held a corner of her hijab over her face. Gail knew Hawkins had brought her here to keep her out of trouble. He may have helped with the registration of her pistol — the weight of it in her purse was comforting — but she knew he was never going to allow her to be in harm's way. This was his operation. He was in his element, and it showed as he moved from group to group trading laughs and slapping backs. And the men and women under his command revered him. As the rear door closed and cut off the room's only air current, Gail turned to see Amena lower the room's lights so that only the podium where Hawkins stood was lit.

"Okay, here's where we're at," Hawkins began. "We believe that there is a strong chance one of the Oktoberfest celebrations across the city has been targeted by Aazam ibn Abd al-Muttalib who, according to our sources, was a commander of ISIS. Our sources tell us he has gone rogue after killing some highly valued targets in Dubai."

A picture of Aazam came up on the screen beside the podium. This picture was slid to the side, and two close-up photos similar to police mug shots were added.

"The two photos on the right are compliments of his stay at Guantanamo Bay in the early 2000s. Each of you will have copies in your portfolio. He may or may not be using a disguise. Do not take any chances with Aazam. He has a reputation for being ruthless, and he's a highly effective soldier. Do not attempt to deal with him alone. Call for backup."

Amena leaned close to Gail and Daanya. "Here's a portfolio so you can follow with the others."

Gail nodded her thanks. She opened the folder, and she and Daanya were face-to-face with the terrorist. The eyes were hostile, yet Gail was surprised at how good looking the man was. *What made you want to hurt others, Aazam?*

"Tonight's festival is at the fairgrounds that is part of Fort Belvoir in Virginia which we feel might be a target Aazam cannot resist," Hawkins continued. "As most of you are aware, the base is the home of United States Army Intelligence and Security Command as well as a number of other divisions." He looked around the room and watched the different agents studying the photos or making notes. "The festival's organizers have agreed to change their security badges to a different color in an attempt to catch our suspects off guard. The new color is green. If any other badge color is seen, handle it as suspect and report it immediately."

How many other facts do they have to memorize? Gail could feel her anxiety growing and forced herself to breathe deeply. Beside her, Daanya took her hand. Daanya's hand felt so warm, like the girl herself. *She calms me and gives me strength, but it's not enough lately. I'm so tired. Please, God, make it end.*

"The following are known to be traveling with Aazam," Hawkins said, and the screen showed Daanya's brother. "Maajid was the front man here in the U.S. before Aazam arrived. We know he's been a recruiter for ISIS for at least two years. This is likely his first operation. He is motivated and a high risk."

The next slide showed a huge black man, his shoulders extending past the frame of the photo like it was unable to contain the giant. “Adham al-Wahab, formally Dandre Brackstorm, is a Marine with two tours of Iraq. He is an expert in all infantry weapons as well as demolitions. He is to be considered extremely dangerous, and although he may be having second thoughts about his involvement, do not underestimate him.”

“What the hell…?” said one of the agents in surprise. Others had also looked up in surprise.

“Brackstorm got involved in an operation that has since been classified. What I can tell you,” Hawkins said, looking across the room, “is he was incarcerated in Gitmo and subsequently cashiered out with a dishonorable discharge. We believe he converted to Islam while in prison.”

Even though she was expecting it, when Dalton’s photo appeared on the screen, Gail’s breath caught in her throat and her stomach dropped. Daanya squeezed her hand, but this time it did nothing to calm her. Gail let out an involuntary groan, and her vision blurred like she was under water, drifting away. She felt Amena and Daanya help her up out of her chair and guide her out of the room and into the hallway. *Pull it together. Dalton needs you!* She pulled in a heavy breath and closed her eyes. From her memories, she grabbed the picture of her family, before Tom had died. The photo of the three of them. Happy times.

Tom, give me strength. I need you to help me save Dalton. She imagined she felt the warmth and love of her family wrap around her, pushing back the darkness. She surrendered herself to happiness of those smiles that were so full of hope and joy. She could see Dalton team winning the league’s championship. *God, we cheered so loud.* Daanya’s arms were around her, rocking her, and she accepted the love from this courageous young woman. Gail’s purse started to slip and she caught it before it fell, feeling the extra weight in it. The gun intensified the strength that infused her. She knew what she was going to do.

After a few moments, she hugged Daanya and pushed herself up. "Sorry, I guess I lost it there for a moment," Gail said wiping at her eyes. She looked down the hallway, suddenly conscious of what someone might think if they found her in this state.

"You've been under a lot of strain, Gail," Daanya said, handing her a tissue.

"So have you."

Daanya gave her a shrug and a shy dismissive wave. "I'm not his mother."

"No, but you love him, just like I do."

The women hugged each other with feeling. As they broke apart, Gail saw Amena slip back into the briefing room. Gail wiped at her eyes with the tissue and patted Daanya's hand.

Gail said, "Thank you. I'll be okay now. You should go back in so we don't miss anything."

"You're not coming?" Daanya asked, her face still expressing her concern.

"Yes, but first I need to find a mirror so I can clean up this mess," she said, displaying the botched mascara on the tissue. As she rose, she said, "I'll be right there."

Gail walked down the hallway towards a sign indicating a unisex washroom. As she pushed open the door, she glanced back in time to see Daanya open the briefing door and enter the room. Gail paused until the briefing door closed, and then she spun on her heel and made for the stairwell. She took the stairs as quickly as she could until she reached the ground floor, her heels echoing in the closed space as she headed for the exit.

Chapter 49

Dalton watched as Aazam attached the final explosives to the fall arrest harness being utilized as the base for a suicide vest. The harness consisted of a waist belt and two shoulder straps made up of nylon webbing. It was the second vest the Iraqi had put together in a matter of minutes. His hands moved across the makeshift garment like a tailor creating a three piece suit. Instead of the ammonium nitrate fuel oil (ANFO) they had used on the bus, Aazam molded and stretched a number of C4 packages in line with the harnesses webbing. This was held in place simply by multiple wrappings of duct tape covering the explosive and the wiring to and from the detonator. Finally, from Adham's bag of equipment, Aazam pulled out a radio remote detonator and taped it along one of the chest straps. There was a simple pull strap detonator on the other side of the harness the wearer could use to ignite the explosive. Dalton recognized that only one of the suicide vests would have a remote detonator — Maajid's vest. Aazam's vest did not have the remote detonator tied in, so it would not explode along with the bus and Maajid if the signal was sent.

Aazam has no intentions of dying for the cause.

"We'll wire this just before we leave," he said, looking up at Maajid. "Don't want any accidents."

Maajid, whose face had gone pale with a green tinge, could only look on in suppressed terror. Dalton started to laugh, and as the situation hit home, the laughter took on a maniacal tone. The two others looked at him.

Aazam wore his "I can kill you in a 100 ways" look while Maajid's face screamed, "I'm not the one that was supposed to be wearing a vest." Both expressions pushed Dalton further into a laughing fit, tears streaming until his stomach cramped. For a few seconds, he worried about pissing himself. The laughter finally subsided, and he felt as if he'd taken some surreal narcotic.
Nothing mattered. Allah would decide.

Now the two others ignored him. Both had their attention fixed on Maajid's laptop as it streamed a live news channel. Dalton walked past the two into the restroom and closed the door. From the sink, he splashed water over his face, erasing the dried tear stains and helping to center himself. Looking into the mirror, he saw a face he could hardly recognize. He had lost weight over the past three months, a mixture of the shitty meals and the exercise regime shared with Adham. The stress helped alter his facial features, drawing more tension in his eyes and mouth. As he contemplated his image, his mind tumbled over different scenarios trying to find a way out of this horror story. Knowing if he stayed in the washroom too long either Aazam or Maajid would come searching for him, he left. With no more than a glance at him, the two were glued to the live feed.

To give himself a way to bleed off the anxiety, Dalton began walking laps around the inside of the warehouse, his hand slapping the outside of his leg to keep count of the number of paces. This had been a regular practice, and the others were used to his habit. On Dalton's second lap, his hand banging away at his jeans, he felt a sharp pain on his upper thigh of his right leg. His pace faltered as he reached down to feel what had jabbed at him. Through his jeans, he felt the outline of a small, hard rectangle which he recognized as the radio controlled detonator Adham had given him just before he had been killed.

Dalton allowed his memory of Adham's whispered instructions about cutting the wires, and slowly, like a spark that grows into an ember, a plan started smoldering in Dalton's mind. He kept pacing around the large enclosure and going over everything Adham taught him about explosives. When he reviewed what he had seen of Aazam assembling the vest, the plan crystallized.

I need a blasting cap.

He couldn't just climb under the bus and grab one of the caps they had installed. In the open garage, there was no way to hide that kind of movement from the others. The bag of explosive components sat open on the table. Dalton made sure Aazam and Maajid's attention was still on the laptop, and he slowed his pace down as he approached the table. As he passed by, he allowed his eyes to dig deep into the bag's contents, looking for the blasting caps. It took two more laps before he was able to spot them without coming to a full stop which might have alerted either of the others.

As he approached the bag on the next round, he kept his full attention of the back of Aazam's head and shoulders, watching for any sign the man was about to turn his way. As Dalton came even with the table, he reached out and drove his hand into the bag, grasping at the blasting caps. His hand came up with a bundle of caps; the batch had been held together with an elastic band. In a slight surprised panic, he quickly pulled two apart from the bunch and hid them in his jean pocket. He shoved the rest into his left hand, allowing his body to shield them from the two men.

Keeping his pace steady, he made another circuit of the garage, having to transfer the bundle to the other hand as he turned to walk the far side of the garage. Coming around again, he used the bus to hide the transfer of the bundle, ready to drop it into the bag. As he cleared the bus, Aazam looked up and glanced over at him.

Dalton forced himself to keep walking and asked, "How long?"

"A few hours yet," Aazam said before turning back to the news feed.

Dalton kept moving around the building, trying to keep his pace and nerves steady. On the next pass, both men kept their backs to him and as he came even with the explosives bag. Dalton gently dropped the bundle back into place as he strode by. He was sure neither man had seen the movement, yet he still tensed waiting for the bullet to hit him from behind.

Two hours later, Aazam crawled under the bus with Dalton. He had Dalton show him how the explosive had been wired.

"A simple series," said the Iraqi, his admiration of the job plain in his face.

"Yes," Dalton said. "We rigged both a manual and a radio remote in case the driver had been incapacitated by the police."

Aazam nodded his satisfaction. They climbed back to their feet and moved to the cab of the bus. Dalton undid the locking nut from the remote receiver and pulled the unit out of the dash so the Iraqi could see it was ready to be wired together. Adham had also waited to finish the wiring to avoid a premature detonation.

"Finish the connection," Aazam told Dalton.

From a tool pouch on the dash, Dalton retrieved a strip of shrink wrap. He cut off two lengths and fed one over the red wires that fed from the series of blasting caps under the bus. Putting the two red wires together with a third length, Dalton twisted the three wires together. Once spliced, he pulled the shrink wrap up over the bare wires so they were covered. From the pouch, he pulled out a cigarette lighter and held the flame under the shrink wrap. The wrap shriveled and tightened over the bare wires creating a waterproof seal that would ensure the wires did not come apart. He repeated the process on the black wires. To the right of the remote receiver, Dalton unscrewed two star screws that secured a standard snap switch to the dash. Pulling this up showed two loose wires. He fished these wires through the hole for the remote receiver.

"Pass me one of the electronic detonators," he said to Aazam.

Aazam turned and stepped off the bus towards the table where the explosives bag sat.

Moving with concentration so he wouldn't mess up, Dalton pulled an orange and black piece of wiring from his pocket and shoved both through the hole where the other wires came from and fed them into a wire strap that was attached to the underside of the dash. These came from the blasting cap he had stolen earlier. He twisted the far ends so they were secure to the wire strap.

Now comes the tricky part.

Dalton's stomach dropped. If he was caught, he was sure he would receive the same treatment as Adham. What scared him senseless was what would happen to his mother and Daanya. He was tempted to just trigger the toggle switch once it was wired up and kill them all.

Inshallah.[14]

He felt the bus move with Aazam's weight and looked up. The man handed him the detonator wordlessly. Dalton bent over the dash and placed the detonator in between his lips. From the pouch, he pulled out more shrink wrap and cut two equal lengths. He gathered the bundle of black wires, isolated the trailing wire, and pulled it together with the black wire from the switch. With his free hand, he took the detonator by one of its orange wires and let drop through the hole in the dash. He made a fuss as if it were slipping, jamming his fingers into the hole. His movements masked his fingers forcing the detonator into the wire strap and grabbing the loose wires that lay waiting, out of sight. Pulling the orange wire into the other group, he spliced the three together and dragged the sheath of shrink wrap over the three wires. Once it shrank, he tied and spliced the remaining wires and dropped the bundles through the hole. It was essentially tied to nothing, having bypassed the detonator all together. Without looking up, Dalton screwed the snap switch back into place and then fished for his crescent wrench and tightened the locking nut that held the remote receiver in place. The remote detonator was live, but the manual would not function; Dalton had accomplished this in front Aazam.

"All done," he said, finally looking up at Aazam.

The Iraqi nodded, "Very good.

"You are a fast learner," Aazam said before turning on his heel and leaving the bus.

Dalton had to fight to keep the relief off his face. Now that it was over, he could feel his hands trembling. Thank Allah they didn't shake while he was doing the work. He was sure he would have dropped the detonator, exposing the fact he had essentially wired the switch to nothing.

Half the threat was gone.

Chapter 50

"What do you mean she's gone?" Hawkins demanded.

"It's my fault," Daanya said. "I should have stayed with her."

Hawkins saw the anguish in her face and realized he had to calm down. He closed his eyes and took a deep breath to help center himself. When he felt himself calm down, he opened them and said in a calmer voice, "Daanya, I need you to stay out of this. Having Gail out there is a huge distraction. I can't afford another."

Daanya pulled back. "You mean I have no choice in the matter."

"No, I'm afraid not." Hawkins turned to Amena, "Assign her to someone. I want her close, but not within Fort Belvoir."

"You can't do this," Daanya said.

Hawkins turned on her, "Not only can I do this, but I will give orders to have you handcuffed if you show the slightest notion to leave the vehicle. This isn't a game."

"Gunnie?" he said into his portable radio.

Tommy Chen's voice came through. "Gunnie here."

"I need one of the detail assigned to Daanya Nasry. I'll brief them when they get here."

"Sending someone up right now."

He turned, looked at Amena, and indicated he needed a private word with her. They walked away, leaving a stunned Daanya to stand alone in the room's center.

Wiping a hand across his face, Hawkins turned and said, "I've fucked up here. I'm way too close to these people. I'm figuring Gail will go after the bus. It's her best bet at catching up with Dalton."

"Agreed."

"You take the bus. I'll take the crowd."

"Don't beat yourself up. I was with her and left her on her own as well." Amena reached over and gave his arm a squeeze. "We're human, Hawkins. Caring is what makes us different than the enemy."

He nodded, "Thanks, partner. Happy hunting."

***

Gail finally abandoned the taxi half a mile shy of the fairgrounds. The bleating of horns was constant and meaningless in traffic that had slowed to a crawl. The festival ground was an athletic field just off the north-south beltway. The off-ramp merged with a two-lane, one-way boulevard that fed the complex that was in the center of Fort Belvoir. The two incoming lanes were jammed tight as ushers armed with flashlights slowly assisted the commuters to the parking areas or to drop-off areas for buses and shuttles.

Running shoes would have been a better choice. Gail's feet had started to ache as she wove in and out of the walking commuters. She squinted against the autumn sundown and vehicle lights. She needed to find a vantage point that would allow her to keep an eye on the incoming traffic. He was supposed to be driving a school bus. That would help cut down the odds.

Using a traffic light, she crossed over, fighting the flow of pedestrians. She moved up against a storefront facing the sidewalk, her back against the wall to avoid the human tide which was pushing towards the center. The problem was she was unable to see the traffic from her position. Glancing right and left, she caught site of an outdoor café that overlooked the street.

Perfect!

She ascended to the restaurant, ordered a coffee, and took a seat along the small concrete wall facing the street.

An employee from the café had commented on her choice to sit outside. "It's starting to get cold outside. The patio is closed for the season," he said, "All the sunshades are in storage."

"That's all right. I find the cold invigorating. I don't need anything else. I just want to sit and watch the lights."

The waiter didn't bother to argue with her.

Probably thinks I'm nuts.

Sitting on the metal bench with the wind at her back, she was happy she had brought a heavier coat. After checking no one was near enough to notice, she pulled the collar up to deflect the wind. Using the motion to hide her intention, she transferred the pistol from her purse to the right-hand pocket of her coat. She pulled the strap of the purse around her neck and let it hang down her left side, out of the way. From her perch, she was able to spy the incoming traffic of both lanes for almost two full blocks. As the vehicles approached, Gail was able to look right into the cabs of trucks and buses and make out the drivers.

It didn't take long before the cold started to seep into her. The wind and the metal bench transferred the cold, and she sat shivering. To fight back, she started doing stretches behind the wall to keep the blood flowing. She would study the traffic, do a short series of stretches, and then check the traffic. If Dalton came this way, she would see him.

Chapter 51

"Alpha is in place," Hawkins said into the throat mic pressed up against his neck

"Bravo in place," Amena responded.

The other teams relayed the same sentiments as they entered the festival with the large crowds. Although Hawkins and Amena thought an attack would happen after dark, they couldn't take the chance. The day had been long, and Hawkins rotated the teams to keep them alert. He moved through the crowd checking faces and body language that might indicate a threat. At times he sat under one of the large tents, a tankard of ale untouched in front of him and half listening to those around him as his eyes moved across the steady stream of people. A couple of times he danced the polka, using the bouncing, twisting movement to mask his observance of the throng around him. The air of surreal joviality strengthened his resolve to end this. He risked bringing a couple of giant pretzels to Amena and Tommy who waited in the crowd outside the gate. He satisfied his hunger with a couple of Bratwurst sausages, the bun overflowing with sauerkraut.

Dusk was not far off.

***

Dalton eased the bus forward, keeping a safe distance from the vehicle ahead of him. The traffic into the fairgrounds was backed up at least a mile. There was a steady stream of red lights alternating off and on as the line stopped and started.

"This will take some time," he said aloud.

"That's okay. There's nothing we can do about it without bringing attention to ourselves," Aazam said.

Dalton looked into the mirror above his driver's seat, eyed Maajid, and said, "Are you sure we'll be able to enter the grounds as a handicap bus?"

"I told you before, there's a drop-off area just inside the main gates. It's all been checked out," Maajid said, annoyed. Dalton wasn't sure if it was due to nerves or the man's conceit. *Probably a bit of both.*

The main gates were not even in sight because of the curve of the road. Dalton was able to gauge the distance to the fairgrounds by the high flood lights that surrounded the inner field of the park.

Although the event wasn't over for another hour or so, Dalton saw party goers covered the sidewalks, coming and going. Some costumed in the typical Germanic style clothing with short skirts and low cut blouses for the women, their hair done in braids. The men were clad in shorts, a white shirt covered by a vest, and the feathered cap. Dalton thought they had to be freezing, but most were jumping and dancing to the German Oom Pah Pa Band music in the distance. From the unsteady antics, Dalton figured they'd had plenty of beer.

As the bus inched forward, the entrance hovered in the distance; it was a dance of pedestrians and vehicles choreographed by maestros with orange batons. Cars would stop and crowds would cross at intervals; this explained the slowness of the traffic.

Standing beside Dalton, Aazam put his hand into his left jacket pocket. It was the pocket that hid the detonator. There was an audible click muffled by the jacket that made Dalton flinch. He realized it was just the power button on the unit, but the knowledge did nothing for his nerves.

It's armed.

Aazam leaned over and wrapped his arm around Dalton's shoulder with a gesture that was almost comradely. His hand settled on Dalton's left shoulder, and he began to squeeze, his fingers digging into the hollow above the collarbone. His other hand, on the right shoulder, ensured Dalton was unable to pull away. Dalton winced, arching his body into the squeeze to alleviate the pressure. It did him no good. The man's hand was like a vice.

"Ahhh." Dalton groaned.

"Maajid and I will continue on foot," Aazam said in a soft voice. "Remember, I will be watching you the whole time. If I even think you are going against my plan, I will use the remote. It may not kill as many as planned, but the effect will be sufficient for my purpose." He gave Dalton's shoulder another squeeze. "And then," he paused for effect, "I will pay your mother a visit."

Aazam released Dalton's shoulder and then patted him almost lovingly on the side of the head. He moved past Dalton to follow Maajid to the steps, turning his head until one eye stared back. Dalton realized it was an indication to open the bus's folding door, and he thumbed the button on the steering wheel.

The Iraqi and Maajid quickly dropped down to the road. Aazam looked back and held Dalton's eyes as he pulled his hand out of his pocket enough to show he had his hand wrapped around the dead-man switch. He need only release the trigger.

Dalton closed the door and surveyed the traffic, both vehicular as well as the wave of pedestrians walking to and from the fairgrounds entrance. When he looked back, both men were swallowed by partygoers.

The lines to enter the festival grounds reminded him of a childhood trip he'd taken with his parents to Disney and Epcot. The people were shepherd through similar fencing that ran back and forth, condensing the line like cattle gates leading into a slaughterhouse.

Keeping his hand low, Dalton pulled the crescent wrench from the hoodie's front pocket. He started loosening the nut that held the detonator radio receiver secure to the side dash. He had to go by feel while keeping his eyes on the traffic. He couldn't risk Aazam seeing him tampering with the explosive connections. While one hand worked on the nut, he used the other to keep the bus moving slowly forward. Once it was loose enough to turn freely, he returned the wrench back to his pocket.

Dalton gave the crowd a once over, looking for any sign of the two men. Keeping his eyes facing forward, he carefully pulled the radio receiver out of its slot, leaving it dangle by the wires. From his sweater, he slowly pulled out the small pair of wire cutters. Waiting until he braked for the traffic, Dalton glanced quickly at the wire to aim the cutter at the two wires coming from the bottom of the unit. With a snip, he cut the source of any electronic spark towards the blasting cap, rendering the manual detonator useless.

The bus moved forward and then braked again. Dalton used this movement to open the driver's window. As his hand came down, he shoved the now useless radio receiver back into its slot. He took his time and tightened the nut to hold it in place. It would look normal if Aazam re-boarded. A quick twist of the crescent wrench tightened the unit back to the dash. He dropped the wrench and froze at a furious banging at the bus's folding door.

Chapter 52

Behind Gail, the café was doing a brisk business. The warmth of the business was a constant tease now as she watched her own breath reflected against the city lights. To fight off the cold, she walked in place, feeling the blood move through her feet and toes. Alternately, she would slap her arms across her chest, tapping the opposite arm with her uncovered hands until her fingers went numb. She would do this while keeping her eye on the roadway.

She almost missed it.

A transport truck in the curb lane with a large display of a Budweiser Beer moved in jerking motions as the traffic stopped and started. The truck's air brakes squealed and hissed as it moved forward. It grated on Gail's ears. *Won't be sorry to see him gone.*

As the truck's trailer jerked past her, she saw the tail end of a blue bus hidden by the transport. The two vehicles had been see-sawing like a pair of cross country snow skies as they moved with the traffic. Even now, the bus disappeared behind the truck's trailer.

Blue? School buses are yellow.

It was the truck's turn to surge ahead, and she saw a handicap sticker on a rear lift door of the bus. On the side, there was part of a name stenciled in white, "Geor—," but the rest was cut off by the trailer. Because of the blue color, she almost dismissed it, but some inner voice, Hawkins would call it her gut, told her to make sure.

She checked her purse and pocket to ensure she had everything, and she ran down the stairs. At the street level, she pushed her way into the crowd and made her way to the front of the truck, dodging people on the sidewalk who were heading away from and towards the festival.

She reached the front of the huge vehicle, but couldn't see the front of the bus. *Damn.* Because of the angle, she would have to get a couple of car lengths ahead of the truck.

She turned to move forward, bumped into a couple heading the other way, and bounced off the tail end of a car. The pair caught her before she fell in front of the transport's front wheels.

"Careful," the man said, "That guy wouldn't see you if you fell in front of his rig."

"Tha...thank you," Gail said, realizing how tragic that could have ended. She looked around and saw the truck had passed her again. Pushing back the fear, she began overtaking the truck. She kept going, passing the next three vehicles. As the line of vehicles came to a stop again, she waved at the driver of the car beside her before stepping in front of him. She crossed and walked back towards the bus in between the two rows of vehicles.

The strong headlights made it almost impossible to see more than a few steps ahead of her. Gail could make out the sides of the vehicles, but the high headlights of the transport and bus blinded her as she moved up the lane. She kept her feet on the yellow line that divided road. The transport moved forward, and the sudden darkness on that side of the road left spots in her vision. Shielding herself from the bus's lights, she staggered forward past the vehicle's hood and stopped beside the door.

The driver was bent away from the door, his attention on the side dash. He straightened and turned. Gail got a look at his profile. Her legs felt like wet noodles. She reached out and put a hand on the glass doors to stable herself. The cold glass grounded her and she brought up the other hand. Gail started to slap at the door with both hands: "Dalton!"

***

"We have contact."

Hawkins recognized Amena's voice and anxiously waited for more information.

"I've got both Aazam and Maajid crossing the street towards the fairground entrance. Both are in dark green hoodies."

"Any signs of the bus?" Hawkins asked.

"I can see a blue bus further up the street. Unknown if it's the one we're expecting."

"Affirmative," Hawkins said, "Tommy, move back to the entrance and cover Amena."

"Roger that. Moving"

Hawkins resisted the urge to run to the entrance. The plan was to keep the greater part of the team spread out inside the grounds. There were at least two suspects at large — Dalton and Adham. There could be more. Hawkins stayed in line at a ticket booth, keeping his eyes roaming across the crowd

"I got eyes on both subjects," Gunnie said

"What are they up to?" Hawkins asked, his voice impatient.

"They're just standing, watching the traffic."

"I think they're waiting for someone," Amena said.

"Are they carrying anything? Packages? Backpacks?"

"Nothing," Amena said. "Wait. Tommy, did you see that?"

"Yeah. Looks like something's bugging Maajid." Gunnie replied.

"What the hell's going on?" Hawkins demanded.

"Something is driving Maajid nuts. He keeps reaching under his sweater," Gunnie said. "He's either scratching or rearranging his underwear."

"Aazam just grabbed him, and you can tell he's not happy," Amena added.

"Could he be wearing a vest?" Hawkins asked.

"Definitely, the hoodie is large on him so he could have something under there," Gunnie said. "Same thing with Aazam."

Shit! There was a pause in the radio communication, and Hawkins looked around his own position. With Bluetooth wireless headsets, it was not unusual for people to be seen talking seemingly to themselves. But people do notice. He saw a couple of people looking at him. He took the time to remember the faces. Who knows if they were innocent bystanders or not.

"Heads up," Amena said, "Looks like that blue bus is what they are waiting for. It's got something written on the side of it. I can't read it from this angle."

"George Washington University," Tommy said. "It's got a handicap logo."

"That's how they plan to get past the main gate," Hawkins said. "Amena, why do you think it's part of the plot?"

"Because Gail is hammering on the front door."

***

Aazam was close to exploding. *These fucking Americans are so weak. They had never faced any hardships in their pampered lives. They like their wars on CNN where they can sit back in the safety of their homes. They allow their government to wage war continuously as long as it is elsewhere. They have no concept of real hardship. They have no idea of what's like to fight or kill just to exist.*

Adham had been the only person Aazam had met he had respected because Adham had known what it took to win. Aazam had not wanted to kill him, but he could not allow him to jeopardize the plan. This was no longer a hit and run mission. This mission called for the ultimate sacrifice. Teams around the globe were waiting for this signal. It would be a bugle call to action to show the West it had no right to interfere in matters that didn't concern it, to bring the horror of war to its shores, and to show that, even with their high-tech weapon systems, the Americans could be brought to their knees.

Aazam would have preferred working with Adham instead of Maajid, the sniveling coward. *Maajid was like those parasites in the leadership roles of ISIS. Cowards who would never lead from the front. No, they hid in the shadows, scared of the American drones. Maajid, too, was happy to give orders and send his people out to die, but he balked at the thought of wearing the vest.* It was why Aazam added the radio receiver detonator — Maajid could not be trusted to follow orders. Now he was whining about an allergic reaction to the nylon in the harness.

"Toughen up. It's time to prove that you're a soldier of Allah," Aazam said, his voice low.

"Hurry. This itching is agony."

"Here comes the American with the bus," Aazam said.

They looked at the bus as it turned into the festival grounds guided by one of the traffic controllers, his light indicating the drop-off area. As the bus made the slow turn, they saw a woman pounding on its folding door and screaming at Dalton.

"It's Dalton's mother," Maajid said, his hand scratching furiously under his sweater.

Aazam cursed. "I'll deal with her. You will enter the grounds and make your way to the far end of the festival. Wait for my signal."

When Maajid hesitated, Aazam grabbed him by the arm, his patience gone, "Do as I say, or I will skin you alive, boy!"

Maajid staggered towards the entrance. When he was inside, Aazam turned towards the bus. It was time to force the issue.

***

"They're splitting up," Amena said.

"Which way?" Hawkins asked.

"Maajid is heading into the fairgrounds. Aazam is heading for the bus."

"I'll grab Maajid. You and Tommy stay with Aazam."

"Affirmative," she said.

Hawkins left the line he had been standing in and radioed to the other agents inside the crowd: "All interior teams, head for the entrance and watch for me. Let me know when you have eyes on me."

"I got you, Hawkins. Golf and Hotel are to the left of the turnstile," one agent reported.

"Good. When Maajid comes in, let him go, but follow close behind me. I want to take him and need you to screen me from the public so we don't raise an alarm."

"10-4. I'll follow your lead."

"Lima team is 30 seconds out," said another agent.

"Roger, fall in with Golf and Hotel."

"Will do."

When Maajid came through the turnstile, there was no mistaking him from any of the other party goers. He was scratching himself like a hound with a bad case of fleas. Hawkins watched as the wannabe terrorist reached into his hoodie trying to find relief. Hawkins saw the flashes of the green harness that plagued the man as he jerked and pulled on the harness. There were bright red blotches on his neck and wrists. If Hawkins hadn't known about the explosives, he would have been concerned about a biological agent. Hawkins watched the man stagger into the crowd, bounce off a couple of people, and move deeper into the festival area.

"Careful buddy. Easy on the beer," someone said

"Someone should cut him off," another person said.

Hawkins allowed Maajid to pull ahead of his position before falling in behind. A glance behind ensured the two agents were backing him up. Seconds later, the second team announced they were in position. Now, it was up to Hawkins.

***

Dalton froze. His first thought as he swung his attention to the door was Aazam had caught him disabling the radio receiver. Seeing his mother at the door banging on the glass with both hands didn't help. He waved her away, but that only agitated her even more.

"Mom, get out of here!" he shouted. He had to make her leave. Aazam would not hesitate to hurt her.

A bright light caught Dalton in the eyes, and he raised his hands to shield his eyes. The light moved off his face, and he saw it was one of the traffic controllers, a military police officer (MP) in uniform, who indicated Dalton could turn into the festival grounds pick up area. He waved at the man and started to pull the bus into a slow left turn, his mother still banging at the door. Seeing her, the MP rushed forward, his hands raised to halt the bus. Dalton had no choice but to stop. It was that or drive over the man.

The MP came around the bus's front end and grabbed Dalton's mother by the arm. He tried to move her away from the bus, but she fought back. Her furiousness surprised Dalton. The MP, still holding her by the arm, rapped the glass doors with his light stick. Dalton hit the open button allowing the folding door to open for the soldier.

"What's this all about?" asked the MP.

"No idea. Maybe she wants a lift," Dalton laughed. "I'm here to pick up a bunch of handicapped students from GWU."

"Dalton, tell him who I am!"

"One at a time lady. You'll get your chance in a minute."

The vehicles behind the bus began to honk their horns, impatient to move forward.

They'll bring all the attention on the bus!

The MP consulted a clipboard and then nodded. "Okay, you're on the list." He kept a foot on the first step of the bus, both to keep the door open and also to keep Gail from getting in.

"Now, what's your story lady?" he said, half turning to look at her.

"He's my son," Gail said in a rush. "Homeland Security is searching for the bus, because they think it's part of a terrorist attack."

"A terrorist attack?" the MP repeated.

"Remember the explosive plant that blew up in Montana?" she said, "And the warehouse in Dallas? It's all related. Please, you must believe me. Contact Homeland. The agent involved is Hawkins. They'll confirm everything."

Dalton started to panic; he looked around, seeking some escape. He needed to get the bus away from his mother or they were both dead. Aazam would detonate the bomb.

The MP looked up and told Dalton, "Shut the bus down. I'll have to check this out." He reached for the radio microphone that hung from his shoulder epaulet.

Before he could speak into the radio, Dalton stepped on the gas pedal, yanking the steering wheel towards the parking lot. The bus surged ahead and the MP fell backwards into the road. Gail tried to grab at the doorway but was pulled off balanced. She fell over the MP and rolled away from the bus. The MP regained his footing only to be slammed by the over swing of the rear section of the bus. It caught him solidly in the back and threw him forward into the roadway where he rolled to a broken heap.

The vehicles that were parked behind the bus plunged forward now that the bus had finally turned, only to squeal to a stop to avoid Gail. The driver of the car behind was unready for the sudden stop and slammed into the first vehicle. Metal crumpled and glass shattered. Dalton watched this in his mirror as he straightened the bus. He circled the drive until the bus faced the street. He opened the door and shut off the bus.

Looking towards the street, Dalton saw two other MPs running towards the collision and the unmoving body of their fellow soldier. *What have I done?* Dalton could see his mother pulling herself to her feet. He saw Aazam standing off to one side. *He had to have seen everything.* Sitting in the dark, Dalton watched Aazam walk slowly towards the entrance, his attention on the street.

Using his feet, Dalton found and dragged the wrench he had dropped to where he could grab it. The last thing he needed was for Aazam to come back and see the wrench. *It might set him off.* He picked it up and put it away in the front pocket of his hoodie, brushing up against the remote receiver that Adham had given him. The detonator was the only thing that might be considered a weapon. Checking to see if he was under observation by Aazam, he pulled it out with one hand while his other hand dug into his front pant pocket to grab a blasting cap. *It could go either way.* Once wired, it would detonate whenever Aazam released the dead man's switch. If he was holding it when that happened, he might lose his hand…if he was lucky.

***

Gail stood ramrod stiff in the middle of the road. She could not see Dalton due to the shadows. *Is he still in the bus?*

Two more MPs raced towards her. One stopped beside her, concern on his face, "Are you hurt?"

She shook her head.

"What happened?" he asked, looking at the wrecked cars before looking back at her.

"The bus," she heard herself say. She watched as the MP, a sergeant, looked towards the lot where the bus was parked. He was distracted when his partner caught sight of the other MP who lay motionless on the pavement, and he ran to check on the injured man. He looked back at her, searching for an answer.

"Bomb," she said, "On the bus."

His eyes widened as her words sunk in.

"Terry!" he yelled, pulling his service pistol from its holster.

His partner looked up. Seeing the sergeant with his pistol drawn, he rose slowly. Looking for threats, he too pulled out his pistol.

"Stay here, Miss," the sergeant said to Gail.

He didn't wait for an answer, but moved towards the bus, the pistol in both hands, tracking for a target. His partner moved parallel with him. Unable to stop herself, Gail moved forward slowly, clutching her purse.

To Gail, it was like the soldiers' movements had been orchestrated. The two men crossed the street together, both with their weapons at the ready. They moved under the shadow of the nearby trees and closed in on the bus. She had just entered the shadows herself when first the sergeant and then his partner collapsed to the ground for no apparent reason. Gail staggered to a stop only to have a hard body slam into her from behind, a hand crushed against her mouth.

"You must be Dalton's mother."

***

Hawkins closed in on Maajid. He could hear the other agents' footsteps coming up behind him and felt confident they had his back. Maajid didn't seem concerned about anything except scratching. Hawkins had timed his approach so the two would meet just as Maajid stepped in between two rows of vendor tents. The rows stood back to back, full of vendors carrying supplies into their booths out of public sight.

As Maajid walked past the entrance to the area, Hawkins seized the man's shoulder and spun him around, jabbing his stiffened fingers at Maajid's throat, crushing the man's airway. The scratching stopped as both hands reached for his throat. Hawkins pushed Maajid backwards into the space between the tents. With a quick kick at the inside of the knee, Maajid yelped as his leg collapsed beneath him. He slammed into the ground and air burst out of his bruised throat. One of the other agents stepped over Hawkins and grabbed Maajid's hands, pulling them away from his throat and over his head. With a practiced movement, the agent tied them together with a plastic quick tie and held Maajid's hands away from his body.

As Maajid was being cow-tied, Hawkins pulled the hoodie over the man's chest, covering his face. He heard the quick zip of another quick tie from behind and knew Maajid's feet had been immobilized. Maajid's chest was inflamed with hives and was scratched raw. Hawkins would have been more compassionate if not for the strips of C4 stretched on the harness. He could see the harness was rigged with both a manual pull switch and a radio controlled detonator with the small antenna following the harness strap. He could not know when Aazam would decide to send a signal to the unit. Pulling a combat knife from his belt sheath, Hawkins used the sharp blade to slice the duct tape around the remote detonator to get at the wires. Once it was fully exposed and he saw the simple setup, it was just a matter of cutting the wires.

Hawkins realized he had been holding his breath.

"You're doing good, boss," the agent in front of him said. Hawkins looked up and saw the sweat on the other man's forehead.

Looking back, he could see the wires running under the duct tape above the plastic explosive across the harness strap on Maajid's chest. He cut the tape at the top part of the strap. With both hands, he grabbed the tape downward in a steady, unified pull. As the tape cleared, it exposed the C4, and Hawkins pulled the blasting cap from the explosive. He cut the cap away from the wires. Using the tape he cut off, he taped the pull switch to the harness in the off position so there was no chance of it catching on anything and setting off any other explosive. He unclipped the waist harness and cut both shoulder straps with his knife. With the help of his partner, they rolled the unconscious Maajid onto his side and the harness came free. Hawkins passed it to the agent behind him.

Into the radio, he announced, "Maajid is neutralized."

To his horror, Amena came back, "Shots fired, two down at the drop area."

Hawkins went cold.

***

Dalton saw the MPs and his mother coming towards the bus, and he cursed under his breath. He twisted the wires of the blasting cap to the remote detonator, shoving the setup into the front of his hoodie. He watched in horror as the two men were cut down as they approached his vehicle. He saw the muzzle flash behind his mother, but heard no report of the gunfire.

Aazam grabbed Gail, and with no thought, Dalton was racing down the stairs of the bus and rounding the hood. He used the large convex mirrors to slingshot himself around the front of the bus.

His mother was fighting back, and he could see she had the flesh of Aazam's arm in her teeth. Blood covered her mouth as the Iraqi twisted to one side so his back was towards Dalton. Dalton saw Aazam raise the dead man's switch above his head, ready to strike at this mother's unprotected head. Dalton grabbed the remote detonator from his sweater and dropped it into the hood of the man's sweater as he barreled into Aazam. Both the Iraqi and his mother sprawled across the pavement, Aazam on top of his mother. As Dalton scrambled to his feet, ready to attack the soldier, he saw a man and a woman coming toward them, guns exposed. Aazam picked himself up with a swiftness that shocked Dalton. His mother lay on her back, her eyes closed in pain.

The woman wore a hijab. "Homeland Security!"

Dalton could see by the disbelief in Aazam's expression that he was also surprised at her appearance. The Iraqi said something in Arabic.

The woman, her gun still trained on Aazam said in English, "I may be Muslim, but I am nothing like you. You have defiled Islam with your twisted rhetoric."

The Iraqi snarled at the woman's words. "It doesn't matter. Allah will decide. America interfered in my country and took everyone I loved, and I will have my revenge," he said, raising the dead man's switch in one hand, the silenced pistol in the other. "Drop your weapons."

When they hesitated, he yelled, "Now!"

Neither Amena nor Tommy lowered their weapons.

Dalton watched as the Iraqi bared his teeth, the hate radiating off of him. Dalton knew the man was waiting to hear the blast of Maajid's suicide vest which would push more people towards the entrance and the bus.

Sirens rose in the distance.

There was no escape.

Aazam said, "Shasmeen," the hatred in his face melting.

He raised the dead man's switch and released the trigger on the remote.

There was a loud bang, and a huge spark lit up the area behind Aazam's head. The concussion staggered the huge man, but he refused to fall. The back of the man's sweater smoked, and he let out a groan as the garment caught fire.

Everyone was frozen in surprise.

The confused look on Aazam's face changed to anger. He looked at Dalton and smiled a malicious grin that sent shivers through Dalton. He raised the pistol towards Gail.

"I warned you."

The female agent yelled, threw herself in front of his mother, and took the first shot in the chest. The second shot caught his mother's shoulder, and she let out a groan. The other agent snapped a shot at Aazam, clipping him. Aazam altered his aim, and the other agent went down as two shots slammed into him.

Dalton lunged forward, but Aazam turned the firearm on him. Dalton froze. He stared down the barrel. Dalton closed his eyes.

A shot rang out. Then another.

He opened his eyes to see Aazam stiffen. Two more shots slammed into the man's chest, knocking him backwards. One last bullet hit the Iraqi and spun him into a death spiral to fall facedown onto the pavement.

He looked over and saw his mother still laying on the ground with the other woman across her legs and a smoking pistol in her hands.

***

The female agent came to slowly, her hand pressed against her chest. She reached under her jacket and tore at the Velcro of her vest, pulling it away to allow her to breathe deeper. Pulling herself off of Gail's legs, she waved to another agent who came racing around the corner and moved toward Aazam, gun at the ready. He reached down, searching for a pulse. After a minute, he looked to his partner and shook his head, pulling out a portable radio.

The woman was speaking to his mother, "Gail, it's over. Dalton is safe. Give me the gun." She laid her hands on his mother's arm so gently that the mere act broke Dalton's heart. His mother looked at her in a daze.

"He's safe?" she whispered.

"Yes, Gail. It's over." The woman pried the gun slowly from his mother's hand

Dalton dropped beside her, "Mom."

Gail's head whipped in surprise and looked at him like he were a ghost. "Dalton."

He grabbed her hand. "Yes, Mom. It's over. You saved me."

She collapsed into his arms

Epilogue

Dalton stared at the ceiling, trying to get his bearings. It took a few minutes before it sunk in that he was in his own bed. He closed his eyes to the surge of emotions, letting them fall where they would. He would have to deal with them one at a time. He had the time now. He knew Hawkins and the people at Homeland Security would want more meetings, and he agreed to cooperate in any way he could.

He sat up and looked around the room he lived in since shortly after his father's death. Brent Smith and the boys from a Shinedown poster watched him without any expression from the opposite wall. He could remember putting it up as a tribute to their music, but for the life of him, he could not remember seeing it, actually seeing it, in… forever. The hockey jersey hanging on the back of the door was the same. That white lettered "Ovechkin" over the number "9" on the red Washington Capitals jersey made him wonder if the big Russian was still team captain. He missed out on so much because of the blanket of grief he'd buried himself under. It was as if he died with his dad.

With that thought, he rose from the bed and began the Fajr prayer to welcome Allah in the new morning. He dedicated the prayers in thanks for the safety of his family and his return. He felt the warmth fill him as Allah poured his love into him.

Dalton opened his bedroom door to see Daanya and his mother drinking coffee at the kitchen table. It felt so strange to see these two women so comfortable with each other. They hadn't even met before he'd left.

"We were wondering if you were ever going to wake up," Gail said, her arm supported by a sling.

"Morning. Is there any coffee left?" he asked.

Daanya rose and said, "Sit down and I'll get you—." She stopped and laughed. She turned and looked at both Gail and Dalton. "You know, I don't even know how you like your coffee."

Dalton felt his cheeks heat up.

"Black with one sugar," he said with a smile. "How about you?"

The smile she gave him nearly blew him away, "Black."

"I know there's a ton to talk about, but Hawkins is on his way over. He should be here any minute," Gail said.

Right away, he felt his apprehension level jump. Daanya reached over and grabbed his hand.

"He's just coming over to let us know about what's happening in the investigation. Nothing's wrong."

Dalton swallowed and tried to relax.

They heard the door below and the footsteps on the stairs. Dalton rose and opened the door on the first knock, catching Hawkins with his hand in midair. His look of surprise turned into a smile.

"Someone looks a little better after some sleep," Hawkins said while stepping into the apartment and making room for Amena.

"You don't look like you got much," Gail told Hawkins.

"No. Busy wrapping up loose ends."

While Dalton went back to his room to grab another chair, Gail put another pot of coffee on.

When they got settled, Hawkins broke the bubble of silence by saying, "Here's what's been happening. Daanya, your brother, cousin, and the others will be charged later this morning. They are all pointing fingers at Maajid as the ring leader, and say they knew nothing about Aazam. Your brother is cooperating and has offered to give up his contacts overseas."

She nodded, but Dalton could see the sadness in her eyes. Regardless of what Maajid had done, he was still her brother. She has lost him as well as the rest of her family.

Turning to Dalton, Hawkins said, "Your information that this was the signal for worldwide attacks turned out to be accurate. We had been following some of Aazam's travels when he had been identified, but we had no idea of targets until the other day. Our suspicions were shared with the other coalition countries, and all but one attack was stopped."

A pained expression came to his face. "You'll probably pick up the news bulletins on CNN about the explosion at the Oktoberfest at Theresienwiese in Munich. Seems that there were two separate teams involved. The Germans had tracked down one group yesterday and a four member ISIS team was killed just outside of the city, so they thought the threat had been dealt with."

"How many?" Gail asked gently.

"Four hundred and thirty dead."

"Oh my God," Dalton whispered, his eyes burning as the numbers sunk in. Daanya pulled him towards her and held him as he wept.

After a few minutes, he felt a strong hand grab his arm and pull him upright. "Okay Dalton, that's all I'm allowing you." Hawkins said. "It's rough and it's something you have to live with, but you have something else that will counter it."

Dalton pulled up his shirt to wipe his face. He looked through redden eyes at Hawkins.

"It was your quick thinking and your determination to stop that bomb from going off that saved us the same fate. Your mom put an end to Aazam, but you did the heavy lifting."

"And not only that," Amena said, "You were right when you said any attack on America by Muslims would have caused more suffering for the American Muslims. We are seeing that play out in Germany as we speak. You've saved more people than you know."

Sniffing, Dalton nodded his thanks.

"The MP you hit with your bus is pretty busted up," Hawkins told him, "but once he was told about some of the circumstances, he agreed to drop all charges. Myself, I think you owe the man a beer."

Dalton nodded.

"But I'm going to ask more from you." Hawkins said, staring at him.

Gail's and Daanya's expressions must have mirrored his own surprise as they all looked at Hawkins with open mouths.

"You have an online presence with the ISIS recruiters. I want to use that with the information we get from Maajid to go after their recruiting system so hopefully we can avoid another attack like this one."

"But won't they know I've been compromised?"

"I'm working on that," Amena said. "We do have a couple assets within ISIS, and we plan on releasing some altered facts that have not surfaced through the media."

"If we are successful," Hawkins continued, "they'll be contacting you."

Looks of worry crossed his mother's face, and Hawkins raised his hand, "No more heroics. I'm talking about an office job," he said more for Gail than for him. "You'll be helping us identify their recruitment centers so someone else can take them out."

Dalton was unsure, and he looked at his mother and then at Daanya.

"Give it some thought," Hawkins said. "Not too much though. You need to decide if you want to drive school bus for the rest of your days or if you want a job with Homeland Security."

"A job." He couldn't believe what he was hearing. He felt Daanya's fingers squeeze his, lending her support.

Amena and Hawkins rose to leave. As he turned to the door, Hawkins said to the trio, "Talk it over and then let me know. You could start..." he raised his eyes to the ceiling as if he had to think about it. "Tomorrow."

If you liked what you read, please leave a review on Amazon, Goodreads, or your blog.

About the Author

After 31 years as a deputy fire chief, Dave Wickenden traded business plans and council reports for creative writing. He wrote and edited the Sudbury Fire Department's *In the Line of Fire* newsletter earlier in his career, and he has enjoyed writing and reading since a young teen.

Dave is a member of the Sudbury Writers Guild. He is active on Facebook and Twitter, and discusses his writing journey on his website. His first novel, *In Defense of Innocence*, was published in the spring of 2018 by Crave Press.

Dave is a father of three fantastic boys and now three grandsons. Both he and his wife, Gina, live in hockey arenas as his two younger sons are very active in minor hockey. The entire family is very involved with fishing and spends many summer hours on the water searching for the big one.

[1] An Arabic expression meaning "God is great" or "God is greater."
[2] Mythical Middle Eastern beings
[3] The afternoon prayer.
[4] A group of countries fighting ISIS.
[5] Bashar al-Assad, the president of Syria at the time of this novel.
[6] Refers to meat prepared according to Muslim law.
[7] Guantanamo Bay
[8] The before dawn prayer.
[9] Meals, Ready-to-Eat
[10] German nationalist movement Patriotic Europeans Against the Islamisation of the West
[11] Translation from Islam Awakened - http://islamawakened.com/quran/60/7/
[12] Daily combat food ration.
[13] Modus operandi, or particular way of doing something.
[14] Arabic expression meaning "If Allah wills it."

CPSIA information can be obtained
at www.ICGtesting.com
Printed in the USA
LVHW02s1617240718
584759LV00001B/39/P